1,000,000 Books

are available to read at

www.ForgottenBooks.com

Read online
Download PDF
Purchase in print

ISBN 978-1-331-32921-3
PIBN 10175057

1 MONTH OF
FREE
READING

at

www.ForgottenBooks.com

By purchasing this book you are eligible for one month membership to ForgottenBooks.com, giving you unlimited access to our entire collection of over 1,000,000 titles via our web site and mobile apps.

To claim your free month visit:

www.forgottenbooks.com/free175057

AND THE

.

BY

.

LONDON

M·D·CCCC·II

"Thus saith the Lord God ; Will ye hunt tne souls of my people, and will ye save the souls alive that come unto you ?

"And will ye pollute me among my people for handfuls of barley . . . to slay the souls that should not die, and to save the souls alive that should not live, by your lying to my people that hear your lies ?

"Wherefore thus saith the Lord God ; Behold . . . I will tear them from your arms, and will let the souls go, even the souls that ye hunt to make them fly."—EZEKIEL xiii. 18–20.

CONTENTS

———◆◆◆———

CHAPTER   PAGE

    I. IN WHICH AN EXILE MOURNS . . . I

   II. HOW THREE GIRLS READ "PEER GYNT" . . 9

 III. CLEMENTINE WRITES A LETTER, AND HER

         FATHER ENCOUNTERS AN OLD ACQUAINTANCE 24

  IV. INCIDENTALLY CONCERNS THE MERITS OF A

         GOOD FIGURE 38

   V. TWO WAYS OF SPENDING AN EVENING . . 55

  VI. A STUDY IN SECRET BIOGRAPHY . . . 68

 VII. CLEMENTINE HAS A FEW SURPRISES . . . 81

VIII. WAYS AND MEANS 94

  IX. A GAME OF POKER WITHOUT CARDS . . . 102

   X. HOW ONE MARRIAGE TOOK PLACE, AND WHY

         MANY DO NOT 116

  XI. OLD WAYS OF FORMING NEW ALLIANCES . . 132

 XII. THE HEART TOWARD THE HIGHWAY . . . 150

XIII. HASTY FRUIT BEFORE THE SUMMER . . . 160

XIV. MR. GLOUCESTER HAS SEVERAL SURPRISES . 170

 XV. WHEN MONEY DOES NOT ANSWER ALL THINGS . 181

CHAPTER · PAGE

XVI. A QUESTION OF UNDERCURRENTS . . . 197

XVII. LA BELLE VALENTINE HEARS THE TRUTH AND UTTERS IT 206

XVIII. FURTHER REVELATIONS OF THE MATERNAL INSTINCT 218

XIX. STUDIES IN SELF-RESPECT 226

XX. PRINCE CONSTANTINE RECEIVES TWO VISITORS ON FRIENDLY BUSINESS 243

XXI. MR. GLOUCESTER DRAWS A CHEQUE . . 252

XXII. THE CONSIDERATION OF SOULS . . . 263

XXIII. TWO WAYS OF PLAYING THE FOX . . 274

XXIV. THE DUTY OF RELATIVES 285

XXV. THE DISCERNMENT OF SPIRITS . . . 298

XXVI. FATE AND THE UNFORESEEN 306

XXVII. DR. FELSHAMMER WRITES HISTORY . . 324

XXVIII. FELSHAMMER SPEAKS 332

XXIX. THREE POINTS OF VIEW 341

CHAPTER I

IN WHICH AN EXILE MOURNS

PRINCE PAUL OF URSEVILLE-BEYLESTEIN had ordered the shutters closed of every room in his vast *hôtel* in the Avenue Kléber, taken to his bed, turned his face to the wall. One of his beautiful friends was dead. Three months before she had been dancing in a cotillon; he could see her still, dressed as La Belle Simonetta, partner to himself, made up, inappropriately enough, as the young Raphael. It had been such a happy idea, and all her own—this *fête* in honour of the Old Masters. And now she was dead of typhoid fever, aged eighteen years and two days. Her tomb should be covered in lilies each day of the month for ever. He would build a marble pavilion to her memory—a pavilion where music should be perpetually played. She had been the gayest creature—a virginal embodiment of *une mye du roy*—always smiling, blushing, singing, or trifling, with light fingers, at the piano. She had been so very fair, so very fresh, so very helpless, so very pretty !

" Poor little child ! Poor little girl ! Poor little

child!" he repeated, again and again, as he lay, sick
from grief, with her miniature (no likeness) set in
brilliants almost crushed in his hand. "Poor little
girl! I was so fond of her! No one was half so
good or so amusing."

The sorrow was real, and in spite of the sentimental libertinism which belonged to his nature, his
household felt that he would not easily recover from
this unforeseen blow,—the first he had ever received
where his affections or his pleasures were concerned.
Some hoped that the period of mourning would assist
the maturity of his moral character. Sobering medi-
tations in solitude, while they produced fits of
impatience, temper, and a kind of indifference to
ordinary ideas, were conducive, nevertheless, to the
development of a man's will and energy. Many saw
in the virtuous Countess's death a stroke of Divine
discipline. Of all Prince Paul's favourites, she had
been the unworldly one, the redeeming angel. The
household were pleased, therefore, at his weeping.
He had a heart. He could be touched. With all
his faults he could love true merit.

"She will be of more help to him in Heaven," said
his aged unmarried aunt, the Princess Wilhelmina;
"she can never grow old or tiresome, and he will
never want to get rid of her. He will remember
when he is tempted that she prayed for him."

Another aunt, equally devout but more experienced, and possessing the common sense which

goes with minds of somewhat ordinary intelligence, went further :

"She was a good influence. All the same, we don't want him to get morbid."

Emotion in their family was a force to be held in check. The two ladies, who were sitting in an ante-room near the Prince's private apartments, exchanged a long glance and tried to think what ought to be done. Paul was seven-and-twenty—the second son of a monarch who had not been driven from his kingdom by the sword, but contemptuously swept out with a broomstick. So the legend ran in a popular song of that day. Educated in exile, where vengeance, deception, and debauchery had seemed the chief, if not the only, employments of the Royal circle, the young man was still amiable and generous. Ambition had lately troubled his thoughts, however, and as he lay tossing in his grief he felt between the cries of "Poor little child! poor little girl!" that the main obstacle in the way of his boldest designs was no more on the earth. He had seriously weighed the possibility of renouncing his princely rank, his discredited claims, and marrying the darling Sophia. All such heroic speculations were now at an end. She was dead—the one hostage he had ever offered to fortune—the sole impediment between him and his worst pleasures, between him and his loveless schemes for power. Surely at her burial some part— the better part perhaps—of himself perished with the

frail slight body—so soon to be dust.   While she lived
the choice of two lives had ever seemed open to him;
in certain moods, the serene, the unselfish, the chivalrous life domestic called him steadily; in other moods,
the exultant, unscrupulous, imperial life of his ancestors—spent in adventures and intrigues, burned in
his veins—not to be restrained without indulgence
of a kind.   He would plot against his foolish elder
brother—a poor creature!   He would raise an army,
march into Beylestein, have himself proclaimed, and
carry all before him with a high hand.   The poor
little dead girl alone had been able to chasten these
imaginings, partly by the sweetness of her affection,
partly by the angelic candour of her soul.   In a sullen
fit he told himself that Fate had chosen to deprive
him of his saving weakness.

"So much the better!   So much the better!" he
murmured, still tossing and still complaining.   "Poor
—poor little child!"

He looked around his room hung with orange-
coloured silk, and resolved to have it all changed
on the morrow.   It should be purple.   But on the
suggestion of Dr. Felshammer, his secretary, he left
Paris that same evening for Salsomaggiore.   For two
days he read novels in bed, and smoked—speaking to
no one.   After that, in the early April mornings,
when the half-drunken masons had ceased singing in
the tavern near the *hôtel*, when the stars were still
brilliant in the sky, and the birds still slept, he would

go out on the balcony and breathe the pure strong air, and wonder why he had not been born a peasant. He fancied he had a great desire to work in the fields, tend vines, and drive white oxen dragging carts of grain. He felt himself being drawn towards the warm green earth—not the earth of the grave and the worm which he trembled at with loathing ; but the earth fragrant, blossoming, fertile, smelling of the grape. All that was dreary in thought fled away ; death itself, remembered in the sunlight, seemed but a calmer development of the joy of life, instead of an ecstatic union with the soil, its inexhaustible health and abundance—it would be a peaceful identification with the everlasting sky.

"Can one get drunk on milk ?" he asked Felshammer, smiling as he spoke. Dr. Felshammer had an imposing figure, but a plain, almost sinister, face. The features had a certain emphatic sensuality, a strong animation, humanly marked by lines of hard thinking, strong feeling, and possibly rough living. Several scars disfigured his spare dark cheeks, and the deep furrows between his eyebrows emphasised his forty years of experience in the world. He was heavily built, with square shoulders, a short neck, and powerful hands. He had been an army surgeon, and now, after a short but highly distinguished service, he was in attendance on Prince Paul, nominally as his medical adviser, actually as his confidential secretary. In ideas he was socialistic with a cynical affection for

the aristocracy, and a contempt for the stupidity—
without charm—of the classes usually described as
labouring. Happy in having found a hero—for he
believed that his Prince was a genius—he asked no
more from Fate, and he wore, habitually, the air of a
man who has chosen his road and his companion and
is prepared as well for the possible misadventures as
the uncertain good fortune of the way.

"Can one get drunk on milk?" asked the Prince
a second time. "These normal things are changing
my whole philosophy. They intoxicate me."

"After morphia, the mud bath!" answered
Felshammer. "When the mud is well settled in
one's system I see no reason why one's heart should
not be accessible to real sane pleasures. Those of the
imagination—delightful in their way—always end so
badly."

"Here I am quite happy," said the Prince. "It
revives my Arcadian ideal of a country landlord
with his double-entry book-keeping and chemical
experiments."-

"That, too, is largely a question of the circulation
of the blood. Your health has improved."

Paul looked at him as though he were a disembodied
intelligence without feelings or humanity.

"Again, there is much in what you say. I am
at times a *solitaire* consumed by the desire of beauty
—more beauty—always more beauty. I seek for it
everywhere—in nature, in art, in souls, of course, too,

in bodies. When I find it I want to keep it for ever." He bit his lip. "How sweet she was!"

"Ach!" said the other, ignoring the last sigh, "the overstrained nervous system! There is a great deal of that kind of thing about. Hundreds, thousands, suffer similarly."

"You call it suffering?" said Paul.

"Saint Teresa's word—not mine. I call it excess of self-consciousness—egoism, that's all. Every one is consumed with the desire of beauty, and more beauty, without knowing it. Especially at your age. The point is your conception of it."

"Naturally," said Paul, thinking of the darling Sophia.

"You," said Felshammer bluntly, "wanted your beautiful countess for ever in the most beautiful scene. The main difference between you, Altesse, and others, is that they will take their beautiful or good when and where they may, and for so long as God chooses!"

"It must be the spirit of contradiction which always makes me long for what I have not. During her lifetime—much as she pleased me—I never had this ache to see her; this needle in my heart is quite new. I am lonely."

"That will pass."

"No doubt, but the best in me will pass with it. That knowledge adds to my loneliness. I miss a better part of myself. This isn't a sentimental fancy—it is a fact. I could never love again. What are you staring at ? "

" That girl on the balcony—to your left."

"Don't you know her ?" said Paul, who had been studying her graceful figure for some time, while he paced the floor; "that is Clementine Gloucester. She was at the funeral. No other woman present could compare with her—not even the Duchess of Annebault !"

CHAPTER II

HOW THREE GIRLS READ "PEER GYNT"

THE PERSON on the balcony was a girl of about two-and-twenty, with a clear rosy skin, dark blue eyes, and coal-black hair dressed in a foreign way with tortoise-shell combs. She had a short upper lip, which just escaped silliness by a blemish, in the shape of a small mole. Although she was English, her countenance had a Florentine mould; the nose was a little short, the brow a little broad, the chin slightly square. When she glanced up in response to the Prince's bow, he thought her smile charming, and her manner perfect.

"She is so distinguished," he remarked to Fels-hammer; "absolute ease, combined with that sureness of touch, look, and movement which you find in real aristocrats or pure yeomanry. Those who come between miss it altogether."

Then alone, without a cigar, he went for a two hours' walk on the highway. There were days and moods which he would share with no one; a mood of

the kind was on him now. Felshammer did not
venture to ask when his Royal Highness might be
expected to return, but he gave instructions to have
the Prince followed at a respectful distance, and he
himself sat down to work at some dispatches in
cypher. One, dated from the English Embassy in
Berlin, ran as follows :—

There is a great commotion in Urseville-Beylestein ;
the Republicans and Royalists have collected a rabble,
and now they wish Prince Paul proclaimed King. They
say that he only can make Beylestein prosperous and
restore peace. But that's a devil of a long story. I hope
he will have the sense to remain in exile. Where is the
fun of reigning over such a crew ? He is too civilised to
make a good monarch in his part of the world. A man
can't be educated at Eton and Oxford, in the best society
of England, France, Germany, and Italy, and then live his
mature years with a pack of mongrels—far less control
them. It isn't good enough, and I don't see why he
should *gêner* himself in the least. By the by, the chief is
satisfied with the new *chef.* He ought to be more careful,
however, with his sauces. They are always too fiery, or
too sweet, or something. But his entrées are rattling good.
Thanks for recommending him. I suppose you are doing
well, so far as comfort and inclination go, in sticking to
the Prince. As to your career, that's another thing. If
you were me, I should stay on by all means. You are
clever enough, however, to take a strong line of your own.
There's an American here, I daresay you have heard of
him ; his name is Cobden Duryee, he has " money to
burn," as they say in the States. He has been ordered
to Salsomaggiore, and I have given him an introduction to

you. He is a good sort ; is anxious to play the traditional Rothschild in European politics. He wants to "back wars"—that kind of thing, restore dynasties. At any rate, there's no harm in your meeting him. He knows that the Prince is no fool. He has ideas about the Medici and the Doges. I think he would like to be an American Doge in the Venetian style. I know it's all rot—in a way. Yet it isn't such rot as it might have been once. Ideas are changing so rapidly, or rather they are rolling back to the primitive point of view. Bismarck saw this coming ; Tolstoi is meeting it. If you and I live as long, we may come to regard it as the regulation scheme—mere commonplace, in fact.

Felshammer's reply to this letter ran as follows :

Dear Hollie,—I will come at once to what you say about myself. I shall remain with Prince Paul. I am no believer in charming weaklings, and I am not a man to devote myself to an irresponsible, fluctuating soul, seeking pleasure only, and shirking all things incompatible with indolence. I am too just, I hope, to be merciless in my estimate of feeble natures—knowing that men are punished—by the law and otherwise—not because they deserve punishment, but because Nature herself makes inexorable war upon her failures. Her legislature is for the robust in mind and body—one or the other at least— and while religions preach benevolence, patience, charity, long-suffering, we know that strength where it meets weakness must prevail, and industry, no matter how wrongly directed, where it meets half-heartedness, no matter how well-trained, must of necessity conquer. If so-called good people had the energy, the nerve, the back-bone, of so-called bad people, the bad would be trampled out of existence. So I shall waste no time on idlers—let them be never so clever—or on the unconvinced—let them be never so adroit in argument. I may wait a little while the young Prince becomes one of the two men within him—a king in the best sense (with an earthly throne or without one, I care not), or an individual—in the most futile sense. If he becomes the latter I shall have done with him. That is no reason, of course, why God should have done with him. Paul, in losing me, might lose little enough, but I want you to understand clearly that I hold definite views of human duty. Passions and enthusiasms leave one ; they depend on our happiness, our health, a host of accidental, non-essential things, whereas you can remember your duty at every turn—on your death-bed, or at your gladdest moment. (Your death might be just such a moment, so the alternative is not so sharp as it ought to be.) I have attended the Prince now for seven years. In that time I have watched his mental, moral, and physical development. So far it is a progression. Do not imagine that I love the man he might be or might have been. Put the thought of might-have-beens, ought-to-have-beens for ever out of your calculations. There are no might-have-beens. There is what has been, what is ; to regret lost possibilities and anticipate probabilities is the vice of dreamers. Therefore I take Paul just as he acts and speaks each day, and give him marks, saying to myself, this is good ; that is less good ; that is bad ; this is worthy ; that is wretched. Without prejudice I examine the total, never asking myself what his intentions were. Who can swear to another's intentions ? I care less and less for what a person thinks or says that he thinks. When I was younger I wasted much speculation on what theologians call the interior life. It is all *trop de bruit pour une omelette.* There is too much fuss about motives, scruples, doubts, misunderstandings, and so on. Tell me what a man does, and I will tell you what he is. What he did not do, or intended to do, is inconsiderable.

At this point his attention strayed to the balcony where Miss Gloucester was now reading aloud, in a clear voice, to two companions, evidently relatives from their likeness to her and to each other. They were girls of nineteen and twenty-four apiece. One was tall, very elegant, sallow and dark. She seemed languid and kept her melancholy glance fixed on the white clouds of the horizon. The other had auburn hair and a white skin. She sat well in the sunshine, which showed her nose and cheeks almost powdered with small freckles. They were not unbecoming ; the purity of her profile, the thickness of the lashes which darkened her hazel eyes, and her long slender throat were flattered by the bright light.

"Cousins !" thought Felshammer. He strained his ears to catch some words of the book, and recognised, with surprise, a passage from " Peer Gynt." It was Peer's last scene with Solveig :

> *Peer :* Where was I, as myself, as the whole man, the
>   true man ?
> Where was I, with God's sigil upon my brow ?
> *Solveig :* In my faith, in my hope, and in my love.

At the conclusion of the act the sallow girl's eyes filled with tears.

"Poor Solveig!" she said; "how she must have suffered all those years!"

"I won't set up as a critic," said the girl with auburn hair; "but, to my taste, the whole story is mad. No one can save another person's soul. I had a friend who tried to do good that way. She is now an invalid, and her Peer Gynt married a rich widow."

"Because one fails, Leonore, that is no reason why all should fail," said the sallow girl.

"A course of conduct based on sentimentality can never succeed," insisted Leonore. "No amount of sentiment, for instance, will make water shoot out flames or fire turn to ice. Life is equally rational. You must learn natures, and not expect from any what they have not got to give. What do you think, Clementine?"

Clementine waited a moment, stretched out her hands, which were beautiful, and said:

"I don't think."

"But you must have some opinion."

"Not necessarily."

"You observe people, surely?" said Leonore.

"I shouldn't call myself observant. If anything guides me, it is feeling. I feel certain moods and thoughts in the atmosphere. Some atmospheres make me happy, others make me wretched; nothing can make me inquisitive. What is it to me what others say, do, or want to do? I believe in influences, of course. But if Peer was saved, it was because he wished to be saved—and not at all because Solveig tried to save him."

"That's agreeing with me!" exclaimed Leonore. "You can help and encourage a desire; you can't call it up where it doesn't exist. Augusta has such pathetic fancies about life."

Augusta flushed painfully.

"I daresay you are both very clever," she answered; "but I keep seeing Solveig waiting on the hill for Peer to come back. And he came back, and he was sorry, and she sang him to sleep."

"Do you suppose he wasn't bored when he woke up?" said Leonore.

Felshammer, fascinated at first by the three voices, reminded himself that he was eavesdropping, and moved his writing-table further from the window. The girls were certainly uncommon; not at all the bread-and-butter misses, the "English roses" of tradition and domestic novels and the London stage. They had been taught to use their reasoning faculties; they were companionable. He, too, had noticed Clementine Gloucester at the Countess Sophia's funeral, and been struck by her appearance. Had he not persuaded Paul to try the baths at Salsomaggiore solely because he had heard that Miss Gloucester and her father were bound for that watering-place? Despising all superstitions, he had, nevertheless, a few fancies of his own which he took for signs and omens when special wishes

assailed his heart.   It made him smile now to
remember that he had said to himself at the church,
" If she takes the seventh pew from the door, we shall
be married some day."   She chose the ninth pew, and
he had been disappointed to an absurd degree, feeling
downcast all the evening as though he had been
defrauded of something which, by every right, was his.
He had a good position, fair means, and an experience
which enabled him to promise strict loyalty to a girl
worth possessing.   The idea of settling down with a
virtuous partner did not alarm him as it did many
younger men, who, having spent their lives studying
a class of fashionable women but too easy to study,
imagined that they knew the whole sex, and were
justified in holding it contemptible except for amusement.   Once, since the Countess Sophia's death, the
Prince had said—

" If I marry it will make me so old ! "

" The Prince is wrong," thought Felshammer;
" wives are not, as a rule, monsters of egoism, vanity,
foolishness, and mediocrity in all things.   But what
can one expect from his early associations ?   No love
between his parents, no respect.   Unintelligent tear-
fulness on one side, energy running riot on the other.
He would do well to avoid relations with the tender-
hearted.   What a mercy that the poor little Sophia is
dead ! "

While these reflections were passing through his
mind another more vehement spirit within him

was wondering how an acquaintance could most conveniently be brought about with Mr. Gloucester.

"Does he care for books, or politics, or would he sooner discuss his complaint? I will ask him his opinion of Napoleon and Bismarck—there is no quicker way of fixing a man's intellectual pitch. 'Peer Gynt' was an unusual book for a girl to choose. I doubt if she understood half of it."

The room suddenly seemed too small and oppressive for him. He locked away his papers and hurried through the corridor down the stairs into the hall, where the porter happened to be sorting out the mail which had just arrived. Felshammer took up his own budget, sauntered out into the porch, and began to cut, with complete indifference, the various envelopes. One letter, bearing a small pink seal, caught his attention. He drew out the contents, and found it began, "My darling Clem." It was addressed to Miss Clementine Gloucester. Here was a fortunate accident. He would send it to the lady with an explanation of the error. Or should he speak about it? While he hesitated, a small basket-carriage, which, drawn by two ponies, was always on hire for any visitor at the hotel, came up to the entrance, the coachman cracking his whip, the little animals shaking the bells on their harness. In a few moments Mr. Gloucester and two of the young ladies came down, evidently to take a drive round the neighbourhood. Felshammer turned pale, lifted his hat, and

made his best bow. Clementine met this advance
without surprise, and also without acknowledgment.
Her splendid eyes rested for a moment on his as
much as to say : "I am sorry you have made
some mistake. I have not the pleasure of your
acquaintance. I am sure that you have not the
smallest attention of annoying us. But we are
complete strangers."

He remained, however, hat in hand, stammering :

"I beg your pardon ten thousand times. This
letter was among mine. I opened it before I read the
address."

At this she smiled agreeably enough, and assured
him, in a musical voice, that it did not matter in the
least. Felshammer gave Mr. Gloucester his card—an
act which flurried the old gentleman because he had
none in his pocket to offer in exchange, and he had
already recognised the newcomer as a member of
Prince Paul's suite. He expressed a hope that they
might see each other again, and stood twitching with
nervousness and irresolution till Leonore got into the
carriage unaided. Then, murmuring, "Dear me,
I am forgetting the ladies ! We are going for a drive ;
dear me ! " he handed the melancholy girl and his
daughter into the chaise, seated himself with his back
to the ponies, gave an order in good Italian to the coachman, and drove off, just touching the brim of his cap
with one hand. He did not wish his soft white hair
disturbed a second time by the breeze. Felshammer

thought he heard him apologising for a bad cold as the party disappeared from sight. Clementine's presence had given him the greatest delight. Trembling with an indefinable sense of exhilaration, he went back to the hall and studied the register. These were the names copied out in the hotel clerk's large sprawling hand :

Mr. Alfred Gloucester.
Miss Gloucester.
Miss Augusta Romilly.
Miss Leonore Townshend.

A reference to Burke soon explained that the girls were Mr. Gloucester's nieces—daughters of his married sisters, Mrs. Romilly and Mrs. Townshend, wives of English officers—one a Hussar, the other a Guardsman. The head of the family was, it also appeared, a very old man, Sir Wentworth Gloucester, Bart., of Trendlesham Hall, Suffolk. Mr. Alfred was his third son, and had married the only child of a French-American Senator from Baltimore, and by her he had one daughter, the aforesaid Clementine. The family was large and probably poor for its antiquity ; there was also a strange absence of distinguished members either in the diplomatic, political, naval, or military world. County gentlemen who enjoyed a local reputation in the hunting field —such were and had been the Gloucesters from the beginning of the race—some time in the reign of Edward I.

"We cannot find authentic records prior to that date," Mr. Alfred would say, with a gentle grief, which found its only mitigation in the knowledge that it gave a proper example to be so scrupulously truthful in matters of the kind. Mr. Alfred was a very handsome man, very devoted, in a helpless way, to his lovely girl. He was a little afraid of her because every one told him that she was clever, whereas he knew himself to be uncontrollably stupid. But he enjoyed his own stupidity, he thought it a sign of good breeding, and he shone as a star in a small circle of extremely pretty inane young creatures whose husbands allowed him to take them about to plays, picture-galleries, cricket matches, and the like. He was always amused to read in *The World* small paragraphs to the effect that "*Mr. Alfred Gloucester, with his fine patrician features of the old school, was pointing out the successes of the exhibition to Lady Tenneway and Mrs. Keston, the two most beautiful women in the brilliant throng.*" He entertained a little at the Wellington Club and at Ranelagh; had week-end parties in July at his home, Eastern Acres, in the Isle of Wight; spent two months in town every season— stopping at Thomas's Hotel in Berkeley Square, which he grumbled at but liked on the whole. Winter he usually spent abroad. Springs he dreaded. His circle of acquaintances was enormous, and he regarded himself as the happiest of men.

"If a fairy came down the chimney this minute,"

he would say to Clementine, "I shouldn't know what to wish for."

He had been brought up by an old north-country woman, and a belief in fairies was fixed as permanently on his mind as the foolhardiness of cutting one's finger-nails on a Friday.

Clementine had been born in Paris, where her mother, as a schoolgirl, had first met Mr. Gloucester. No one at St. Aelred's had ever seen the lady, but, from her portraits, she had been fair to look at. Clementine's remembrance of her mother was slight, and the influences of her childhood were those of the artists' colony in Paris. She had met in easy fashion nearly every European celebrity at the house of a great painter in the Rue du Bac. Her dream now was to have a home of her own where she could see and hear all that was interesting, all that the newspapers would never print. A delight in knowing secrets, having them, and keeping them was strong in her blood. One secret, however, which concerned her own life had been carefully concealed from her. Mrs. Gloucester was not dead. She had left Mr. Gloucester three years after their marriage to become a dancer of Greek dances illustrative of Theocritus and others. The dancing continued till the lady was past forty, and her renown—as La Belle Valentine—world-wide ; then she retired and lived sumptuously in Vienna as Madame de Montgenays. She never troubled either her husband or her daughter. If La Belle Valentine had hours of bitterness they were not squandered in remorse over any neglected duty. She lived to " keep her figure," and no other consideration ever agitated her mind for long. Reckless, unmoral, self-absorbed, and highly artistic, she was the pride of dressmakers, and the pensioned love of two rich Russians. Clementine always observed the official anniversary of her mother's death, and, when she was at home, decorated daily with pious wreaths the marble tablet to her memory over the family pew at the parish church of St. Aelred's. Gloucester, a man of frivolous mind, had persuaded himself that he was in reality the heart-broken young widower he had played so well after the separation from his wife in 1882. His very greatest friend, Mrs. Sylvester, knew the whole story, and always assumed, nevertheless, with exquisite tact, that Alfred was an inconsolable mourner for the loss of a perfect companion. Clementine, as a little girl, had been a good child with a gay disposition and pretty ways. She could steal on to a knee, and, perched there, sit like a flower on its stem, scarcely moving. She inclined towards caresses, and was fond of touching or stroking or petting those whom she found sympathetic. Yet, with all this, she was known to be somewhat cold—self-sufficient without being ungraciously selfish. Now at two-and-twenty she was well educated, observant, rather sarcastic, and far too impulsive in spite of her calm demeanour. There are two kinds of composure. One is morbid and arises from a feeble or fatigued vitality. It betokens a genuine lack of interest in all things and is the least pleasing form of egoism. The other kind, which is magnetic, is the sign of complete sanity—a heart at peace and a physical organisation without weakness. This last was the composure characteristic of Miss Gloucester. She had never experienced a strong emotion, a violent sentiment, a really unhappy hour. Her face, in spite of its fitful and almost mocking beauty, seemed as unalterable in its lines as some calm portrait by Leonardo da Vinci. By no effort of the imagination would one picture her as older, or tearful, or laughing, or melancholy, or impassioned. What was she thinking of? An unwavering disdain of small ideas shone in in her eyes. Mr. Gloucester was never clever enough or profound enough to wonder how she would have treated the history of La Belle Valentine.

CHAPTER III

CLEMENTINE, on returning from her drive, wrote the following letter to her friend, Miss Ruth Hollemache:

MY DEAR RUTH,—When we left London I heard the birds trying to sing through the fog in St. James's Park. On the night we arrived here the whole sky was filled with stars; it was a June morning by moonlight. Papa said, "Dear Italy!" But he thought the drive from the station to the hotel was far too long.

I hear that Prince Paul has come, or is coming, for the cure. I used to know him rather well when Aunt Emmeline was at Osborne with the Queen. Papa and I stayed with the Bernards at Cowes three years in succession; the Prince was always on the Duke or Naples's yacht. I met him at a lunch given by Mrs. Lorimer. I was about sixteen and very plain, or rather unsettled-looking. I liked him in a dim way, but there was always a certain restraint because of his position, and people ran after him, making themselves very vulgar, I thought. He is handsomer now than he seemed in those days; he is tall and dark, with a pointed chin and cold, hazel eyes. In fact, the eyes are distinctly peculiar. They are almost

24

like onyx eyes in a statue or bust.   The effect is startling.
Papa says that the Prince's elder brother is so sickly and
dissipated that he cannot live, and this one is certain to
make a name for himself even if he is never restored to his
right place in Beylestein.   How interesting it will be to
watch his career from a distance and trace in the actions
of the man the little conversations we had together, as boy
and girl, on history !   Will he be able to carry out any of
his ideals ?   Now that the poor Countess Sophia is dead,
I may say that it was always a certain surprise to me that
she attracted him so much.   She was exquisitely pretty,
of course, and so angelic, and the most perfect dancer I
ever saw ; no one could help loving her, but, dear and
sweet and good as she was, I could never imagine them,
somehow, being real companions.   He was serious and
sombre, whereas she was a delicious sort of talking baby.
You know how Leonore prattles when she is in a fluffy
mood.   Well, the poor Countess was far more childish,
and continually so.   I suppose she amused him.   But
could such an affection have lasted ?   I admit that I do
not understand love.   I find it impossible to get interested
in novels.   They seem to me absurd and unlike life.
Papa is pleased because I do not read them, and he tells
people, I know, how sensible I am.   But am I sensible ?
Am I not rather deficient in sympathy or common feelings ?
When I saw the Prince almost fainting with grief at the
funeral, I could only think, " How very strange ! " and I
merely wished that, if I myself were dead, I could know
that some one mourned as much for me.   This, I assure
you, was my one emotion.   I find something quite inhuman
in the thought now I recollect it at this interval.   And
yet I did see how sad it all was.   Write soon, my dear
Ruth, and believe me,

Yours affectionately,
CLEMENTINE.

After signing this she slept till it was time to dress for dinner. Mr. Gloucester and his party always dined in the restaurant of the hotel, because the *table d'hôte* made his head ache, and he liked especially prepared dishes. Chicken broth, lamb chops, and rice pudding he demanded in every climate. When he entered the restaurant that evening he was overwhelmed to find Prince Paul and Felshammer waiting on the threshold. The Prince's manner was irresistible. Would Mr. Gloucester and the ladies take pity on him and be his guests? He had taken the liberty of counting on their kindness; the table was laid; flowers were placed at each of the five plates; the lights had rose-silk and filigree silver shades. His Royal Highness had begged dear and amiable Mr. Ritz to have some music played by local musicians.

"There may be great talent," said Prince Paul, smiling with delicate irony. He was amazed at Clementine's appearance. She did not seem to him a beautiful girl, but a girl with an undeveloped fascination. "In five years' time," he thought, "she will make mischief!" During the meal His Royal Highness talked incessantly. He was a bad listener at all times, and, although he always caught what was said, he maintained that it was seldom worth catching. He spoke to Clementine of the influence of colour on life.

"In England, for instance," said he, "all rooms

should be as brilliant as you can make them in order to counteract the greyness of your atmosphere. But I don't mean by brilliancy gilding and lustres. I mean Oriental colours—the most vivid greens, reds, blues, pinks, and mauves. Chinese mauve—you know it? Use wood—wood is always beautiful—and have it inlaid with ivory, tortoiseshell, copper, silver, or enamel."

He asked Mr. Gloucester a question about forestry in the British Isles.

"A thing you neglect altogether," he added, before Mr. Gloucester made his timid reply—

"I admire trees very much, sir—an English oak now, or a beech—I have seen beeches in Norfolk which I won't describe lest I should be accused of exaggeration. And in Berkshire there is Savernake! A picnic in Savernake! Clementine has planted some poplars and sycamores at our little place. She likes poplars. They form a protection and they grow quickly. Ah, they are not the poplars of France!"

He was habitually nervous, but during the Prince's conversation he had observed two ladies enter the room and sit down at a table close by. He recognised, by an instinct of terror, the younger of the couple, and nearly sank into a fainting fit. The sense of good manners—stronger in the unhappy gentleman than any emotion—prevented such an accident. Madame de Montgenays was the lady's name, and they had not met for eighteen years. She had altered entirely; the nut-brown hair was now of ebony blackness, her fresh complexion was now artificially white—a very smooth waxen white. She had shining grey eyes and vivid red lips, the upper of which had an elaborate cupid's bow well defined by a brush. She did not appear to be more than five-and-thirty, and her slim, supple figure was still that of an unmarried girl. No corset interfered with her admirable grace of movement; she wore a white lace gown, one row of superb black pearls around her throat, pearls in her ears, and a bunch of heliotrope in her belt. Her companion was elderly, well dressed in silk, and implacable. She spoke in undertones, ate without pleasure, and was the one of the two who took wine. This she appeared to enjoy, although she sipped it with extreme moderation. Mr. Gloucester remained as still as a fallen horse till the dinner came to an end. When the Prince rose, he staggered to his feet (controlled by a lifelong training in propriety) and managed to follow the party from the restaurant into the hall.

Felshammer, who was the last to leave, bowed discreetly to Madame de Montgenays, who gave him a rapid signal. Bowing, he went up to her, shook hands with a certain tenderness and a great demonstration of respect. He hoped that he did not appear to force the latter.

"Tell Mr. Gloucester," said Madame de Montgenays, "that I want to see him. He can get away while they are all listening to that crazy band. My room is No. 61."

Felshammer hid his astonishment, and the lady, showing her excellent teeth, gave him the impression that she was laughing.

"It is not a caprice," she observed; "it is not a case of love at first sight! But he must come. Tell him quietly."

"Which of the three young ladies," said the companion, in a deep voice, "is his daughter?"

"The one who sat at the Prince's right hand," replied Felshammer.

"Is that so?" said Madame Montgenays, exchanging a glance with the other woman. "Is that so? I guessed as much, but I wasn't sure. I heard that her mother was almost ashamed of her when she was little—couldn't bear to have her round."

"She is good-looking enough now," said Felshammer, with resentment.

"She's got some style about her, anyway," said the lady. "Now go and give the old man my message. Break it to him gently."

Felshammer bowed once more and hastened after his Prince. He had decided that La Belle Valentine and Mr. Gloucester were acquaintances of long ago; that, although she was too prudent to wish for an introduction to the daughter, she wanted, in some obscure feminine way, to make matters difficult for the father; an old grudge, a womanish determination to assert herself, no excuse would be too trivial for a person of her type once bent on gratifying vanity or spite. Gloucester had passed her by without the faintest acknowledgment. The secretary shrugged his shoulders, and soon found an opportunity of delivering the message. Gloucester received it without flinching.

"Did she say anything else ? " he asked.

" Nothing else about you. I knew her very slightly. We met once in Milan."

Gloucester seemed relieved, but offered no information. Ten minutes later, when the party were all seated on the Prince's balcony, Felshammer saw him steal away, looking miserable, yet holding his fine head erect, and moving his feet with decision. As he went up the stairs he rubbed his face and his hands with his handkerchief. "The most painful moment of my life," he murmured to himself, "and wholly uncalled for."   Conquering a horrible dread, he knocked at the door of Madame de Montgenay's sitting-room and was instantly admitted by her maid. He had just time to notice that some splendid pieces of old brocade had been thrown over the hotel furniture when his wife came in.

"We needn't shake hands, Alfred," she said at once, conscious enough with perfect good-humour of the aversion he felt to the meeting. "This is a rehearsal of the resurrection. Let us sit down."

Once he had thought her American accent piquant; now it seemed vulgar, odious, rasping. She had always considered him a weak, effeminate creature—

"a pretty boy"; she made no attempt to conceal her scorn.

"If he had only blown somebody's brains out— even mine!" she would say.

"I will tell you right away that I'm not going to bother about Clementine," she said, "but she's certainly a success. I'm real glad. I haven't got the maternal instinct. I don't know why, but I simply haven't, so I won't say that I want her. As for seeing her and saying, 'I am your long-lost parent'— no. I am one of the few women who are poor actresses, and who are still not stagey. I'm as natural and unpremeditated as I ever was. The stage hasn't spoiled me. I loathe scenes. What I want is this— you must clear out of Salso. I'm here on business. My friend, Cobden Duryee, is working out a deal with Prince Paul. Cobden Duryee has known me all my life; he wants me to marry him; he says my record is as good as his, anyway. He's a very wealthy man; he doesn't care two snaps for society, and he's dead in love with me. He thinks I just about win it."

She looked at Gloucester and chuckled kindly:

"If I had a mind to, I could almost make you sue for a divorce. You could get one in the States for incompatibility of temper. He'd marry me."

"Not a divorce so late in the day as this surely," said the wretched man, "for the child's sake. It has been for the child's sake all along."

"I believe in being white," observed the lady,

"and so I am not going to press that point. But I want you to understand that it is a sacrifice on my side. As Mrs. Cobden Duryee I could have a perfectly magnificent time. He adores me; he knows all about me; he only says: 'Val, you don't know enough to go in when it rains! That's been your trouble, my dear child.' I am always a child to Cobden. A man who can talk and feel that way commands a woman's allegiance."

She fastened her glorious eyes on his pale ones, and curled her tinted lips while his trembled.

"What's more," she went on, "he says my soul is the purest he ever met. When other people talk about purity I have to smile. They don't know what the word means. They seem to think it's being dull and driving honest people to the eternal dogs! Well, will you go away to-morrow and take Clementine? It isn't decent—our all being here together. It's making a burlesque of the whole business. Besides, I won't have Cobden mortified. And I must stay whatever happens."

"We'll go," said Gloucester, "we'll go, of course. It's most extraordinary, I'm sure, our meeting in this way."

"Not at all. The wonder is that we don't meet constantly. Have I changed much?"

"Yes," he said, "you have changed. I shouldn't have known you, perhaps. You look very young for your age."

"Don't forget that I'm fifteen years younger than you are. But, it seems to me, you were born tired." She surveyed his delicate, handsome features, his fine clear skin, his white hair perfectly brushed, his slight figure, languid, frail, timid.

"Mercy!" she exclaimed. "Will any one tell me why we married? How did we ever stand each other for one second?"

"I suppose I was attracted by your vivacity. I couldn't pretend to know what you saw in me."

"We didn't even dance well together—it was like a whirlwind and a pond lily! You were considered a good dancer too. I wasn't happy at school—that would account for a good deal. It's too bad, anyhow. We have almost ruined each other's lives."

"Almost?" he repeated, looking up with hatred— "almost? Is anything left of me? I have gone to pieces absolutely. I exist for no one but the child."

"Then I'm glad she was born. That's as true as I'm alive, Alfred. You were always good to me and I haven't a single thing against you. Clementine is going to give you trouble, of course. But I don't think she will cut up. She's the kind that marries three or four times and is a model wife to each one while he lives. There's a steadiness about the square chin. Send me her photograph."

He stood up, walked to the door, bowed.

"We shall leave in the morning," he said; "you shall have a photograph."

4

" Thanks."

And so they parted. Madame de Montgenays went to the looking-glass and practised several expressions — some tender, some vindictive, some haughty.

" Say, Mabel l " she called out.

Her companion, the large lady, came in from the adjoining bedroom.

" Did you hear every word ? " asked Valentine.

" Yes."

" Could I have said more or less ? "

" I never, in my life, met any one with such tact. It was superb ! "

" Pshaw ! Was it ? Well, I didn't prepare a syllable. I just spoke from my heart."

" It couldn't have been better. The tears came into my eyes when you mentioned Cobden Duryee."

" No ? Did I speak so well of him ? "

" Well ? " said Mabel—" well ? Wait till I tell him about it, and see what he thinks."

" Are you going to tell him ? " said Valentine ingenuously. " Had you better ? "

" The idea ! You can bet that I will tell him ! He ought to know how he's appreciated."

" Mabel," said La Belle Valentine, " if it weren't for Cobden I shouldn't be a bit happy—not a bit. I believe I'd pass out. I should just lose my grip. And it isn't because he's rich either. And he's as homely as a mud fence. It's because he understands

me, and never says mean things when he's mad.
He'll get so mad sometimes that he almost kills me,
and yet he has never once—never once, mind you—
said a single thing he might have said. That old
pancake who was here just now doesn't say much,
but he looks at me as though I were mud under his
feet."

"Who cares," said Mabel, "for that silly old fool?"

"I don't," said Valentine; "and I've been
Quixotic about Clementine—absolutely Quixotic!"

"Noble, that's all. Unsurpassed nobility!"

"I can afford to be noble," replied Madame de
Montgenays, drawing herself up. "I have nothing to
lose by it. I don't have to look in an etiquette book
to find out whether I am being noble in the correct
way. I'm individual—I am a personality, thank the
Lord! Now come and brush my hair. I told
Hélène that she could go to bed. It's a mistake to
let her hear so much!"

All this time Clementine and the Prince were
sitting side by side on the balcony while the brass
band played vigorous airs from "Rienzi" and
"Othello." They had exchanged ideas and glances
—long meditative glances which stirred, fascinated,
and absorbed them to the degree where self-consciousness ceases altogether. Their young clear voices
trembled; neither heard with any distinctness what
the other said; her body, without her knowledge,
swayed towards his; his towards hers; the secret

forces of attraction had mastered their wills; they spoke lightly enough, they realised nothing, but the impelling deities were at work in a silent, invincible way.

"I remember you long ago at Cowes," Prince Paul said more than once. "I thought you the strangest little girl—so earnest. You wouldn't dance with me."

"I dance now."

"You scolded me for wasting my time. You said I was too fond of pleasure."

"I must have been impertinent as well as strange!"

"No, I liked it. I always felt happy when I saw you. Once you lent me a book—one of Ruskin's. I was very ungrateful—I didn't read it. In those days, when I read at all, I preferred Zola and Shelley. What a mixture! How absurd people are! But I have decided to lead a life of action; there has been enough literature. Give me Tacitus now and an unexplored country. Let us found an Empire! I ought not to joke about such a serious idea—because I am serious on that subject.

"Why not on all subjects?"

"Most subjects collapse when you make fun of them. Don't you know that? Some day I will tell you my philosophy."

"Can't I hear it now?"

"It would take too long. Besides, I may be wrong,

and I want to be quite sure that I am right before I
try to convert you."

"When will you know that you are right?"

He looked at her and made no reply for several
minutes. She thought he had forgotten her presence.
Then he said :

"Perhaps you may be able to help me. Will you
—if you can?"

"O yes! I suppose it won't be for ages. We
both have to watch things. Then, afterwards, we
can compare notes."

"But why must we wait for ages? I wish you
hadn't said that. I believe in the strength of things
once said."

"You are full of beliefs!"

They both laughed, but he repeated :

"I wish you hadn't made it ages. A year or two
would have been enough!"

When Clementine said good-night and went to her
room she seemed to be moving on wings. The two
other girls ate chocolates in their small *salon* and
discussed the events of the evening, but she locked
her door and sat at her window, looking at the sky
and meeting, in fancy, Paul's eyes again and again.

CHAPTER IV

INCIDENTALLY CONCERNS THE MERITS OF A GOOD FIGURE

MR. GLOUCESTER took a sleeping-powder after his interview with Mme. de Montgenays, and when he awoke the next morning with a numbed brain it was some time before he could remember why he felt miserable.

"Have you got the toothache, Wedge ?" he asked his valet, in the hope of tracing his own depression to something infectious and impersonal.

"No, sir, but Miss Townshend has sprained her ankle. She tripped over some matting."

"Sprained her ankle ? Then we can't leave Salso to-day. It is quite impossible. Send for a doctor. No one can see me till twelve o'clock."

He turned over, and sank again into a doze. La Belle Valentine had already heard of Leonore's accident.

"It is just Alfred's luck," she exclaimed ; "everything always happens for his convenience." But she maintained the good-humour which had helped to keep her cheeks as smooth as porcelain for five-and-forty years. On her return from the bath-house, she met Felshammer.

"Cobden Duryee arrives to-day," she said gaily. "He has got a letter of introduction to you from young Frank Hollemache. Keep a look-out for him. He's a rough diamond, but he can pull every rope in the States."

Felshammer, gazing after her divine figure and admiring her gait, thought it a shame that she was so horridly vulgar. Commonness jarred upon him to a poignant degree that day because he was enjoying a good many fine reflections about Clementine's brow —the sweetest brow, and Clementine's upper lip— that silly, provoking upper lip, and Clementine's voice —that husky, low-pitched, most caressing voice. It was a new recreation to amuse himself by this conscious indulgence in sentimentality. He laughed at his own fancies and improvised little poems which were ridiculously bad. All the same, he was not quite at ease. The saying to oneself a pretty brow is unquestionably pretty, but what of that? what does it matter? is simple. One can repeat it quite often—as often as the brow occurs to the memory or the imagination. To find an adequate reply is the difficulty. What does it matter? It may matter a great deal. He did not mention her name to the Prince. Both men lurked about the hall in the hope

of seeing her, but they heard that Miss Gloucester
was devoting herself to her cousin. She would take
her meals upstairs. The Prince sent her some
magazines with his compliments. He received a
charming note of thanks in reply. This he did not
show to his secretary. Felshammer, black with fury,
began to think the girl an insufferable coquette. It
was hard to like her. Were girls, in any case, ever
interesting? Why did men marry? For a home
and for children, of course (any fool knew that), but it
was never for companionship. "I am a man's man,
after all," he informed himself. "Women bore me.
She would bore me, I believe, if I saw much of her.
I doubt whether she has more than a rather charming
face. It is a charming face! If a mere face could
satisfy one's heart," and so on, and so on. He knew
that this was insincere. Not a word of it had a
genuine thrill. He was suffering from a violent
infatuation—one of those forms of desire which, without warning, enter a stubborn nature, and, without
encouragement, endure. The idea of sanely loving
some appropriate person at a fitting moment was
acceptable enough to him, but to find himself suddenly
jealous of the Prince, driven into rivalship with him,
criticising him with actual malice, was humiliating,
odious, almost painful. If he could have brought his
reason to admit that there was any real danger of a
quarrel—or worse, a gradual estrangement—on the
subject of this girl who had strayed uncalled-for into

their path, he might have found some excuse for demanding a short leave of absence. This danger, however, was just the thing he refused to acknowledge. Already he had reached the stage when a mere sight of the girl herself was infinitely more important than any consideration or claim ; he told himself that he wanted to see now what would happen. Probably nothing, he said, aware that he was trying, by an affectation of indifference, to ward off the cruel disappointment. Prince Paul, on his part, had been fascinated by Clementine, was still fascinated, and took an artist's interest in his own emotions. The normal vanity of the male was flattered, too, in his case, by the girl's evident interest. His temperament quickened under kindness, responding to it as a flute does to a dexterous touch. Felshammer, harsh, authoritative, and loving power over others, was, on the other hand, stimulated by Clementine's indifference. It excited his love of domination ; he would show his mastership ; bend her spirit to his will ; happiness or tenderness in affection was not what he sought ; for him—authority, a right to govern some body and subdue some soul.

Clementine had appeared at a decisive moment. The Prince was becoming rebellious. Felshammer could still manage him to a considerable extent, but the time had passed when the secretary's glance of approval or word of discouragement could influence Paul's actions. The devoted man felt this ; he redoubled, trebled his efforts, and so still carried the day on important points. Yet his pride suffered from the very necessity for these unusual exertions; he foresaw the final equality of wills between the Prince and himself, and, following an instinct rather than any process of reasoning, he sought an opportunity to retire, while in the ascendant, from a position he could not hope to hold. If it was amusing to govern a capricious, clever young man, it was not a dull change at least to bend the humours of a brilliant girl —a girl, plainly, with a career before her.

"I'll do it !" he exclaimed to himself. "I'll marry her. I'll show her that I won't stand any nonsense !"

By chance he saw her crossing the corridor from her own room to Leonore's.

"You look tired," he said brusquely.

"I may look so—I don't feel so," she answered, with a certain annoyance.

"It is a mistake to keep indoors on such a day."

"I like to make mistakes—they rest me."

"That is because you are perverse. But I am perverse too. We ought to agree."

"We don't," she said firmly; "we could never agree. Any agreement between us is not to be imagined."

"That does not dismay me in the least."

"Why should it ? " she asked, beginning to detest him. Fear was not in her character, or, without feeling any repugnance for the individual, she might have been afraid of a determination stronger than her own.

"I am sorry," exclaimed Felshammer, with his eyes fixed on her beautiful brow, "you don't understand me."

"Why should I? I don't know you. I believe I shall say something rude in a minute. You ought to feel that we cannot get on at all."

"I never feel as I ought."

She wished, or thought that she wished, to join Leonore without any further delay. But she did not move; she studied his face and noticed characteristics which in another man of better manners she might have respected.

"Your frankness is magnetic," he said. "I have never met anything of the kind in a woman. It is boyish—little-boyish—for one finds it in very few men. It means such courage."

"I must say," she admitted, "that if there is one thing I despise it is social tact. But courtesy is another matter."

Felshammer on all occasions had one natural gift in his favour—this was a courteous voice. The abruptness of his conversational method found its mitigation always in his persuasive and musical tones. Uncouth as he seemed to Clementine, she could not think him impertinent. But she passed him at last, and, entering Leonore's room, closed the door sharply behind her.

"Why were you so long?" asked Leonore, who

was stretched out on the bed while a maid brushed her auburn hair.

"I met that Dr. Felshammer," replied her cousin; "he's a bear."

She repeated all he said, adding: "It's so intimate, and I hardly know him. I must teach him his place."

"What is his place?" said Leonore.

"He's a chance acquaintance. I don't want to know what he thinks of my frankness, do I? I am not interested in his opinion of me, am I?"

"Why should you be?" exclaimed Leonore.

Women of scrupulously truthful nature ask rhetorical questions when they cannot or will not admit a fact. The two girls stopped talking about Felshammer and discussed the Prince. Leonore called him handsome. Clementine said she did not admire him in that sense. But he was, of course, a good-looking man.

"Very original, too, I should say," observed Leonore.

"Dreamy," suggested Clementine.

"Not altogether dreamy either."

Then they tried to define the especial peculiarities of temperament conveyed by the term dreaminess.

"Perhaps dreamy was not the best word," said Clementine at last.

"I wonder whether he is capable of a great love?" said Leonore.

Clementine, with unconscious hypocrisy, tried to think that this was a point she had not yet considered.

" Psychology is so interesting," continued Leonore, " and I could speculate about a character for hours."

Encouraged by this scientific attitude in her companion, Clementine made a few remarks to the following effect :

" I think that the Prince believes himself to be independent of other people. The love of freedom is so strong in him that he would resent any human affection which might interfere with his liberty. He would always fight his own feelings, and live, as far as possible, by reason alone. I see this plainly. Intellect is his idol, and his soul is quite frigid towards everything else. He is all but heartless."

" And yet you like him ! " said Leonore.

Clementine met her eyes gravely.

" For his spirit," she replied ; " for his hatred of pretence."

" I think it is for his figure," said Leonore.

" Other men have figures."

" Rarely such a good one."

Clementine made no hurried contradiction. She walked to the window, and, as it happened, Paul was walking on the road toward the town.

" I daresay there is something in your idea," she owned ; " one is influenced, of course, by the shell."

She watched him out of sight, being too simple to move away when she was so entirely pleased to remain.

" Let me know," said Leonore, " when you don't like him any more."

"I shall always like him," replied Clementine, with decision—"always. Nothing could make the slightest difference."

"Suppose he had his leg shot off and his nose broken?"

"I shall always see him as he is now."

"That is the right thing to say, I know," answered Leonore; "but is it the true thing?"

"I wouldn't say what I didn't feel if it were ever so right. This isn't because I am too honest to pretend. I am merely too lazy to act," she added hastily. "I want to be myself in peace, and I don't care whether I am inconsistent or not—that isn't half so bad as being uncomfortable."

Augusta joined them then, and Clementine went back to her own room, where she could brood without interruption over her recollections of Prince Paul.

Paul, meanwhile, was making the acquaintance of Mr. Cobden Duryee. The American financier was a tall lean man with a florid complexion, a harsh black moustache, eyes that glanced swiftly, lips that moved slowly, and a jaw which seemed made of cast iron covered with parchment. Paul noticed his admirable hands and feet, his perfectly-cut clothes. He spoke with a slight New York accent, and had the manner of one accustomed to make his own terms in every circumstance of life. After a short conversation Duryee came at once to the point.

"I want your Royal Highness to settle for a while in the States—not as a social figure, but as a man of affairs. I have spent the last three months in Urseville-Beylestein. It is a fine country, but when the science of economics and commerce degenerates into the game of politics the era of decadence usually is recognised. Your people have ceased to feel the dignity of work ; they hanker after officialism, empty distinctions, little posts, the praise of the press. It has ceased to be a nation—it is a large parish controlled by little ideas."

"My poor country !" exclaimed the Prince.

"You can't save it," said Duryee, "and it is quite contented. Journalists are writing up the scenery and buying railroad shares. It will soon be a paradise for hotel-keepers and bead-sellers. The valley peasants have started a bead industry already—a Jew from India is giving them points—and the hill population are taking lessons in folk-songs from a Berlin singing-teacher — for the summer season. They are also building a gambling saloon in order to attract a bright crowd. Beylestein, in fact, is coming along splendidly. All the best couriers have taken it up. No, sir, I wouldn't bother about Beylestein if I were you. The old notions about monarchy were great—simply great, but they are as dead as Alexander. You must start fresh. Come and manage one of my steel foundries. I have no children ; it's just as well, for I am a con-firmed neuropath, and I have suffered from insomnia, depression, and dyspepsia ever since I was thirty. But I am a very rich man. I should like to build one beautiful city—and I want a king for it—a Doge, a born one. Think it over."

Not knowing what to make of his singular new friend, the Prince said:

"This news about the bead-making and the railroads interests me very much. Do tramways run through the lovely valley of the Dormer?"

"Not yet. But a syndicate from Vienna has bought the whole valley—there was one proprietor only who refused to sell his estate. He owned about five acres on the best site, and he kept them for an old charger who carried your father on his last ride through the capital. He wanted to bury that horse where the view caught the rising sun. His neighbours thought him sentimental. So did the syndicate. Well, the horse was poisoned, and the sentimentalist met with a queer kind of an accident on a lonely road. He didn't recover. Don't ever worry about Beylestein. I see life the way animals do, sir : to them it is very pleasant or very disagreeable, but never comic. That's the sole reason why I can't laugh over the development of Urseville-Beylestein."

Paul stretched out his hand toward an emerald and copper cigarette box, pushed it in the direction of the millionaire, and by a gesture indicated the polite hope that Mr. Duryee would smoke. He found it impossible to speak, because he remembered the old charger.

He had a white star on his forehead and he answered
to the name of Charmides.

"Your father was a king," said Duryee, putting a
cigarette into his mouth, but rejecting, mournfully, a
light ; "mine was a Presbyterian minister way up in
the country. You can't forget His Majesty, and I
don't forget the Doctor. He used to pray for me
every evening at half-past nine. Well, every evening
at half-past nine, sure enough, I begin to feel lone-
some, and, in a way, home-sick. But I struck out in
a new line although I had five ancestors in the
ministry. I said to father at the end of my first year
at Yale : 'This has got to stop.' He said : 'What,
my son ?' I said : 'I'm a financier. Everything in
me pulls that way. I want to work in an office.'
The old man was disappointed at first, because he had
it all fixed up that I should be a minister too, and
finish his edition, with notes, of the Prophet Amos.
He slept on my statement, however, and came down
smiling the next morning. 'Go ahead,' said he, 'it
may be that the Lord has employment for you in
Wall Street. Your mother thinks it's about time for
one of the Duryees to make money.' And she was
right, sir. Now, why can't you follow my lead ?
Start something new. People talk about merchant
princes. Be a prince merchant."

Paul removed a ladybird which had settled on the
sleeve of his coat and put it outside the window on a
fruit-leaf. This took time, because the leaf had to be

5

taken from a dish of peaches on the sideboard. Paul ordered peaches all the year round. Duryee watched each of his graceful, languid movements, and finally caught Felshammer's eye. Felshammer had been present during the whole interview.

"Ladybird, ladybird, fly away home.
Your house is on fire ; your children will burn !"

said the American, with religious solemnity in his tone and resentment in his glance. He felt that Felshammer disliked him.

"Are you serious?" asked Paul, watching the insect.

"What about?" said Duryee, equally indifferent.

The Prince, piqued by Duryee's change of tone, showed more vivacity, and said :

"The American proposition."

"Oh, that !" replied Duryee, with good-humour. "I was serious enough about it. I never go crazy."

"I want to hear more," said the Prince ; "it isn't altogether a project in the vein of comic opera !"

"First, you ought to work in a lawyer's office for two years. I am a lawyer myself by profession. How can any man get along unless he knows technical right from technical wrong ? The old Romans understood education. Law is the essence of it."

Paul threw back his head, straightened his shoulders,

and then sat on the edge of the table, supporting himself on his hands while he looked Duryee in the face.

"You want me to renounce Urseville-Beylestein ? Felshammer is appalled."

Duryee accepted this information with a slow movement of the jaw as though he were testing his powers of mastication.

"Dr. Felshammer has the European's dread of Americanitis. He forgets that we get our worst characteristics from the discontented, ill-used European who goes to the New World for a chance to breathe. He brings with him a good many crude, possibly vulgar notions—the result of oppression, injustice, suffering, and the abuse of authority in high places— the contempt of the well-to-do for the shabby unfortunate. But such poor devils are not American— although they may tinge American life and thought."

He rose to his feet ; the Prince accompanied him to the door of the room and, fascinated by his personality, walked with him down the corridor to the lift. Felshammer followed them, biting his nails as he went and full of forebodings.

La Belle Valentine was waiting impatiently for Duryee's call. When at last he tapped at the sitting-room door and called her name she forgot that she was graceful by profession ; she tripped over a foot-stool and saved herself from a fall by permitting him to catch her in his arms.

"Why, Cobden," she exclaimed, "is that you? O say, Mabel, it is Cobden!"

She shed tears of real joy; she gazed at his iron and parchment face with the rapture of a girl admiring the heroic ideal of a first love.

"How young you keep!" observed the financier. "You don't change a bit, do you, Val?"

"Never for you," she said. "I couldn't fool you anyway."

"That's why you like me," he said grimly.

"Of course."

She sat at his feet; she wound her arm round his knees.

"This," she remarked, "is my idea of perfect happiness. I was afraid you wouldn't get here. I worried. Don't you ever go back on me, Cobden, because I could not stand it. Have you seen the Prince?"

He repeated a little of their interview.

"What do you think of him? Is he a superior Willy Wimble?" she asked.

"He must meet some men of the right sort," said Duryee. "I think he has seen enough of women for the present. He wants a bracing environment."

"You funny old thing! You don't want him to meet me!"

Duryee stroked his own chin, and then patted, very softly, her charming shoulder.

"You have missed it, pettie," said he; "he can meet

you as often as he has a mind to.   You are intelligent;
you have sized up the value of most things.   I mean
he has seen enough of silly women."

"Lucie arrives this afternoon."

"So I understand."

"You know," she said presently, "that Clementine
and her father are here?"

Every reference to Mr. Gloucester invariably made
Duryée speechless.   A strong sense of justice kept
him always aware that Valentine's husband had been
altogether ill-used.   He did not like him ; he had
called him a "dude" some time before that word
came into general fashion as an epithet for the agreeable foolish among well-born men.   But, although a
"dude," Gloucester had shown unusual loyalty toward
his wife, and his touching, if timorous, affection for
the child had thrown her mother's selfishness into a
light beyond the reach of any softening haze.   The
financier could explain La Belle's conduct on reasonable grounds—she lacked the maternal instinct, and,
granting this defect, it was a merit, he thought, that
the flattery-loving creature, quite conscious of an unsympathetic failing, affected no sentiment she did not
feel.   Nevertheless he sighed when she mentioned
Clementine.   It reminded him of the irremediable
blot on his idol.   Why did she call his attention to
it ?   Couldn't she understand how it jarred ?   And
she did understand ; she was neither tactless nor blind.
But she longed greedily, with an incessant desire, to

be loved for herself as she was, in spite of all her faults, in spite of her history, in spite of a nature, to its depths, unlovable. This was her triumph over life and her joy in living. Cobden knew her temper, her vices, her age to the hour of her birth, the many changes of her hair, the variations of her wonderful complexion ; he knew everything, and still he adored her.

"You can't beat it," she would say to Mabel. "I want to ask every woman who is mean to me and thinks herself winning it all along the line : 'Tell me this—does your husband know you as well as the Devil knows you ? Would he love you just the same if he did ? Answer me that.' I want to see just how I stand and where I stand. I want to be sure of my ground."

Duryee glanced round the sitting-room, noticed the pile of theatrical newspapers from all parts of the world, the countless photographs signed of royal and other personages, of famous "stars" in their most popular *rôles*, of himself in cap and ulster, in evening clothes, in fancy dress as François Premier, in a golfing suit.

"It looks home-y, doesn't it ? " she said, delighted.

CHAPTER V

TWO WAYS OF SPENDING AN EVENING

FELSHAMMER did not attempt to vindicate his antipathy for Duryee. He owned that the man was genuine, but he held that genuineness in the wrong direction was far more dangerous than insincerity striving, by means of histrionics, for the noble course. Yet when Prince Paul asked his opinion of the financier, he found himself understating his objections to their new acquaintance. He wound up by admitting : "I admire him. He is as hard as nails." When he left Paul he realised that, so far from remaining at any rate neutral, he had strongly encouraged the American's influence. It was vain to blink facts. He wanted the Prince to leave Europe; he found him, for the first time, in his way.

"He will dazzle that young girl. Naturally enough, she will feel flattered by his notice. He cares nothing about her ; once his vanity is gratified she may jump into the first pond or spend her youth

forgetting him—if she can. He will say—and the
whole world will say : 'She ought to have known that
it was hopeless.' In theory we all think alike on
these points—extenuating circumstances occur to us
only when we care for the individual or individuals at
stake."

Thus he analysed his own mood, but as he possessed
robust health in conjunction with a highly-trained
self-consciousness the fact that he knew why he said
and thought certain things in no degree disturbed, as
it does in many reflective temperaments, the ultimate
execution of his ideas in action. The suddenness of
his passion for Clementine now seemed to him normal,
pre-ordained, and unalterable. A man must settle
down ; a man worthy his sex .must have a hearth,
whether happy or the reverse ; once pleased, he must
be determined in courtship, concentrating on the
business as a life and death-bed affair. Clementine,
legally secured, could then take her share in his
existence, making his mental, spiritual, and physical
interests—now scattered curves—into a perfect circle.
Did not the wedding-ring symbolise this mystic fusing,
by the spell of wifely love, of the separated elements
in human nature ? " Clementine suits me " was the
conclusion of this transcendental soliloquy. A sincere
lover of poetry, he became sentimental too, and
" Clementine suits me " also summed up the many
metaphors by which nightingales, roses, spring,
blossoms, and the moon did their usual service for the

translation of primitive decisiveness into picturesque uncertainty.

When he next met the Prince he called his attention to the beauty of a young person who sat with La Belle Valentine and her companion at a table near them in the Restaurant.

"Duryee has asked me to supper this evening," said Paul. "I hope La Belle will be there."

"He and his party clash with the Gloucesters," observed Felshammer carelessly ; "it is a pity that they are all here together."

Paul looked again at the young person. She seemed about five-and-twenty. Although she had very curling flaxen hair and dark-blue eyes, there was something so indolent underlying her evident vigour, such a curious vivacity in the full mouth and the movement of the nostrils, that, in spite of an almost classic profile, she suggested irresistibly an African type. She displayed her teeth, which were dazzling, when she talked, but her heavy eyelids seemed oppressed by a constant need of sleep, and she kept them half-closed the greater part of the dinner.

"She might be an allegorical design for Sloth," said Paul. But he was interested because she was uncommon and indifferent to his presence. The head-waiter was asked to discover her name. It was found that she was Mme. de Montgenay's guest and had been described in the register as the Hon. Mrs. Basil Hollemache.

" It must be our Hollie's sister-in-law," said
Felshammer.   " I remember that his brother made an
odd marriage."

The Prince could find nothing better to offer than :
" How small the world is ! "

" I remember Hollie's telling me that Basil took up
with some mysterious girl whom he met most
informally at Naples.   At Naples, sir !   This must
be she."

" What was Basil?   Where is he now ? "

" He has suffered all his life from religious mania,
and so they gave him the family living.   He is now
in a Home."

" I wonder," said the Prince, " whether she has
anything to say for herself.   She doesn't look
stupid."

" There is a rumour, according to Hollie, that her
father was Lord M——."   He mentioned the name
of a well-known diplomatist.   Paul was more amused
than ever, and Felshammer, from long knowledge of
his character, did everything possible to stimulate his
curiosity.   Clementine was not once mentioned.
With the Prince little flickers of love blazed up and
went out in a day.   It had always been to the interest
of the exiled court to encourage this illuminative, if
fickle, temper ; caprices he might enjoy to his heart's
content, but the fairly durable ascendancy of any one
woman was something which his supporters could
not permit without strenuous opposition, or con-

template without the bitterest misgivings. In the sporting art of substituting at precisely the crucial moment one dangerous alluring study for another Felshammer had proved himself an unprejudiced and supreme tactician. Unprejudiced because he had never once been actuated by an egoistic motive, and supreme because he had never yet failed to accomplish his purpose. But now his judgment, for the first time, trembled with personal feeling; he was so anxious for success that Paul, curiously sensitive to all emotional under-currents, became irritable and perverse.

"I am getting sick of this place!" he said abruptly. "I shall either go on to Florence or visit America with Duryee."

As he spoke he looked from the corner of his eye at Felshammer, and in that flash of distrust, not missed by the secretary, a silent antagonism sprang into life between them. It affected the Prince with a kind of cynical wretchedness. He had been disappointed so often in human nature that a lost illusion seemed to him but a commonplace of daily experience.

"He, too, has at last an axe to grind," passed through his head. "I wonder what it is? Has Duryee got hold of him?"

He continued acting, but talked more pleasantly, discussing the news of the day and making caustic jokes about his advisers in Urseville-Beylestein. After dinner he went to the millionaire's private apartments,

arid did not ask any member of his suite to accompany
him.

Felshammer seized the opportunity to inquire about
Miss Romilly. He went himself to the door of the
Gloucesters' sitting-room, and was asked to join the
party at whist. The game bored him, but Clementine,
looking sad, he thought, was there, and he did not
hesitate to accept the invitation. No one seemed in
a mood to play. Augusta could watch herself in a
little glass near the table, and this kept her amused
for the first round. Presently, however, she began to
yawn. Mr. Gloucester, weary after his excitement
of the previous evening, could not keep his eyes open,
and trumped his partner's king.

Felshammer accepted with stoicism this glimpse of
a traditional evening in the home-circle. It was
cheerfully endured as a necessary part of the courtship
of Clementine. The girl was too intelligent to
suppose that he could have found the smallest entertainment with her father, even at his brightest, and,
although she was the last as a rule to detect attentions
offered to herself, there was a fire in the secretary's
eyes and restrained ardour under his calm hearing
which she could not ignore.

Outwardly she could and did appear unconscious,
yet within she resented his admiration, quivered under
it with a sensation of fear, with a desire to escape,
with an instinct that his love was kind but his power
sinister. The game went on—Felshammer, with the

disadvantage of a reluctant partner and a bad hand, was winning most of the tricks. He smiled at Clementine once and she felt herself turn pale. She had never before come into contact with any dominating, resolute, and passionate disposition ; her relatives and intimate friends had all been people who were violent, if they ever were violent, in their tempers only—in squabbles with lawyers, servants, and each other, but their affections were mild and domestic, their wills grumbling but never invincible, their tastes could be removed by argument, their desires suppressed or concealed at the first whisper of an acknowledged authority. She knew herself no match for determination of the uncompromising Teutonic mettle ; a weight fell on her heart, she was unable to think or to feel ; a numbness came over her whole being, and she followed the game mechanically, as much dazed by Felshammer's peculiar influence as though she had taken heavy wine. At ten o'clock they had finished the rubber.

"One keeps such early hours at dear Salso," observed Mr. Gloucester, with an apologetic voice and an air of saying good-night.

"Where is your Prince ? " said Augusta, rubbing her eyes. She was altogether sure that Felshammer took no interest in her or her appearance, and she asked the question with instinctive malice.

"He is playing poker, perhaps, with Mr. Duryee and Madame de Montgenays," said the secretary,

watching Clementine.   He missed, therefore, the
look of agony which passed over Gloucester's now
livid face.

"Mme. de Montgenays is the beautiful lady, isn't
she?" said Clementine—"the one who sat at the
little table?   I should like to know her."

Her father tried to think of something to say—
something to change the subject. But his tongue
clave to the roof of his mouth, and he sat twirling his
shaking thumbs and wondering what he had done to
deserve such misery at his time of life.   And he began
to associate Felshammer with the misery in question.
He had brought him the hateful woman's message;
he had just dragged in her name most unnecessarily—
a person, in any case, who ought not to be so much
as hinted at in the presence of his innocent girl.   The
girl, too, by a fatal accident, was standing at an angle
when the resemblance to her mother—all but im-
perceptible to strangers—was terribly clear to the
nervous old man.   What could he do?   Clementine
began to praise Mme. de Montgenays; she looked
fascinating—who was she?   Every one in the hotel
seemed to know about her.   They waited about the
corridor and in the hall to see her pass.

"She is called La Belle Valentine," said Augusta;
"she used to dance.   Barker told me."

Barker was their maid.

"I wish you wouldn't talk to servants and people!"
exclaimed Mr. Gloucester, finding his voice; "it's a

shocking habit. You are not to do it! If Barker comes gossiping to you, I will give her notice."

Augusta made no reply, but she managed to say under her breath to their guest : " Dear uncle is not himself this evening. He is never like this."

" But he is right, all the same," replied Felshammer. Mr. Gloucester's fit of exasperation had given a note of intimacy to the talk which the secretary was not slow to emphasise. He sat down and gave his views about the management of servants as though he had been appealed to, as a near relative at least, to support the head of the family. It was half-past ten before he left them, and, although they all felt relieved at his departure, Clementine, when the door closed upon him, was conscious of a flatness in the atmosphere and a loneliness in the room.

Prince Paul, meanwhile, had spent his time in a very different manner. Mr. Duryee's small party were in brilliant spirits. La Belle Valentine, being entreated, actually danced a cake-walk to Mrs. Hollemache's accompaniment, in sparkling style, on the banjo. But this rare entertainment took place towards midnight, after several games of poker and a good many delicious cock-tails prepared by the sympathetic Mabel. What makes an evening gay? Is it the talk? an accident of temperature? the actual company? On this particular occasion everything seemed perfectly delightful. The room had been transformed by glorious stuffs, bowls of flowers,

exquisitely bound books, splendid trifles in silver and
bronze and gold, rare pieces of china. Mr. Duryee
always included a number of such things in his
luggage ; a wandering man, he liked to invest hired
apartments with as personal an air as private property
could give them. La Belle Valentine was on her
best behaviour. Paul, as the hours advanced, found
himself believing in her innocence ; such liquid
eyes, such fine chiselled lips, such a subdued, all but
reproachful smile, such a tranquil brow, surely went
with potential if misunderstood virtue ? And Lucie
Hollemache ? She was so assertive in her mysterious
languor, so pleasant in her idleness, so uncritical in
her slow, affectionate glance. She was one of the few
women whose faces do not look sad or perplexed in
repose. Animation, in fact, did not suit her, and
when she laughed the effect was unnatural, even disfiguring. While she played the banjo, her features
were lit up by some curious emotional power from
within—just as a flame or any number of flames will
show through tinted glass. The flames may move
and vary, but the glass remains changeless. In conversation she showed a dry, rather subtle humour ;
but silent by preference, she said little and listened
admirably. Duryee told stories, and at poker showed
his knowledge of human character by winning the
Prince's money. Paul played a good game, and in
beating him Duryee used all his wits—which pleased
the young man. He could be won by the homage of

the brain—never by the agency of a cheque-book. Perhaps this was why he enjoyed that evening with peculiar zest. His companions treated him less as a social superior than an intellectual one. They led him on to talk, weighed his words, and were openly impressed by the force of much that he said. But how gracefully it was done! Sometimes one or the other ventured to differ from him. Duryee protested that he would have to think over this idea, get at the bed-rock of certain propositions, see how some scheme worked out in practice. It was all very stimulating, and, when at length they had to say good-night, Paul resolved that he should see a great deal more of these new acquaintances. They were such a change after exhausted, fussy, time-serving courtiers. As for Clementine or the dear Countess Sophia, they never once came into his remembrance. Darlings both, no doubt, but experience had to be gained. He found out from a member of his suite that Felshammer had spent the evening with the Gloucester party.

"Poor fellow!" said he, in fits of laughter: "I feel for him. I can't imagine anything duller on earth."

The conversation between the several ladies who had contributed to the events, tedious and otherwise, of that night was not insignificant.

Augusta sat at the foot of Clementine's bed and studied her serious face.

"Do you think you will sleep well, Clem?" she asked.

"No," said truthful Clementine; "I take too much interest in my friends to be happy when I know that mischief is brewing."

"What mischief is brewing now?"

"Why did Prince Paul go alone without Felshammer to Mr. Duryee and those women? I saw that Mrs. Hollemache—she's handsome and horrid."

"Then the Prince won't like her."

"O, yes, he will! Men will forgive any fault in a person so long as she can make a meal pass pleasantly. They don't want wonderful characters— they like people who are civil at dinner."

"How do you know that?"

"I feel it all over me."

"Do you like Felshammer better than you did at first?"

"Not a bit better. Yet he is far more trustworthy than Prince Paul—far more faithful. Doesn't that show that it isn't character always? It is something else, something indefinable."

"I see," said Augusta slowly, "why you seem to understand men—you judge them by yourself."

"I'm sleepy now," observed Clementine. But her cousin, on leaving the room, noticed several books on the bed. As she stood on the threshold, she looked back and asked:

"Why are you studying guide-books?"

"I want to get away. I want to go to Florence. I want to look at pictures. I am tired of people."

Augusta closed the door softly and went away smiling. She was engaged to a good-looking, clever chivalrous young man in the Treasury—an old Blue, one who had taken high honours, a marvel. Clementine, dear impossible Clementine, was too eccentric and uncertain to attract the men who made, undoubtedly, the best husbands. Augusta, once locked in her own little room, kissed the edifying photograph of Mr. Jim Hazeltine, L.LD., F.S.S., put his last precious letter under her pillow, undressed, and said her prayers —mentioning Jim several times disguised under various interests, and expressing a hope, in conclusion, that poor Clementine might learn to be happy in a reasonable way with a suitable individual.

La Belle Valentine and Lucie were more laconic.

"What do you think of Prince Paul?" asked Valentine. "He isn't a patch on Cobden, of course."

"He has brains," said Lucie, "and he's magnetic."

"Mercy! I don't think he's got a particle of magnetism. Now Cobden——"

"Cobden, my dear," said Lucie, "is not the be-all and end-all of everybody's existence. He's superb, but there are others!"

Valentine smiled good-naturedly and patted her friend's shoulder.

"You can have them," she replied; "I'm willing."

CHAPTER VI

MRS. BASIL HOLLEMACHE before her marriage had moved a great deal in sporting and gambling circles under the protection of her parents, Captain and Mrs. Gaveston. The gallant Captain was a gentleman who had left his regiment under painful if obscure circumstances. One heard rumours of a conspiracy, and complaints to the effect that, without money, slander could not be fought to the bitter end. He had kept a certain number of friends, however, and it came to be assumed among most people that he could say a good deal if he chose, and had been made, very cruelly, a scapegoat. " But for my son, my wife, and my daughter—" he would observe, shaking his head with the agony of thoughts too appalling to be formulated. For the rest, he drank to excess, although he never appeared intoxicated. His life was a state of chronic torpor. Handsome in his youth, he dyed his hair before he was forty, put on stays, and curled his moustache with the tongs. Some one had bought

him a decent annuity, he paid as he went (to use his
own phrase), his wife enjoyed a separate but more
indefinite income, his son received an ample allowance
from some mysterious trustees, and they all lived
together on the kindest terms in Savile Row.   Rents
in Savile Row were not at that time what they are
now, but the address was a capital address, all the
same, and the house was frequented quietly by well-
known persons, chiefly of the male sex, from every
class of society.   Mrs. Gaveston's little dinners and
suppers, followed by singing, gossip, cards (in which
the Captain could never be prevailed on to take a
hand), were much appreciated even by those who, it
might be thought, had the world and its best amuse-
ments at their feet.   Lord Munalley, P.C., K.P.,
G.C.B., &c., would now and again figure at these
simple entertainments, and bring little Lucie sweets
(but, naughtily, he could seldom remember her name),
and delight the heart of little Charlie with rare foreign
stamps, beautiful crests for his album, and shining
coins fresh from the Mint.   Whenever Lord
Munalley called he was invariably unexpected.   Mrs.
Gaveston, who was interesting rather than pretty, with
irregular features and raven hair brushed straight back
from a low brow, would advance gravely, saying :
"You are indeed a stranger !"   But these happy
days and evenings did not last.   When Lucie and
Charlie reached respectively the ages of sixteen and
fourteen they found themselves orphans.   Lord

Munalley, too, passed away—he was an old man
long before the children knew him. The dear com-
fortable house in Savile Row was let ; its treasures
were sold, and Lucie, with her brother, had to regard
Messrs. Gregory, Hawkins, Hawkins, and Palmer, of
Lincoln's Inn, as her guardians. The head of the
firm informed her that, in accordance with the wishes
of his late client, Charlie should finish his schooling at
Eton, and proceed to Oxford, where it was hoped he
would qualify for a good position later on at the Bar.

"You," he continued, looking thoughtfully at
Lucie and comparing her mentally with a certain
early portrait (by Lawrence) of Lord Munalley,
"you"—and his voice softened as he traced the
undeniable curves of a genuine Munalley nostril—
"you, my dear Miss Gaveston, may travel, if you
like, with a companion. I can recommend several
ladies for such a post. There is, for instance, Miss
Travers, the daughter of the late Dr. Travers, an
eminent man in his own profession. As for finishing
your education—every young lady, no matter how
gifted, must of course be finished—you can have the
best masters."

"And my allowance ? " asked Lucie.

"Your allowance," said he, looking at his notes,
"will be seven hundred a year—exclusive of your
companion's salary and expenses. When you are
one-and-twenty you are to have a thousand a year.
It is strictly tied up," he added ; "the capital can't

be touched. Your brother will have exactly the same fortune—to a penny—and on the same conditions."

"Dear papa!" said Lucie, with swimming eyes. She had always been honestly attached to Captain Gaveston. "Dear papa! Who would have thought he was so business-like?"

Mr. Gregory simpered, and the interview came to an end. Lucie eventually went to Italy with Miss Travers, but they could not agree, and Miss Travers was supplanted by a Baroness von Trier. The Baroness was a lady who wrote an admirable letter. On paper she was the most prudent, the most austere of women. Messrs. Gregory, Hawkins, Hawkins, and Palmer felt that she conducted her correspondence with them on model lines; she became their ideal pattern of female intelligence. Her photograph, too (sent from Heidelberg), gave the best possible impression. She was tall, spare, agreeable in visage, white-haired (she had borrowed a *toupée* from her mother for the sitting). They engaged her for their ward, and no girl could have fallen under a worse influence. In the first place, she was wholly frivolous. Passionate natures make mistakes frequently, come to ruin not seldom, but flippant people have often a great deal of shrewd sense in the conduct of life. Their hatred of peril and pain makes them instinctively far-seeing. The Baroness was judicious, therefore, in this calculating way. Without the borrowed *toupée* she looked about thirty-seven. Her hair was sandy and she had a look of Dürer's *Eve*. From morning till night she poured her silly experience and sharp counsel into Lucie's ears. The two trapesed through Europe (no one could get better value for her money than the Baroness) ; they stopped always at first-class hotels, and made the best sort of acquaintances only.

"Rich vulgar people won't think us worth while or smart enough," she would say ; "our chance is with *la crème de la crème* only—those who are too sure of themselves to be snobs."

At Naples, when Lucie was nineteen, they came across the Dowager Lady Hollemache, who was there with an invalid son. He was at death's door ; the unhappy mother was too glad to have his last hours soothed by Lucie's faultless sympathy ; the Baroness read him bits from Heine and the whole of Goethe's "Hermann and Dorothea." The poor young man was a good German scholar, and many feared that he had overtaxed his brain by a too profound devotion to Teutonic metaphysic. His manner, talk, and gaze at times were very wild. But he liked Lucie ; presently he needed her ; finally he swore he would marry her. He got better ; he cursed and raved at the Dowager ; he seized her chaplain—an inoffensive good soul who followed her ladyship everywhere—by the shoulders and thrust him from his room, shouting : "I'll soon show you whether I am dying !"

Such monstrous behaviour could not be kept a

secret from the other inmates of the hotel. As the
chaplain murmured, it was the general opinion that
such a dangerous character ought to be locked up.
Who could wish to read of the tears, expostulations,
threats, insults, and abuse which formed the overture
to Lucie's married life? For, of course, after his
mother cut him off with two hundred a year, the
romantic Miss Gaveston married him. He got rid of
the Baroness—which was a wise move—although the
lady declared that but for her efforts he could never
have found a wife to pay his bills or support his vile
disposition. The young couple were together for
three years. They were really attached to each
other; no cross word ever passed between them;
Lucie's conduct was impeccable, and Basil had no
reason to regret his passionate choice. Yet, such is
the irony of appearances, that in spite of their great
and genuine affection, the unfortunate man fell a
victim at last to his constitutional melancholy, and
the poor wife—still a girl in years—was blamed by
every member of the family for a collapse which had
been inevitable from the beginning. If anything had
delayed the blow or given the afflicted man an idea
of normal human joys it was the time he spent with
Lucie. But the Hollemaches were too glad to find
an excuse for their relative's mania, and, when it
became common knowledge that Basil was under
the care of two keepers at a Home, rumour, on the
highest authority, added, as a qualifying clause, that

his wife's heartlessness had driven him there. She found herself in London without a single friend. The people who would have received her were not themselves received in select circles. This was the moment for the Baroness von Trier. She wrote announcing her willingness to forgive the past and reassume her former position.

"*You loved him, he loved you,*" was one passage in that fatal epistle; "*this is my own reply to all my own questions, some of them rather bitter, I admit, on the subject of your strange unkindness to me—your devoted, if dependent, friend.*"

"This woman," thought Lucie, made cynical by injustice, "in spite of her faults, had the sense to see that my poor darling and I were all the world to each other."

She drove to the Baroness's lodgings (curiously enough the lady was in England on private business); they embraced, cried, and talked for five whole hours. A week later they left England for "dear Lucerne," where Lucie spent six months, telling over and over again every conversation and incident which had transpired from the moment of the Baroness's pathetic departure till her magnanimous return. During that period of sympathy and fatigue the companion never once lost courage. Ever cheerful, interested, and consoling, she heard the eternal "he said," and "I said," and "they said" of domestic reminiscence without any flagging of the spirits or diminishment of attention. The stories, or rather chronicles—for they were strictly epic in character—seemed always fresh so far as the inexhaustible listener was concerned. Lucie was the first, the only one, indeed, to grow tired. Suddenly she stopped talking. She began to take long slumbers twice a day and in the evening she yawned over French novels. The Baroness suggested a change, and they went to Berlin. There they stopped at a *pension* kept by an officer's widow, and became acquainted with a few celebrities—friends, it was understood, of the late Baron von Trier. Lucie really enjoyed herself in Berlin. For the first time in her life she began to feel genuine. Lady Hollemache's loud whisper : "And who, pray, was Mrs. Gaveston ? Didn't she play old Smokie at Baden-Baden ? Wasn't she photographed with her tiresome hair hanging down her back ?" had made Mrs. Gaveston's daughter extremely thoughtful. But in Germany there was, to begin with, no mistake about the Baroness's authenticity. She was well connected ; her late husband had been dissipated, stupid, unpopular, but he belonged, beyond a doubt, to the old nobility. The Baroness was not liked because she was regarded as a vain and worldly woman ; she was also poor, but no one had ever attacked her reputation or denied her actual social rank.

"If I had only the merest apology, an oaf, an imbecile, for a son," she would say, " how these good ladies would welcome me ! It is the greatest misfortune to be a middle-aged, penniless, respectable widow without a son."

Things were going on in the pleasantest way when her brother-in-law was appointed as an Attaché to the English Embassy there. He was a good-hearted man, but he had his mother's version of the Basil marriage. When Lucie's name was mentioned to him by a Grāf at some very grand dinner-party, he felt himself, as he declared, in a painful position. He really did not know, he wrote home, " which way to look or what to say." But he found out Lucie's *pension*, and, too prudent to call upon her, sent her a carefully expressed letter :

Inasmuch as my dear mother is, reasonably or unreasonably, so much estranged from you, I feel sure you will understand why I am at a loss to know precisely the right course to adopt. But as some error in judgment is, perhaps, in such distressing circumstances unavoidable, it must be, I think, in my mother's favour. You will, I know, have the generosity to admit this. What, therefore, is to be done ? It is scarcely likely that we should meet, as I am hedged about with strictly official duties and acquaintances. Yet here we are in the same city. I should never, of course—and here you may rely on my discretion—give myself the pain of, or place you at a very grave disadvantage by, mentioning any definite reasons for my mother's attitude, yet neither of us wish to set people guessing. It would be unfair to all parties concerned. With perfect confidence in your good taste and sense I put the circumstances before you and await your reply.

Lucie, on receiving this, was for showing a proper spirit and teaching Frank Hollemache a lesson. She would not budge—no, not an inch. What had she done to be so insulted ? What business was it of his whether she lived in Berlin or in Timbuctoo ? What next ? But the Baroness took a strictly impartial view.

"Behave well, and he is gentlemanly enough to appreciate it. Then, when the old termagant dies, he may come round."

"Who cares two snaps whether he comes round or not ? " cried Lucie, pale with anger.

"If he chooses he can make it most disagreeable for us, and what can we two women do against society ? Nothing."

"Very well," said Lucie, "this ends it. Henceforth I shall go only among people who won't be so good that they will have to drop me when they hear ill-natured lies. I will not know a creature who isn't notoriously shady, and they may all judge me, if they please, by my associates. I shall be absolutely defiant."

And she kept her word. On leaving Berlin she went to Vienna, where, by degrees, for it is difficult to get a firm footing in any set, no matter how unprejudiced it may be, she made a number of friends— including Mme. de Montgenays. La Belle Valentine had a sound instinct ; she could recognise virtue when she saw it.

" That little Mrs. Hollemache is silly," she would say, " but good—as good as wood (gold is not good). I like to have her around."

Lucie had known this protectress for about a year when she appeared at Salsomaggiore as her guest. The Baroness von Trier, of course, could not approve of any intimacy with such a doubtful character. She found another engagement, and wrote to Frank Hollemache : " *Dear Lucie is becoming headstrong—not to say heedless. I have lost my influence, which I hope was a good one, and as I still wish to keep her affection and my own first impressions of her nature, I am resigning my post.*" He never answered this ; he thought her a cat ; but, when he met her taking tea at the Russian Embassy, and actually chatting on intelligent terms with the Ambassador, he made himself civil, and discovered that she was a superior sort of woman. But a still greater surprise was in store for the young Attaché. The illustrious Cobden Duryee invited him during his first leave of absence to join him on a little tour through Hungary. They halted at Vienna, and behold ! at a brilliant supper given by Mme. de Montgenays in honour of her dear old friend Cobden —Cobden, who as a little boy had used to carry her satchel to school—Hollemache sat several places from his own sister-in-law. She occupied a seat between the Crown Prince of Alberia and the First Consul of Urseville-Beylestein. Lucie was at last very happy. It is true that she saw few members of her own sex— .

except nuns. La Belle Valentine held the strictest
views about the women she would admit into her
house ; but the men who came were the most distinguished in Europe. They treated Mme. de
Montgenays—so far as Lucie could judge—with the
utmost courtesy. Perhaps it was known that she
controlled the financial and other interests of Mr.
Duryee. It is certain that all were anxious to stand
well in her favour, and the one ambiguous criticism
ever passed upon her was this : "If only she had never
met Louis Napoleon ! Such a pity !" Hollemache,
meeting his relative under such auspices, decided to
unbend. He bore a strong resemblance to his brother,
and this softened Lucie's heart. She forgot her
proper pride, she smiled affectionately, she spoke with
a gentleness which touched the pompous but not
insensible young man and roused his better nature to
something approaching enthusiasm. He felt ashamed
of his letter ; he longed to make amends. He went
so far as to ask her pardon (not crudely, but in veiled
language) if he had ever inadvertently or in a blundering way in the objectional character of trustee hurt
her feelings.

"It is beastly to be a trustee," he explained ; "one
has to be so impartial that one becomes a brute. But
one doesn't mean it really."

Later on he spoke of her to Duryee as a perfect
brick ; her marriage with so delicate a man as Basil
had, no doubt, been a mistake—a mistake due to love,

and youth, and inexperience. But she had behaved
most awfully well, and any one could see at a glance
that she was a lady in every sense of the word.
Having delivered all this, he felt he had done the
right thing. He wrote a prudent version of the affair
to his mother, who sent one comment back by return
of post :

"*Lucie is the kind of woman who will always deceive
men. They respond to hypocrisy as reptiles do to music,
and they love paint. They think it means a heart.*"

CHAPTER VII

CLEMENTINE HAS A FEW SURPRISES

THE morning after the dull whist, Mr. Gloucester, looking very ill, took Clementine for a walk. They went, without speaking, through the picturesque old town, with its market-place, its narrow streets where children, goats, and dogs played together on the cobble-stones, and past the quaint church full of peasants at prayer. Presently they came to the open country and a winding high-road. Then Mr. Gloucester found his voice—a forced, weak voice which seemed strange to Clementine.

"I have had a worrying letter," said he. "Haxsworth"—the name of his agent—"seems to have made rather a muddle of things. I can't make head or tail of this long yarn he has sent me. But a lot of money has been used, I fancy, in an irregular way. I wish I had a good business head. I thought Haxsworth was a treasure, and I left it all to him. I shall be blamed, of course."

"It is your own capital."

" No, my darling, it is yours."

" It comes to the same thing."

" No, no! Do you think I might consult Fels-hammer? I hear he is wonderful at law and accounts. He is a professional actuary—as well as a heap of other things. He would give a friend's advice, and that's what I want—a friend—some one who has nothing to gain."

Timid and trusting natures, once deceived, invariably become more suspicious than the sceptical. One unkind doctor will make them detest the whole medical profession, and a single encounter with some dishonest person will drive them to a really vindictive misanthropy. The gentle Mr. Gloucester now felt that he hated the entire tribe of lawyers; they were all bloodsuckers, knaves, and liars; they all sought his life, he knew; daily they murdered hundreds by tormenting communications, and not a soul was ever the wiser. His eyes brimmed over with tears at the idea of the perishing innocent families—done to death and ruin through the worries of a legal correspondence.

" It will kill me!" he said to his daughter. " Kill me!"

She did her best to comfort him, but, as he could remember neither dates, figures, nor facts, she caught a little of his own despair. He kept repeating: " I don't know what I have done to come in for all this at my time of life, when we were so happy, and everything seemed going on beautifully. It is very hard."

"But, papa, every one must expect a little anxiety sooner or later."

"I don't know what I have done!" he said once more.

"I hate the idea of consulting strangers. Dr. Felshammer is a stranger."

"Far better than any so-called friend, my poor darling—far better. Wait till you know the world," said the unhappy gentleman; "wait till the creature you have fed turns round and rends you." His sighs were sobs; their curious sound haunted Clementine for days.

"Shall we be poor?" she asked. "Are we poor already—very poor, I mean!"

"As poor as rats."

This was a blow, but her idea of the rat-degree in poverty depended on her aunt, Mrs. Romilly, who constantly compared her position with that of insecure domestic vermin because she could not afford a box at the opera and a house at Ascot for the races. Clementine saw her own dress allowance reduced, their travels cut short, a house or so sold, a smaller suite of rooms at dear Thomas's in Berkeley Square, fewer dinners at Ranelagh, perhaps no suppers at the Wellington. They might have to let Eastern Acres furnished for six months. How horrid! She would not let her poor shattered papa see that this final possibility seemed almost more than she could stand. He groaned at her cheerfulness, and the more she dwelt on the bright side of his difficulties the more desperate he became. As a matter of fact, he was a penniless man at that moment, and he had been swindled out of Clementine's fortune, bequeathed to her by her mother's father, the rich French-American Senator.

"Do let me talk to Felshammer! He's young; he is up to all their dodges. I know he is only ar acquaintance; but really at such a crisis, and far away from home, it is excusable to trouble him."

"You are right, of course," said the girl.

This note of perfect confidence was like balm applied with a dagger on the man's wounded heart.

"No, no! I am much at fault," he faltered; "my judgment is not suited to business. But you like Dr. Felshammer, don't you?"

"I am sure he is very clever and very strong."

"That's just it—he's strong; he's a fighting man, and I am not. My dear, there is the omnibus returning empty from the station. I am very tired. Let us stop it and drive back."

So they got into the omnibus, and, without speaking, stared out of opposite windows at the charming landscape till they reached home. Mr. Gloucester went to his room on arriving in the hope of getting a little sleep before lunch. Clementine lingered in the courtyard to watch a boy who had brought some performing mice. They walked on a tight-rope, and played tambourines, and valsed.

Felshammer saw her from his window and hurried down.

"You have walked too far," he said, with his usual abruptness, as he came up to her. "You're quite pale."

"I am worried. Papa isn't well. He wants to ask your advice about something."

"Come over here to that seat and tell me about it. Is it his health?"

"No—it is his agent. He has an agent, you know, for our little property."

After some hesitation she told him that Mr. Gloucester, five years before, had formed the acquaintance of a rising young solicitor in their county; he was the town clerk's son. Mr. Gloucester knew nothing at all about the management of an estate or the laws with regard to land. Mr. Haxsworth had been in the habit of spending week-ends at Eastern Acres. Her father would show him his prettily bound books, his small but choice collection of eighteenth-century prints, his tiny cabinet of cut gems, very curious and valuable, his roses, his pug-dogs, his few and genuine antiquities from Pompeii. And in the evening he read Lamb and Thomas Love Peacock and Horace Walpole's Letters aloud to Mr. Haxsworth. Papa, it seemed, always thought it indelicate to discuss financial matters with a guest. Besides, he did not understand them, and he did not wish Mr. Haxsworth to find out the full extent of his ignorance.

" And what sort of man is this Haxsworth ? " asked Felshammer.

" A man about thirty—rather good-looking in a common way—with a quiet manner. Papa calls him gentleman-like—which means, of course, that he isn't a gentleman."

" And you—what do you think ? " asked Felshammer quickly.

" I had to be civil to him because he was papa's discovery, but I never liked him. He would be quite honest, I believe, with a man as sharp as himself. My poor papa's simplicity has tempted him. It is like leaving a purse full of gold on the high-road. Many who would never steal it would pick it up and keep it without trying to find the owner."

Felshammer, already in love with her appearance, now felt the fascination of her compassionable good sense. He was leaning forward in order to gaze more earnestly into her eyes when the sound of a short, quick, familiar step on the gravel made him spring to his feet. Paul had joined them. Clementine blushed to the roots of her hair ; her lips took a deeper red ; Felshammer saw that she was actually trembling with emotion at the mere sight of the young Prince. And he began to hate Paul as he had never in his life hated any man. It was a hatred which rose like a flame from his heart ; it seemed to scorch his throat, and it had the taste of blood. This revelation of his own capacity for brutal feeling made him as pale as the girl became when her blush died away. Felshammer, unable to command either his rage or his tongue, muttered some excuse and left the two together. His first clear thought, an hour later, was : " Now I understand Cain ! "

Paul, however, took his seat by Clementine, and looked affectionately after the secretary's retreating figure.

" He suffers from moods," he said, smiling, "and his manners are bad. I have told him so. He doesn't mind. He declares that manners were invented as a refuge for the malicious and an easy game for fools. I think he is right. Do you know that I have decided to go away—to America ? "

" To America ! " repeated Clementine, reminding herself that she had no right to care so terribly where he went.

" Yes. I shall often think over our talk about ' Peer Gynt.' Everything you do or think will affect my soul, and all I do and think may affect yours ! Is that the idea ? "

He spoke in a light tone, quoting idle words which they had exchanged at the dinner-table ; but something in his glance was more serious, more tender than he was aware of. Destiny is no miracle-worker, and the event which is mistaken for a sudden development is no more than the final visible touch to a gradual hidden process.

"So you are going to America?" said Clementine. "We, I think, are going home. Papa has been obliged to change his plans."

"I want to see whether Duryee's notions are true," replied the Prince, still engrossed in himself. "Duryee maintains that we are so undiscerning in Europe that when a clever fellow happens to be born in the working classes he goes straight to the New World or to the Colonies. We do not know how to make use of him, and therefore, while the strong leave us, the weak and inferior ones—without spirit or ambition —remain."

"I wish I were a man!" exclaimed Clementine. "I should like to be the private secretary to some great statesman."

"I am nobody," said the Prince, "but if we had lived a few centuries ago you might have dressed up as a page and travelled with me all over the world. Would you have enjoyed that?"

"No. I could never enjoy being dressed up as somebody else. I hate a false position. I should like to be a boy in reality, but as I am a girl I don't want to be a sham page. Viola, on the stage, always looks ridiculous to me. And Rosalind is as foolish, so far as her appearance goes. No man or woman could be deceived by them."

"I call you extremely serious," said Paul, smiling. "I am afraid that your soul will make mine rather melancholy. My main delight now is in things which are artificial. Suppose I change? I sha'n't know myself. It will be awkward."

He thought it was impossible not to be fond of this sombre, picturesque child. But he dreaded another honest attachment. Had he not suffered enough on account of the darling Sophia? He compared them both with Lucie Hollemache. Lucie he could never love; Lucie seemed facile, worldly-wise, tearless—O, above all, tearless—and she was very amusing. That is to say, she had the peculiar attractiveness of a sleeping kitten. One always expected her to wake up. Lucie was going to America. There would certainly be a delightful party on Mr. Cobden Duryee's very famous steam yacht.

"And you are going back to the country?" he said, turning again to Clementine. How pretty she was!

"Yes—back to Eastern Acres."

"You won't forget me when you get to England? Perhaps you will write to me sometimes?"

No, she would not forget him, but letter-writing was another matter. This piqued him.

"But I want you to write," he explained.

"It will all depend on whether I have anything to say," replied Clementine. To herself she was saying: "Here is some one I must never see again."

When he asked her whether there might be some chance of their meeting, later on, in London, she answered without hesitation:

"We shall go straight to Eastern Acres."

He showed his disappointment, which gave her a fearful happiness and a still greater determination to avoid him eternally. She caught sight of Augusta waving from her bedroom window.

"I'm afraid I am wanted," she said. " Papa is not very well."

Paul walked with her to the lift, and, trivial as the incident seemed, he always thought of her as being borne away from him in that silent machine. What did she mean; why this sudden reserve? Why the cold voice and the kind, almost beseeching glance? She had character, that was clear. Later on he made some remark on the subject to Felshammer at luncheon. The secretary fairly snarled with irritation, and he ate nothing.

There are two ways of loving—one is joyous, active, sane, without questionings and without bitterness—the young and beautiful love which makes life charming and is its recompense. The other sardonic, agitated, complaining, more full of tears than laughter, makes its victims idle, cowardly, cruel, and capricious. Felshammer's passion for Clementine had long passed the bounds of a sane affection. Somewhat cold as a very young man, he was now indulging, with all the strength of maturity, the dreams and frenzy which are the undoing of youth. He was learning each moment some fact about a force in human nature which he had heretofore thought an overestimated thing. The newness and strangeness of the experience but deepened its intensity, just as one who begins gambling or any vice in middle life will fall more completely under its spell than any other. It was as though the devil had entered into him, and he knew it, and welcomed the invader because he felt an energy in loving, a vindictiveness in hatred, he had never imagined possible.

That afternoon, while Mr. Gloucester was seeking peace in a second sleeping-powder, and Augusta was writing to her Jim, and Leonore was reading "The Blessed Damozel" (her favourite poem), Clementine heard a sudden sound of horses and voices rising from the courtyard below. Madame de Montgenays and Mrs. Hollemache, dressed to perfection, attended by the Prince and Mr. Duryee, were stepping into the little pony carriage. A large omnibus, surrounded by porters with luggage, gesticulating maids, and valets of debonair mien, was being loaded with trunks. The manager presented bouquets to La Belle Valentine and Mrs. Hollemache ; he bowed obsequiously to the millionaire, and with irreproachable courtesy to the Prince. Felshammer came out, followed by the rest of the royal suite. What did it all mean? Another vehicle, driven at a furious pace by a shouting coachman, clattered up to the door. The pony carriage started. Madame de Montgenays blew a kiss to some one on the balcony and called out, "*À demain!*" fell forward, and balanced herself by catching the Prince's arm. "A thousand pardons, Altesse!"

His Royal Highness laughed aloud. Clementine trembled from jealousy. Then the omnibus followed, full of the maids and valets, and swaying with the weight of immense boxes. What did it all mean? The secretary, grim and sulky, threw himself into the chaise, looked up straight at Clementine, lifted his hat, and bowed as he had never been seen to bow to any Imperial Majesty. "*À la gare!*" He, too, and his companions were soon out of sight. Clementine stood leaning against the shutter of her window. Had they gone? Was it then at an end so soon? She must have stood there for nearly half an hour, immovable, disconsolate, and confused, when the page-boy, having tapped at her door and hearing no answer, entered with a letter on a salver. How she sprang forward with colour once more in her cheeks!

But it was not the Prince's handwriting, and she opened the envelope sadly. Felshammer had scrawled these words in pencil :—

"I will write from Paris. I don't know what possesses H.R.H., but he is leaving at once. A caprice. Duryee has bewitched him. I will write from Paris. —K. F."

The girl tore the note into fragments.

"It isn't Duryee," she said to herself. "O, I know it isn't Duryee! It is that woman with the sleepy eyes. Poor little Countess Sophia ! How soon he has forgotten her ! "

And she paced the floor at the thought of Paul's inconstancy to his dead love.

CHAPTER VIII

THREE weeks had passed. The Gloucesters were now in London living at the back of Mrs. Romilly's house in Chester Square—for she herself was out of town, and she did not wish her best rooms occupied. But Mr. Gloucester, thankful to be spared hotel bills, climbed five flights of stairs to an old dismantled nursery, and ate without murmuring, when he had any appetite, the bloaters, rabbit-pies, and steak-puddings prepared for him by the charwoman. His health was failing fast, and daily interviews with his lawyer left him haggard and sleepless for the night. When the charwoman presented her accounts he looked very grave and told Clementine later that expenses would have to be reduced. "I haven't the money," he said piteously. She undertook the housekeeping herself, and Mr. Gloucester soon had reason to praise her good management. Once more he had roast chicken and cutlets and rice-pudding—she cooked them with her own hands. As for her

94

own diet, she declared a preference for milk and buns. He did not see her steal out one evening with a little packet containing a ruby bracelet—one of his own presents in happier days. On reaching the pawn-broker's shop she looked for some time at the brooches, umbrellas, tea-pots, and old rings in the window. Presently, with a gasp, she darted in, and, assuming a firm voice, actually drove a good bargain. Her papa needed champagne. It was not a moment for the refinements of timidity.

"The stones are perfect," she said; "they were chosen by a great connoisseur. I shall certainly redeem them—so the more you advance the more interest you will have."

After some grumbling, but with much respect for her intelligence, the man gave her thirty-five pounds —in the circumstances a fair loan. Money-lenders, notoriously alert to the deceitfulness of female beauty in business transactions, are always impressed by plain dealing.

"You won't have to do much of this!" thought Mr. James Metcalfe to himself, counting out the bank-notes. He was not a Jew, but a Presbyterian of strong religious views, with an admirable Scotch wife and seven docile children—the eldest destined for the Ministry. Clementine thanked him as he took the trouble to bow her out of the shop and watch her walk down the street. He was an expert in discerning the uncommon case—not uncommon because she was a lady in appearance, but because she had told the truth about the rubies. And he knew that if she lived she would redeem them. Among other qualities, he had recognised an indomitable determination to succeed.

"No, my lady," he repeated, "you won't have to do much of this!"—and he went back to lock away the bracelet. He could think of five customers for it straight off. Perhaps he sighed; the resolute, strictly considered, are not always the most remunerative clients.

Clementine found that Dr. Felshammer had called during her absence, and was waiting for her in the oppressive apartment which Mrs. Romilly called a "snuggery." Remembrances of Salsomaggiore, the sunshine, the music, the brilliant dinner-party, the Prince, swept over the girl with a suffocating violence. She had not wept for months. But now she fled up the staircase to the bath-room, where she sobbed wildly, stifling the sound in the coarse bath towels. It was not romantic; it was not the way in which she would have wished to weep over a hopeless love, a royal lover, and domestic misfortunes. Romance, however, depends on the soul, and not on upholstery. When she had finished crying she went down, careless of her altered appearance, and greeted Felshammer as kindly as she could. He held her beautiful hand— absorbed, in one passionate glance, her face.

"I have just come from Southampton," he said;

"straight from Waterloo here. I saw them off—the Prince, Mr. Duryee, Madame de Montgenays, Mrs. Hollemache. The yacht is superb. They have gone!"

"Gone!" said Clementine, taking a chair in the corner, far away from the wretched fire of cheap coals. She could not feel cold enough; all she asked was to be numb, wholly numb from head to foot.

"And I thought they would never get off! Now I can devote myself entirely to"—he paused—"Mr. Gloucester, if he will let me. He is too chivalrous for these rascals."

"Haxsworth has robbed him of everything. Papa gave him what is called a power of attorney."

"That is a pity. But don't get discouraged."

In spite of her desolation, her anxiety, and an unconscious wish to remain wretched, Felshammer's presence gave new vigour to the girl's spirit. The Prince's secretary had no sense of humour, and, however precious this particular gift may be, it is a question whether those who possess it love the best or make the truest friends. Terror of the laugh and a knowledge that the laugh can be justified is often a paralysing misfortune, oftener still a restraint on confidences, but oftenest of all it gives an ironical sting to sympathy. Clementine could not analyse her relief for the fact that Felshammer did not appear to hear the angry tones of the charwoman squabbling with her husband in the scullery below them, did not seem

8

to notice the odour of onions which filled the whole
house, did not have contempt for the half-furnished
room (Mrs. Romilly had locked all her nice things
away), did not feel the great, great change between
the serene gaiety of her former life and the squalid,
humiliating gloom of poor relationship, pawn-ticket
in pocket, at the back of Chester Square on
sufferance.

"I am not discouraged," she said. "I mind
nothing for myself. I am nervous about my father.
Wait till you see him l I hate poverty in England,
where the mere decencies of life are made impossible
on a small income. Here to be poor is not a discipline—it is a degradation. We could be happy
enough in Dresden or in Touraine."

"I had no idea that matters were so serious."

Mr. Gloucester had stated his case after lunch on
Felshammer's last day at Salsomaggiore, and had expressed himself as greatly reassured by the interview.
The secretary had discussed the affair from every
standpoint, and discussed it in vain, for the old gentleman either never told or could not remember the
whole story. Felshammer, not at all realising the
actual circumstances, and knowing that the mind of
a country squire is given to exaggeration, did not
attach any importance to Gloucester's panic, and
treated it as a humour to be pacified for Clementine's sake. Indeed, he had been intolerably bored,
and more than once during the course of Mr.

Gloucester's narrative, he had wondered how such a fussy, doddering, tiresome person came to have such a fascinating child. But to see her now, wan and list-less, to find her humiliated by a harsh reverse, to hear a bitter note in her husky, caressing voice, to know that she was suffering, touched his heart to its depths. He thrust his hands into his pockets, walked up and down the room, and directed his glance, each time he turned to face her, towards the little mole on her upper lip. This he considered a defect, though not unpleasing.

"You will find that it is all right?" he exclaimed.

"It is kind to say so, but the affair is beyond flattery. The money has gone." She did not look at him, but studied a tabby cat which was arching itself on the window-sill outside.

Wishing that she possessed a more feminine soft-ness, he asked: "Are you sure you understand business?"

"I may not understand business; I know that we have nothing. I am afraid, too, that papa will be blamed, and he is not able to bear criticism."

"It is an absurd theory that the party who loses must be in the wrong. What are your plans for the moment?"

"We must let Eastern Acres."

"I see," he said, adding, with characteristic abrupt-ness: "I want your father to dine at the Travellers' with me. I'll call again to-morrow."

" Please do."

She went to the front door with him, and then he walked back with her to the little sitting-room.

" We are too polite," she said ; " or perhaps you are merely absent-minded ? "

Long after he had gone she kept smiling, and, with every cause for depression, she was irresistibly cheerful—running up and down the stairs forgetting why, looking out of the windows thinking of no one and nothing, yet sensible of some great relief. At moments she would sigh ; once she heard herself say, " But he is not like Prince Paul. I wish he were."

Felshammer had resolved to let nothing stand between him and his wishes. A materialist by instinct and an adventurer in disposition, he could scheme when the humour seized him with audacity, eagerness, unhesitating perseverance. And he was one who lived for the moment only and this world always. He would have thought it a piece of extreme folly to bring the question of eternal possibilities into any calculation, nor did he care to consider too closely a future which comprehended more than seven days of time. Three vehement motives were now directing his soul ; one was the infatuation for Clementine, the other was a desire to assert himself in some new way, the third was a sudden perception of the indispensability of wealth to a man who has to fight for what he wants. He had always taken a contemptuous view of money ; for, having inherited a moderate fortune, he lacked that embittering experience of poverty which is the common ordeal of the ambitious and the cause of such innumerable moral failures. Broadly speaking, a man is independent whose purse is so, and the pride which Felshammer displayed in all his human relationships was—while a genuine quality—a quality greatly assisted by the knowledge that he had satisfactory private means. These same resources, nevertheless, proved each year somewhat confined for his position. Court life, even spent in exile, is costly. Fashions every season became more extravagant, and an income which had seemed handsome to his father—a successful timber merchant in the fifties of the last century—required in the nineties too much carefulness in the spending to be regarded as much more than a provision against positive discomfort.

"I'll do it!" he thought, as he left Chester Square. The touch of Clementine's hand still lingered in his, and the brightness of her eyes still shone before him, lighting the way he cared not whither.

"I'll do it!"

CHAPTER IX

A GAME OF POKER WITHOUT CARDS

AT eleven o'clock the next morning Felshammer drove to the Prince's London agents, Messrs. Sachs and Bickersteth, of Lombard Street and Suffolk Street, Pall Mall. Their clerk was expecting him, and he was ushered at once into a small office (panelled with mahogany in the Empire style) where the partners were sitting. After a welcome of the utmost cordiality from both gentlemen, they invited him, through a narrow passage, into a fine room beyond, furnished with a number of deed-boxes bearing impressive names, and a few choice objects of art or historical value—including a chair once the property of Pope Leo X., as Mr. Sachs declared when he offered it to Felshammer.

" We still conduct occasional transactions on behalf of the Vatican," added Mr. Bickersteth—" if I may say so without indiscretion."

Mr. Sachs shrugged his shoulders in an amiable way.

Sachs, among financiers, came of a highly distinguished stock. One Sachs, in direct line with
himself, had lent money to the great Cecil, and
another had been a general merchant during the
reigns of Ferdinand and Isabella in Spain. The
Bickersteth respectability dated only from the time of
the first Duke of Marlborough ; but, although this
made him meek in the presence of Mr. Sachs, it was
not contemptible as a record in the City.

"I have called this time," said Felshammer, admiring the Pope's chair and accepting it with easy
reverence, "on my own affairs."

"So we thought," said Bickersteth. "We said so,
didn't we, Oscar ? "

Oscar Sachs was small, smooth, polished, and
vigorous. He wasted no strength, however, in words,
but used his head as much as possible when he wished
to express agreement or dissent. Prince Paul always
declared that Sachs had inherited this nod from the
ancestral accommodating goldsmith, who had, in his
case, caught it from his famous client, Lord Bur-
leigh.

"I want to make money. I want to go into
business," said Felshammer. "Now that the Prince
has gone, they are not dying to have him back, and,
to be candid, I myself am not sorry as I thought I
should be to lose him. He needs a change. Nothing
but danger can come from persisting in his present
policy—which is no policy at all. It is not that he

shows contempt of public opinion, but ignorance of it. A different thing, you will agree. Cobden Duryee was right. Urseville-Beylestein has been put on its legs again, and it is marching straight to the Stock Exchange."

"We don't require Mr. Cobden Duryee to come from America in order to tell us that," said Bickersteth. "We have known it all along."

"Well," said Felshammer, "I know more about Beylestein than any one; and, if there is money to be made there, I intend to have my share."

Sachs tried a new pen-nib on his own excellent thumb nail.

"Beylestein has had a set-back," he explained. "When the Rothschilds withdrew their offer for the Largs district it created a bad impression. Responsible backers became shy of the whole concern. What are they, after all, but sheep? The Prince ought to have closed with the Rothschilds at once. He carries his system of procrastination too far."

"Yes, we thought so distinctly," said Bickersteth; "he missed an opportunity which won't occur again."

"Have you ever travelled through Largs?" asked Felshammer.

"We sent our expert—Mr. Campsey. His report was not altogether satisfactory, was it, Oscar? That is why we urged His Royal Highness to get rid of the province. Vulgarly speaking, it is a fancy article."

Mr. Bickersteth was good-looking, florid, middle-aged. He was not a bad painter in oils, and he had also acquired, by the aid of an old confidential clerk, considerable knowledge of financial affairs. At the Bank of England he was regarded as "no fool." "Bickersteth," a Governor now and again would remark, "is really no fool." Moreover, he followed the arts, and shone at dinner-parties if one wanted light but competent conversation at the right side of a peeress. His method at Lombard Street, when he met subordinates, was to convey hard truths in a familiar manner. This made him popular.

"Largs," he continued, "is not precisely another name for market-money."

Felshammer saw that Mr. Bickersteth regarded him as a subordinate—a subordinate, too, whose influence was not all it had once been at headquarters. From that moment he resolved to master Bickersteth, humiliate him, harass him. "I should like to see him a little paler and thinner," thought the vindictive secretary; "he has too easy a life."

"You had better change your expert," he said aloud; "it is true that I advised the Prince to dawdle over Rothschilds' offer—if he had refused outright he would have offended them for nothing. Why offend them? They are admirable people. As it has happened, no one has to put his pride in his pocket. The matter is simply 'off.' You can have Largs on a lease of twenty-one years for nine hundred thousand pounds."

"All I can say is," replied Bickersteth, "I wonder you stop short at the million! But I am afraid——"

"Yes, I am afraid too," said Sachs.

"Not that we wish to discourage you," added Bickersteth.

"You couldn't if you tried," replied Felshammer, "because you don't know what you are talking about. It isn't worth quite a million yet—it is worth exactly what I asked for it. And I shall get my price."

Bickersteth, with good-humour, asked:

"Will you be paid in cash or in a term of years?"

"Seriously," added Sachs, who thought that Bickersteth sometimes carried banter too far.

"I want a lump sum down, and the rest pretty soon either in hard money or the equivalent of hard money —something I can sell in the market."

"You have got your terms all cut and dried," said Sachs.

"I do not come here by appointment in order to think out my propositions while you wait," said Felshammer. "Why did the Rothschilds want Largs?"

"We don't say that Largs is valueless—we say it is not worth nine hundred thousand. Isn't that our point, Oscar?"

Oscar nodded.

"It is worth that to me," was Felshammer's reply.

The three men sat for a moment in silence looking at each other and blinking.

" What will you do with it ? " asked Sachs.

" What would the Rothschilds have done with it ? "

" We don't know," said Sachs.

" But we can surmise," put in Bickersteth. " They intended, doubtless, to develop the place and sell it back eventually, at a profit, to the Beylestein Government. That's fair enough, too, because it is a pure gamble. The Government won't risk a farthing."

" It is not in a position to do so," said Felshammer.

" Then it must pay those who are willing and able to back a highly speculative enterprise."

" I'm glad to hear that you think so," said Felshammer, drawing a letter-case from his pocket ; " but you haven't answered my question. What would the Rothschilds have made of Largs ? Railroad stock ? "

" I daresay. Wouldn't you say so, Oscar ? "

" Probably."

Felshammer asked them whether their expert's name was Campsey—Henry Denzil Campsey. Yes, that was the man—a man in whom they placed the utmost reliance.

" He has great influence," added Sachs.

" It seems to me, too, that he has a great deal of influence ; whether he always uses it to the best advantage I cannot say," replied Felshammer. " He advised you, for instance, that the Largs district was not altogether promising ; he told you that you had better close with the first fair offer."

"Well, practically," said Sachs, becoming more interested.

"I happen to know," continued Felshammer slowly, "that it was Campsey himself who urged the Rothschilds to withdraw, which they did. Campsey then wrote to Hermann Gessner to secure it at any price, but to offer as little as possible on the ground that the Rothschilds' action had created a prejudice against the investment. A neat touch. You see, it is an oil region, and it's larger than the State of Pennsylvania. Do you smell petroleum? Read that."

His own hand shook a little as he took out Campsey's letter to Gessner, which he gave to Sachs.

"Gessner," said Felshammer, "is more daring than the whole gang. He pays big prices and he has bought Campsey."

Mr. Sachs and Mr. Bickersteth studied the Campsey document, looked at each other, shot out their lips, sucked in their cheeks, looked at Felshammer.

"I am free to confess," said Bickersteth, with an indescribable loftiness of tone, "that I do not understand these modern methods of transacting business. I have always regarded Mr. Campsey as a person of experience and respectability."

"I," said Sachs, "would not have believed Campsey capable of such conduct. Have you told the Prince?"

"No," replied Felshammer slowly, "I have not

told the Prince. It would mean several changes. He would say that he paid you to guard his interests. I think you could still guard them—if you had some one with a real knowledge of Beylestein in your firm. Am I clear?"

"I think you have been quite successful in putting your case clearly," said Sachs.

Both he and his partner were now livid. They were honest, unimaginative, self-satisfied men who had grown careless and over-confident from a success which they owed to tradition and by no means to their own efforts or their own intelligence. The old-fashioned way had made their business—an inherited one—and given them their connections—also inherited ; they refused to mix with the new generation of financiers, and sniffed when the rising firms at Frankfort were mentioned. Frankfort gossip seemed to Messrs. Sachs and Bickersteth perfectly absurd. As for Gessner—

"He is not a stayer," they would say. "Who is Gessner? The Rothschilds are good enough for us. What do you think?"

"Too much was thrown on Campsey," continued Felshammer. "It was a big deal, you must remember. I am not a capitalist, but I paid three thousand pounds for that letter to Gessner. It is worth far more than three thousand pounds to you"—and he restored it to his pocket-book.

"If it is genuine," said Sachs, clearing his throat,

"I won't deny that it is marketable in a strictly limited sense."

"The Prince," Felshammer went on, "had a letter from you yesterday urging him strongly to close with Gessner—Gessner offering a far lower sum than Rothschild. That didn't show good judgment on your part—in view of this fresh information."

"We did our best. We acted, as we thought, in the Prince's interests," said Sachs.

Bickersteth added :

"You must bear in mind, Dr. Felshammer, that we were misled by Mr. Campsey."

"Yes," replied Sachs ; "grossly deceived by Mr. Campsey."

"But it is your business to make it impossible for Mr. Campsey or any one else to mislead you. The Prince pays you to keep your eyes open. You seem to reason as though the City were Paradise, and every man there was above temptation."

"All legitimate investigation and legitimate precautions we take, and are, of course, delighted to take. But we have never stooped to bribery," said Bickersteth, looking towards the letter-case. "We do not want to begin it. Not that we grudge the money—it is the idea."

"Yes, the idea," said Sachs—"not the money."

Felshammer buttoned up his coat and laughed aloud.

"You are supposed to be substantial people," said

he, "and you have still got an immense pull over new-comers. On the whole, I'd sooner be in your firm than in any other I know. But if this particular story got about—coupled with a few others of the same kind—people would begin to get anxious. They appreciate honest men, but honesty is not enough. A bishop, for instance, ought to be virtuous, but he must be a good administrator unless the diocese is to go to pieces. So in financial matters. Employ a trustworthy agent if possible, but get a sharp one in any event."

"I cannot admit the least negligence on our part," said Sachs firmly, "and it is worth noting that Mr. Campsey is in the employ of the Government. He is the greatest living authority on land values. Our good faith——"

"That's just it. There has been too much good faith. You must be in the very centre of things and know every move."

"There is no use, Dr. Felshammer, in going on in this way with us!" exclaimed Bickersteth, showing spirit because he was terrified, and because he had already decided to accept the secretary's terms what-ever they might be. "And I am not aware that the Prince's interests have suffered. Mr. Campsey's negotiations have proved ineffectual."

"Thanks to me," said Felshammer.

"What do you propose?" said Sachs.

"I should like to be a partner in this firm. I can't

plank down capital, but I will undertake to stand permanently at the wheel."

"From all I am able to gather from your disposition," said Sachs drily, "we should soon find ourselves a pair of dummies."

"Have a fourth man, if you like—one who will bring money," said Felshammer, "and hold his tongue."

"A permanent man at the wheel with a casual *quorum* would, in point of fact, be the real head of affairs," said Sachs. "We couldn't possibly agree to that. But——" He paused.

"Oddly enough," observed Bickersteth, "we were looking about for a new manager, weren't we, Oscar?"

"Write me your suggestions on that line," said Felshammer quickly. "I wish to have all the facts before me. Meanwhile, I can't afford to keep three thousand pounds locked up in this letter of Campsey's."

"The first two years' salary in advance," murmured Sachs.

"I prefer to call it the first year's *bonus*," said Felshammer.

Mr. Sachs and Bickersteth showed a just irritation.

"I call this pressure!" exclaimed Bickersteth. "I do, indeed. It is not what I should have expected from you. I can't help saying so."

"Your expectations are apt to be too idealistic!"

said Felshammer grimly. "It isn't Quixotic—if you mean that, and it is not the style of Monte Cristo. But my case is a good one and the ground is fair. The fact remains—you have not been sharp. You don't want to lose your best client, and I want to get on a little faster in this world. You haven't seen the real point of the matter even now. Why should Rothschild, or Gessner, or any of these firms have the Largs district ? With your connections and record—so far, and my knowledge, why can't we strike oil on our own account ?"

"And the Prince—what about the Prince ?" said Bickersteth, dropping his voice. "Is he to know ?"

Felshammer took his exact measure in that one remark.

"I suggest the Prince," said he loudly, "as the fourth man. He will not interfere with us. Of course he is to know."

Sachs burst out laughing, shook him heartily by the arm, and considerately waved Bickersteth toward a very handsome Spanish mahogany cabinet.

"You will take something ?" said Sachs. "There's some wonderful sherry just sent us by the Grand Duchess of Wesen. We haven't opened it yet. I must congratulate you on your ideas. They will give us a lot to think about for the next few days."

"My address is the Travellers, till Wednesday morning. Allow me !"

His attention had been diverted to Mr. Bickersteth,

who was now fumbling in his pocket for a knife with which to cut the string of a small basket. Felshammer cut the string himself, and noticed a card attached to it bearing the following name, address, and inscription :

With MR. HERMANN GESSNER'S *compliments.* 18B, Grosvenor Square, W.

The sherry proved the finest he had ever tasted. He suggested drinking the health of the Grand Duchess of Wesen, and he reflected inwardly on the fact that men who are conventionally truthful in large transactions will lie in the cause of snobbery, or accept bribes when they are not too valuable to be in strictly good taste.

"And now tell us," said Sachs, remarking Gessner's card and tearing it off carelessly in the hope that Felshammer had not seen it—"tell us how you got hold of Campsey's letter! That would be worth hearing."

"As good as a play!" added Bickersteth, much restored by the wine. "Such a thing doesn't happen once in a blue moon."

"I should call it a fairly common occurrence," said Felshammer; "but, if you like, you shall hear all about it after we have settled down."

When he had gone Mr. Sachs and Mr. Bickersteth gave their clerks and callers a bad day. The two

gentlemen were considered "upset" about something.
But the chief accountant felt consoled when he heard
them wrangling with each other.

"They are only human after all," said he; "they
are just like everybody else when you come to know
them."

CHAPTER X

HOW ONE MARRIAGE TOOK PLACE, AND WHY MANY DO NOT

MR. COBDEN DURYEE was on friendly terms with Hermann Gessner, and he had recommended to his service young Charlie Gaveston, Lucie's brother. Charlie was a delicate youth of luxurious tastes, but he had a perfect manner, a handsome countenance, and the ingenuous charm which had been his mother's supreme attraction. Out of amiability and the wish to please Duryee, who was beyond the usual favours, Gessner appointed Charlie, whom he considered at first sight a safe fool, his private secretary. Charlie, in the character of safe fool, was allowed to hear conversations and read letters many of which would have been the ruin, or made the fortune, of an experienced clerk. But he was not intelligent; he obediently wrote down, copied out, or repeated word for word what he was told to write, copy or report. Matters of great importance literally went in one ear and out the other, impressing his memory, which was remarkable, but leaving his imagination untouched, his sense dormant. Gessner treated him generously, carefully as an invaluable machine, paying him well and liking him with a semi-paternal affection. The Mun-alley story was a help too ; Gessner had the German liking for romance. All went well and was well till Charlie at his club made a friend of the secretary, a Major (retired) who had a dashing daughter. This dashing daughter (one of seven) was perfectly respect-able, but she had a passion for the Turf. In the course of a fearful scene, during which Charlie restrained her with difficulty from eating some smelling-salts, she confessed to the loss of something more than three thousand pounds. She was not pretty ; she was not wicked ; it was a case, not so uncommon as the cynical might think, where virtue was the most dangerous weapon she could employ. And she employed it well. Her remorse was real ; her tears were real ; her odd, expressive face disfigured by weeping would have wrung a harder heart than Charlie's. Besides, she had grace and fire in addition to her Irish chastity. Charlie swore that she must and should be his. He would give himself the blessed right to pay her rather large bets. She slipped out of the house one morning after this distressing inter-view and the two were married at the registrar's. Launched thus into matrimony, the young couple spent the hours and enthusiasm usually sacred to the honeymoon in somewhat harassing discussions on

financial points and very wearisome letter-writing to
lawyers. Charlie's capital was strictly tied up. His
income, combined with his salary from Gessner, was
always anticipated for months in advance. He had
always lived carelessly among rich people, and,
although he was not extravagant in comparison with
other members of his set, he could not save, and
he did not know how to economise. The dashing
girl, whom he now had the privilege of calling his
own, showed herself adroit at this early crisis, and, in
spite of the fact that he was driven to associate her
most disagreeably with his first bitter experience of
money worries, she managed to keep his affection
by deserving it. Good-humoured, gay, resourceful,
and witty, she made his chambers in the Albany
so bright that he could scarcely believe that he was
anything so dull as a married man. Her friends—a
host of accomplished persons, mostly of her own
nationality—rallied to her support; he spent lively
evenings in a charming circle, where he heard the
best songs, the cleverest conversation, the finest music
he had ever listened to. He had the same dogged
fidelity in loving which was considered so eccentric in
poor Lucie, whose indifference to all men—except
Basil Hollemache—had become a kind of family
grievance. Charlie admired his wife, was proud of
her, devoted to her; frankly, he thought her poverty
a drawback and her bills awful, but she had abnormal
elegance, and she was as true as a die.

" We must scrape through somehow, Libbie dear!" said he.

It happened shortly afterwards that Mr. Gessner had occasion to go to Paris, and, liking young Gaveston, took him as a member of his suite. Mr. Gessner never travelled with less than three secretaries, a valet, a footman in livery, and a courier. Gaveston, to the disgust of the old staff, had charge of Mr. Gessner's private correspondence, and was treated in every way as an especial favourite. Gessner had an invalid daughter but no son. Charlie's airy gift in conversation amused the old banker; the stupid fellow's greenness in business matters disarmed him, his delicacy of mind, colouring, and temper seemed peculiarly lovable to a man who detested most women, finding plain ones grotesque and pretty ones exacting. Charlie, without being effeminate, had feminine tact and grace; he brought charm, without danger, into the sombre magnificence of Lombard Street. Gessner however, was close-fisted, particularly with those whom he liked, because he was morbid on the subject of disinterested friendship, and no one in the world could influence him, because he was jealous of his own will. Charlie, obeying a sound fear, was never foolish enough to confide his trouble to Mr. Gessner. But he met Felshammer at Cobden Duryee's during the Paris visit, and he told Felshammer his entire life— omitting only what may have seemed discreditable to Libbie. He took, for instance, the whole re-

sponsibility of the bets.   Libbie in the narrative shone
out only as his good angel, the noblest, the best of her
sex.   Felshammer recognised at once a young man
who, not persevering enough for an independent
career, was too proud for a servile one—the kind of
young man who was good-hearted, easily deceived,
easily broken, and as easily mended.   Such persons are
often very useful, and Felshammer soon found a use
for him.   Charlie never discussed Mr. Gessner's
affairs ; he did not understand them to begin with,
and, in the second place, he would have considered
any breach of confidence a dishonourable thing.   But
one night the Prince's secretary invited him out to
dinner.   The host, by assuming a knowledge which
he did not possess and taking things for granted
which he merely guessed at, extracted a great deal
of information from his guest—after he had once
persuaded him to take far too much iced champagne.
Charlie, indeed, when it was all over, and the jolly
evening was ended, and he found himself at his hotel
somehow or other in bed, had little recollection of
anything he had said.   Felshammer, nevertheless, had
heard about Campsey—which was all he wanted
to know, inasmuch as the Prince was already
considering the offer from Gessner for the Largs
district.

The morning after the dinner, therefore, Charlie
woke up with an insane headache to find Felshammer
sitting by his side reading *Le Figaro* and smoking a

cigarette. Greatly bewildered, the foolish youth was no match for that citizen of the world. He found himself being reminded of statements he ought not to have made, and pinned down to promises he ought never to have given. One was an undertaking to produce Campsey's last letter—or, failing the original, a copy. And he (Charlie) was to receive three thousand pounds for his pains—just the sum he wanted for Libbie's bets. Was it a dream?

"If I said I would do it, I suppose I must see it through!" observed Charlie, wretchedly hoping that Felshammer would respect him for such a Quixotic sentiment. "I must stand to my guns, of course. We Gavestons always keep our word—at any cost."

Felshammer did not smile; the little vanities and false sentiments that chequer human weakness always seemed to him more curious than amusing. He looked at Gaveston inquisitively—much as a doctor would observe in a patient the manifestation or development of any expected symptom.

"I never doubted that you would see it through," he answered gravely ; "it's a case of *noblesse oblige*."

"It isn't quite square all the same," faltered Charlie. "Gessner would call it a mean, shabby trick."

"Gessner is willing to take advantage of the Prince's ignorance," said Felshammer, whose eyes flashed at the thought. "It is not for Gessner to prattle about meanness or shabbiness. If you deal with these men as you would with gentleman of strict and rigorous codes of honour, you will come to smash. With them it is always war, and always, in one disguise or another, 'sharp practice.'"

Two weeks later Charlie paid Libbie's bets—not through his bankers, but by an arrangement with Libbie's godmother—a woman of some means—to whom Felshammer sent a cheque. It was supposed to represent the proceeds of a small transaction in freehold property—the godmother owned a little estate to the south-east of London. She did not understand business, but she could grasp it sufficiently to know that she was to call something a sale which was not a sale, because it would mean not a penny's loss to her and a very great convenience to Libbie, of whom she was exceedingly fond. She made one condition. Did dear Charlie know and approve? She could not encourage wives to play tricks on their husbands. Oh, yes, Charlie knew and approved thoroughly. It was Charlie's suggestion, in fact. So it was all arranged in a friendly manner.

Felshammer, with a copy of Campsey's letter in his despatch-box, was able to advise Prince Paul to great advantage. His Royal Highness, on leaving Europe for the United States, left the settlement of the Largs affair in his secretary's hands absolutely.

"Are you wise, I wonder, to trust him?" said Duryee.

"He would sooner rob and ruin himself than

swindle me out of a farthing!" replied Paul. "I
should be an idiot if I didn't trust him. He might
shoot me—but he would never cheat me."

Felshammer was a man of inspirations; he did not
prepare schemes, mature them, and execute them with
care. It is quite possible that but for the sight of
Clementine in trouble he would never have proposed
himself as a partner in the firm of Messrs. Sachs and
Bickersteth. The idea came unsought as he looked
round their imposing offices and observed their contentment and realised the undeniable wealth and
influence which contributed to the support of such
serenity. At first he had intended to frighten them
only, and make them pay him handsomely for his
astuteness. Then the bigger notion entered his brain,
and, as he drove away from Suffolk Street, he felt that
he had made a decisive stroke—perhaps the great
stroke of his career. He dined alone at his club,
went to the play, and walked past Clementine's
window in Chester Square before he could settle
down for the night.

"Love may not last long," he said to himself,
"but while it lasts there is nothing so amazing."
He remembered all the words she had ever spoken
to him—not many, and some of them more than
cold. The voice he could not recall—for a voice
seems to defy the memory and is the most elusive
of all personal things. Yet he thought it the most
enchanting voice he had ever heard.

" Furthermore," he said, continuing his meditation,
" if I save her father's life and make her the richest
woman in London, she will never look at me as she
looked at Paul when he offered her a box of chocolates." This certainly appealed to his ironical sense
of humour, and did not humiliate him, because he
considered all girls very wretched judges of men, and
very foolish in the bestowal of their love. There was
just that touch of pity in his passion for Clementine
which the enamoured immortals of classic poetry felt
for the human objects of their interest.

The window, however, which he was watching
with such tender concern was not Clementine's at
all. She slept at the back of the house, and at that
very hour she was talking with Augusta Romilly,
who had come to town that day to see the dress-
maker. The girls were together in a large four-
posted bed, and for two hours they had discussed the
various ways of wearing a wedding-veil, till Augusta,
exhausted, fell asleep, leaving her cousin to watch the
shadows cast by the night-light on the ceiling and to
wonder what other ornament she could most advan-
tageously pawn. It is often held that it is better to
have trouble in one's youth than in one's middle-age;
the fresh heart, it is thought, is stronger to bear grief.
But this is not the case. A fresh heart is also an im-
mature one; it is tender, impressionable, unseasoned,
altogether too delicate for hard blows. No sorrow is
so bitter, because it is so little expected, or so un-

mitigated, because it is so little understood, as the sorrow in a young mind. The world at once seems squalid, Providence unjust, and when the sense of suffering injustice begins to dominate a soul at its first flight the wings grow heavy, the way looks dark with unknown terrors, and the ultimate goal is considered as some probable mockery, cruel and desolate. Clementine resented the social law which gave Prince Paul full liberty to make himself charming to irreproachable women, whom, nevertheless, he could not marry, and who would be blamed if they presumed to fall in love with him. Her pride was up in arms at a notion of any inequality in breeding which was based on something neither in nature nor in logic. Official rank she could appreciate easily enough ; etiquette, where etiquette reduced social jealousies and obligations to a system, she considered an indispensable thing ; can one play a game without rules ? But that love should be treated as a game seemed to the high-spirited girl revolting. Nor did it occur to her, as a quick way out of all her pressing difficulties, that it might be possible to make a good match. No ; she and her poor papa would go away to some little town in France, live simply, and die decently.

Sleepy Augusta, on being called the following morning, said :

"Some brides wear myrtle. A myrtle wreath looks very well, but orange-blossoms are more appropriate, and one can only wear them once. I wonder what you will wear when you marry, Clem ? "

" I don't think that I shall ever marry," said Clementine.

" That's perfect nonsense, of course," replied Augusta ; " but it will be your own fault if you don't."

"I suppose it is called a fault," said Clementine drily, "if one doesn't marry."

Augusta was too gentle to own this, and she felt also that as she was engaged herself, whereas Clem was still free, it was only kind to drop the subject. So she said :

"O you funny old Clem ! I wish my hair was as pretty as yours ! "

Mrs. Romilly appeared after luncheon, on her way to the station, in order to have a chat, as she said, with Alfred about his affairs, and tell him that she would soon be requiring the house for spring-cleaning.

"We come up for the season in May, you know," she observed.

Mrs. Romilly was tall and gaunt. She always looked cold, and her skin seemed stretched too tightly over the bridge of her nose. Habitually she wore a short serge skirt, a black silk blouse, a stiff collar, and an emerald and pearl brooch which Queen Victoria had given to her mother-in-law, the late Mrs. Adolphus Romilly, daughter of Lord Breechmere.

"Poor dear Alfred," said his sister, putting two cans of Brand's Extract (which she had bought as a little present for him from the Stores) on the table, "you are in a pretty pickle! I feel for you. Can nothing be done?"

"I am dining with a man named Felshammer to-night," replied Mr. Gloucester; "he writes in a hopeful strain. He says he believes he can offer one or two useful suggestions."

"Who is Felshammer? Married or single, rich or poor?" asked his sister rapidly. "Clementine must marry. As she won't have much money after this, she can't give herself airs, or expect to pick and choose. I have always thought that she was too ambitious for words in her ideas. Her chance now is with some man of means who wants to get on socially—a brewer, or a stock-broker, or tea, or wine —or something like that. It happens every day— there you have a prospect within the range of proba-bility. But as for anything else—don't prepare for miracles."

"How quickly you talk!" answered Mr. Gloucester. "I hear only half you say. I am very sorry, but my brain has been so tired that I can't follow you."

"Good gracious! This will never do. You must rouse yourself, my dear Alfred. Lethargy soon grows upon one. Who is Felshammer? I hope he is not another swindler. You are so facile with swindlers. From what Augusta tells me, I can see that Clemen-

tine had her head turned, completely turned, by
Prince Paul.   It is the greatest mistake to encourage
girls in these friendships with Royalties.   Americans
go in for it, I know; but remember the Emperor
and Valentine.   Did that association make for any
one's happiness?   Very well, then; if this Dr.
Felshammer is taken with Clem—and Augusta
thinks he is—don't play the fool, my dear man;
an unmarried daughter soon begins to look rather
like a failure after five-and-twenty," and so on, and
so forth.   Mrs. Romilly did not leave her shrinking
brother till Mrs. Townshend, from Aldershot, appeared on the scene of action.   The sisters kissed,
studied rapidly each other's toilettes, and exchanged
"Tut, tuts!" behind Alfred's bowed back.   Ada
Romilly and Louise Townshend never agreed on
any subject, but as Ada had nursed Louise through
a dangerous malady, and as Louise was paying for
Augusta's trousseau (Romilly being hard up at the
moment), they did not like to quarrel.   So Mrs.
Romilly left Louise alone with Alfred, although she
felt convinced that Lou would do a lot of harm by
talking religion, praising Prince Paul, and showing
the whites of her eyes at the first murmur of common
sense.   Louise had been what is called sweetly pretty,
and she was still most charming in appearance.   She
was wistful, untidy, picturesque, and good—a divine
woman.   Other women and all children instinctively
sought her hand—not because it was strong, but

because it was sympathetic. At her approach, the word "darling" formed spontaneously on male or female lips. Weary, heart-broken Alfred called her "darling" now, while the tears which Mrs. Romilly had frozen melted pitiably and rolled down his cheeks.

"Darling Lou," he said, "you are so good to come!"

"I can't tell you how much I feel for you," said Louise; "it is something awful! But God means it for the best, I am sure. Dear Clemmi will soon learn to despise the unmeaning and artificial habits of living which we are all brought up to consider indispensable to our happiness. *All seek their own, not the things which are Jesus Christ's.* She will feel out of it at first; yet, when she is offered love, she will know that it is for herself only—and what a blessing that is! I hope she won't want to earn her living, because she is not cut out for anything except a domestic life, the life of the wife and mother. But, even if she doesn't marry—and a poor girl must face this possibility always—isn't it far more dignified to remain single and true to an ideal—of course she will have an ideal—than to marry for convenience or be married to a fortune? Don't you agree, dear Alfred?"

Both sisters were voluble, but whereas Ada expressed a practical mind in sharp tones, Louise was sentimental and had an odd sing-song voice which her husband called soothing and absurd.

"Do you think that Clementine cares for Prince Paul?" she asked. "Not in any forward way, dear, but simply—almost without knowing it herself—as the very nicest girl would, if she saw much of such a fascinating man. It would be tragic, I admit. All the same, how much more interesting, really, than any mere commonplace attachment!"

"I don't know what you and Ada are talking about," said Mr. Gloucester. "Clementine never mentions the Prince. He is nothing to her, I am certain. She admires him, and finds him agreeable, and all that sort of thing; but, believe me, she cares no more about him than I do for—for whom shall I say?—the caretaker here, if you like."

"Perhaps Leonore is wrong. Then what about this Dr. Felshammer? Is he suitable?"

"Why any man?" exclaimed their brother irritably. "Haven't you said that she can't expect offers now that I have lost her dowry, poor child? I suppose her beauty, and her talents, and her sweet disposition count for nothing."

"Young men nowadays are very self-seeking. They don't seem to fall in love as they did when I was a girl. I don't mind telling you in strict confidence that Leonore hasn't had a single offer. Men dine and dance, but they are not proposing right and left—especially in good society."

"Then more shame to them! Leonore is well rid of such poor creatures."

"Oh, I quite agree!" said Mrs. Townshend. "And you must realise that the same idea applies to Clementine. Leonore is also considered very pretty and attractive."

She did not stay much longer, but she had made him happier than he had been for some time, because she left purposely behind her, in addition to a ten-pound note (a sum put aside for her summer mantle), a large roll of papers and magazines, including the *World*, the *Art Journal*, and the *Studio*, his favourite light reading.

CHAPTER XI

OLD WAYS OF FORMING NEW ALLIANCES

A WEEK later Mr. Bickersteth informed his wife that
the new manager, Dr. Karl Felshammer, would dine
with them. The Bickersteths had no town residence
of their own, as they preferred to hire famous mansions
from peers who were embarrassed or anxious to augment
a daughter's dowry. For that year Mr. Bickersteth had
secured Carlington House, Park Lane, from the Duke
of Edenborough, and there Mrs. Bickersteth, with a
state formality to which no duchess could pretend, lived,
moved, and had her being in what she liked to call
"a hidden way."

" Our home life," she would say to her friend Canon
Galesworthy, " is very, very old-fashioned. Ernie and
I have such quiet tastes ! "

The facts were that she had no children living ;
her strength had failed, and she was not fond of what
is called society. She came of too sound a Quaker
stock to care for any host of fashionable acquaintances

132

who would feel that they did her great honour in using her house as a *rendezvous* and assisting her to squander Mr. Bickersteth's money. Money was squandered, it is true, but it went in the gratification of her own taste for gowns, laces, jewels, and pomp. An imaginative creature, she saw herself always as a lonely empress (the late Empress of Austria was her ideal woman), and when this magnificent solitude was disturbed by callers of superior social rank she resented the intrusion, and found all contact with the inhabitants of an outside world discouraging, depressing, and detestable.

"And do you really wish me to meet this Dr. Felshammer?" she said to Mr. Bickersteth, turning from him to look, in turn, at the two pictures by Greuze and the two by Watteau, a Ruysdael landscape and a lovely Poussin, the Manets and the exquisite Daubignys which hung on the faded guilt leather panelled on the walls of the historic morning-room.

"Yes, we shall have to see a good deal of Dr. Karl," replied Bickersteth ; "he is Prince Paul's right-hand man. The Prince is under his thumb."

She said, "Very well," and was not interested. Men appealed to her as little as women.

Felshammer, cynically amused on his arrival at Carlington House by the imperial splendour and circumstance affected by the banker's wife, was astonished to find himself ushered, after passing

through a gallery and three large saloons, into the
presence of a striking personage about five-and-thirty,
who was standing by the fireplace of a small octagonal
boudoir without windows.   The lady was of medium
height ; her figure was unusually supple and well
proportioned ; she wore white velvet trimmed with
sable ; a diamond chain, once the wedding gift of a
Spanish infanta, hung round ·her waist ; her neck and
arms were bare.   Neither pretty nor beautiful, nor
fascinating nor pleasing, she possessed, nevertheless,
great distinction.   A smooth olive skin and black hair
added to her foreign appearance ; her features would
have looked classic in marble. They seemed irregular.
She had deep, very dark hollows, probably due to ill-
health, under her eyes, which were brown and
melancholy, proud in expression, and, though full of
fire, full also of an irremediable fatigue.   Felshammer
observed these points‾ by degrees ; the first characteristics which impressed him were the dark hollows
under her eyes and the gracious indifference of her
smile.   Bickersteth was at the piano playing, with
exaggerated feeling and far too slowly, the accompaniment to Schubert's Serenade.   He rose when
Felshammer entered, presented him to Mrs. Bickersteth, and said—

"I told you there would be no party.   It is so
much pleasanter by ourselves.   Rachel, you must
know, once travelled from London to Portsmouth
with Prince Paul.   There was a great crowd, and he

carried her pillow to the boat. His manners are perfection. You thought so, didn't you, Rachel ? "

Pride and anxiety were mixed in Bickersteth's
glance whenever he looked toward his wife. The
profound affection he felt for this being, whom he was
utterly unable to understand, showed itself in various
ways, but chiefly, to a man of Felshammer's penetra-
tion, by the nervousness of his speech and the trans-
formation of his whole personality in her presence.
Manner, bearing, mien—all were changed, subdued,
not by fear, but by the desire to please. The real
weakness of his character became far more evident
than it was at Lombard Street, where the habit of
authority and the traditions of the firm provided him
with an artificial strength. During dinner Mrs.
Bickersteth talked seldom, but always admirably.
She had read solid books in three languages ; her
knowledge of foreign affairs was most unusual ; she
cared evidently for things only, and not at all for
people. Felshammer soon realised that he had never
before met a woman quite so well informed, so wholly
lacking the sense of humour, so strangely picturesque,
yet so deficient in the ordinary feminine charms of the
most commonplace member of her sex. Intellectual
vitality had perhaps exhausted her physical magnetism.
Of the latter, she had none. Her individuality filled
the room, just as a fine work of art, whether in
painting or sculpture, will dominate its surrounding
atmosphere ; she was at once a restraint and an

attraction. When the dinner—the best Felshammer had ever tasted in England—was ended, Rachel left the two men, and, complaining of a headache, said good-night to both.

"She is a great sufferer," explained Bickersteth, reseating himself after watching her unconsciously as she walked away down the long corridor. "She has never recovered from the death of our two boys in one week. Women, I suppose, feel these sorrows as men do not, but my wife's devotion to her children went beyond all reason. The doctors were of that opinion; it amounted to a mania. They absorbed her life. In one way the terrible loss may have been a blessing in disguise. Naturally, I shouldn't mention this if you were not bound to hear about it, perhaps less accurately, from other people."

Was he jealous of his own dead sons? The fretful bitterness underlying his words could not have been an unintentional revelation of feeling, thought Felshammer. Clearly Bickersteth wished to be regarded as a man with a grievance, a man to be pitied not envied, excused not condemned, one who, bearing every outward token of fortune's favour, had, nevertheless, a sword through his heart.

"He gives me the key to his character," said the secretary to himself, changing the subject adroitly to City affairs, and deepening, in consequence, the good impression he had already produced on his host. A confidence should never be received either as a surprise, an indiscretion, an apology, or a hostage. It is something understood yet scarcely heard, something unforgettable yet too little our own to be trusted even to the memory ; uttered, it must be as though it had never been told ; at each rehearing it must seem more distant and delicate.

Five days afterwards Felshammer called on Mrs. Bickersteth and found her considering the purchase of some old Venetian lace which had been spread out before her over a screen.

"It is very beautiful, isn't it ?" she said quietly. "Do you care for such things ?"

No ordinary interruption was ever permitted to disturb either the current of her life or the course of her ideas. A story was told to the effect that she once made a very pompous Lord Mayor read aloud the greater part of Shelley's "Epipsychidion," because he happened to call when she was studying it.

"Yes," said Felshammer. "I think that women should wear as much lace as they can afford. It makes young ones seem ethereal and old ones sublime."

"I agree," she answered slowly. "I have a whole collection of lace dresses myself. You don't look the kind of man who would notice clothes or jewels, but you do notice them all the same. I wonder why ?"

"Because they are lovely to look at !"

"I am wondering how you will like living in England," she continued, gazing at him with unemotional but marked interest. "Have you many friends here? Do you want to have friends?"

"My sole object for the next few years will be to make money. A person who is concentrating all his energies on money-making is not agreeable socially, is he?"

"You want to make money," said Rachel; "is it for spending or keeping?"

Her directness, free from any hint of vulgar curiosity, was so much like his own that he felt as though they had been well acquainted for years.

"I hope to spend my fortune after I have made it," he answered.

"Not on yourself, I suppose?"

"Not altogether on myself."

"I am a Quaker," said Rachel; "but, although my people rarely spoke of money, I am sure that they thought about little else. They were all rich and in earnest and kind; we lived perpetually with the value of money and the fear of God before our eyes. Looking back, I see how dull and calm it was."

"But sane."

"Too sane! It was saner than life, if you understand me. It made every emotion seem over-violent and unreal by contrast. If I had any strong feeling, I thought it couldn't be true. You see, it was an education based on the principle that existence has two dangers only—debt and eternal punishment. This would not be the case even if the whole world were a Quaker colony. So I am no longer a consistent Quaker. My husband "—she hesitated, then repeated—" my husband says I am a rationalist. What are you ?"

"A rationalist also," said Felshammer. "I agree with Huxley. 'Of moral purpose, I see none in Nature.'"

She began to move, with great deliberation, as though they were chessmen, some silver and other trinkets, snuff-boxes and Japanese baubles, on the table by her side.

"Then I wonder how we shall both end ?" she said at last. "I am always wondering about the end."

"Doesn't the present interest you enough ?"

"It does not interest me in the least !" She waited a little, but he offered no protest. "I am glad," she went on, "that you don't tell me, as most people might, that I have everything mortal could wish for."

"I wouldn't be so presumptuous. Besides, I couldn't be so blind."

"You have heard about the children ?" she said quickly.

"Sorrow is in your face."

"I suppose it is. Who are your friends ?"

"They know me very little. They are a Mr. Gloucester and his daughter."

As he spoke the word " daughter " their eyes met. Rachel lowered hers at once.

" Clementine Gloucester ? " she asked.

" Yes."

" I know her. She is very pretty, a brilliant girl.
If she is in town I should like to call upon her. I
pay few calls."

Felshammer told her a little about Mr. Gloucester's
difficulties.

" But they are passing difficulties," he added ; " so
don't appear to know about them unless she herself
says something—which is unlikely."

" London is a hard place for a brilliant girl with
no money."

" No harder than any other place."

" It is obvious," said Rachel, " that I have more
than I need, while she has nothing that she deserves."

" Don't   pity   her ! "   exclaimed   Felshammer,
nettled.

" I   am   pitying   myselt.   You   have   missed   my
point ! "

" It sounded like pity ! " he insisted.

" You are quite right ; but it was self-pity. Won't
you admit that men are sometimes obtuse ? "

" They are often wrong ! "   He felt sorry, and an
ambiguous retort was the nearest thing in his nature
to the admission of a mistake. But Rachel remained
the same, placidly indulgent, because so slightly
touched by the sentiments or words of any one. The
secretary's rough ways pleased her, if anything could
be said to give her pleasure. She knew no man well,

because men were afraid of her, and she took no pains
to encourage them. Felshammer without encouragement treated her rather as an intelligence than as a
woman, and to her inexperience this seemed an
approach to the Platonic friendship of which she had
read in biographies. All the love of her soul and body
had gone to her children and was now in the dust
with them. The cleverness which was hers, cleverness inherited from five generations of acute financiers,
craved male companionship nevertheless; there were
days when her mind seemed like a ball whirling
through space and seeking, vainly, some wall to beat
against and rebound from; or like an arrow sent with
great impetus, yet without aim, into an atmosphere
where neither rising nor falling but only unresisted
flight was possible.

"Here," she said "while I keep alone, the world
looks large, and I can believe that people understand
human nature. The first hour I spent in society and
the first words I hear at a dinner or during some call
show me that we are cramped, bigoted, and false in
nearly all our relations with others. To be rescued
from narrowness, and for ever, is all I ask of the
future life—if there be such a thing. Personally, I
don't want it."

"Because you aren't well," replied Felshammer.

"No, that is not the reason. I had the same idea
as a girl when I was strong, and they used to say I
had everything before me."

"But you have told me that you had a dull girlhood. Youth wants romance, tumult, passion."

Colour rushed into her face as she heard these expressions, which seemed to her too vehement, and, distressed she began to fold up the lace. Felshammer wondered then at the transparency of her hands, although her sudden vivid blush had entirely escaped his notice.

"I had a short girlhood," said Rachel. "I married before I was twenty, and my marriage, of course, was entirely one of affection on both sides. My view of life has not been affected by individuals." The last sentence was added in a colder voice.

Felshammer, unconcerned, met it with :

"That's probably true enough."

"Are you, by any chance, going to the Oscar Sachs' to-night?" she asked.

"Oh, yes, I must! I have not yet met Mrs. Sachs."

"She is much admired, and she gives a great many parties, but I don't attend all of them. I must be there to-night, as Ernie says, 'for the look of the thing.' Isn't it irrational? She knows that I dislike entertainments; every one who will see me there knows the same fact. And yet I go because it would be thought unfriendly if I stayed away! The smallest and the greatest feelings we possess are sacrificed to this very 'look of the thing.' How silly and how tedious!"

"Still, your presence is bound to give pleasure."

"If you care for lace," she replied, with a rigid countenance. "I shall be wearing some very curious old Brussels point. For those who like beautiful things it will be a certain compensation for my unutterable dulness."

Felshammer had invited Mr. Gloucester to dine with him that evening for the third time, and afterwards they were going together to Mrs. Oscar Sachs's party. The music there, it was hoped, might distract him a little from his perplexities. But at the first dinner Felshammer had learnt the folly of endeavouring to help a man who could only show determination when he was being advised for his own good. Gloucester, by suspecting the motives of his firmest friends, now sought to atone for the implicit faith which he placed in a rascal. He began to take a childish pride in looking wise over the most innocent suggestion, and whereas he had once signed recklessly, without misgivings, papers of the highest importance to his estate, he could scarcely be induced now to write a line to his favourite sister.

"I am surrounded by vultures," he told Clementine —"vultures and jackals."

When Felshammer reached his club, he found a telegram awaiting him to the effect that Mr. Gloucester was unavoidably detained. Mr. Gloucester was dining at that moment at Holland Park with an acquaintance whom he had met through the agency of his new man of business. He was more terrified of this personage, a Mr. Keeping, than he had ever been of Haxsworth at his worst; he trifled with Keeping, shuffled, equivocated, procrastinated, coquetted, but he knew that in the end Keeping would have matters arranged in his own way. Keeping, for instance, had sent the telegram to Felshammer.

"Chuck him!" Keeping had said. Mr. Gloucester protested, murmured that such a proceeding would be grossly uncivil.

"But you must meet Bingham. It is imperatively necessary, believe me. Every day now is precious. This is a matter of duty, not pleasure."

Mr. Gloucester talked with boldness on the obligations of common courtesy while Keeping wrote out the telegram, rang for his office boy, and had the message carried to the post.

"It's really too bad! I hope he won't be offended," said Mr. Gloucester, offering Keeping his cigar-case, as the door closed on the boy's retreating figure.

Keeping chose a cigar, fingered it, held it to his nose, cut off the top, held a match to the end, and drew three long whiffs before he made any reply.

"O, that's all right!" he said at last. "You must take things quietly, Gloucester."

It had come to this; his man of business addressed him as Gloucester. But the moral strength which surrendered to Keeping's will was also beyond the

stimulus of offended personal dignity. Resentment
overflowed in his heart and rose scalding to the
sockets of his eyes. Outwardly he showed the
uncomplaining shame of one who has drifted, from
no motive, into a false position.

Bingham proved to be a plausible, good-looking
person, for whom Keeping had conceived one of those
curious infatuations which are so common between
scoundrels and their dupes. Keeping, who was
shrewd and scheming but quite honest according to
moderate standards of rectitude, had been dazzled by
what he considered the brilliant financial genius of his
friend Catesby Bingham. Bingham's ringing laugh,
his intimate anecdotes about aristocratic society, his
resource, above all his success, for he handled a large
amount of money in the course of the year, fascinated
the commonplace solicitor, who was the average
well-to-do man of the average conventional world.
"Bingham," he would say, "always makes me think
of Sherlock Holmes." The cleverness of Sherlock
Holmes was Mr. Keeping's ideal of ingenuity
amounting to the miraculous.

Gloucester himself began to feel, half-way through
dinner, the charm of Catesby Bingham's glossy ease.
If he was not well bred, he came so very near it that
he would have passed in polished circles for a polished
person who had mixed perhaps a little too much with his
inferiors and had become a shade coarse.

He walked part of the way to Chester Square with

Mr. Gloucester, and the following conversation occurred between them. Bingham said—

" By the by, have you ever heard anything about East Reefs ? "

" No, nothing," replied Mr. Gloucester.

" I can give you a tip. You can make twenty thousand pounds as certain as anything. You may regard it as made."

" I had better not begin to spend it ! " replied Gloucester, but he began to tingle at the idea.

" No, no l I'm not ragging ! " continued Catesby Bingham. "If you like to apply for four hundred East Reefs between this and to-morrow night, I can tell you of a market for them at treble the price and treble that again."

" But if I apply for these shares, where am I to get the money to pay for them ? " said Gloucester.

" It is morally certain that you can part with them within forty-eight hours. You'll only have to pocket the difference."

" Or pay the loss ! " said Gloucester, who had gained some knowledge of business since his troubles began.

" Or pay the loss, of course. But there's no chance of that."

" I don't like the risk."

" I'll take the risk. It is only upon those terms that any man in his senses would give you such advice." He caught hold of Gloucester's arm, slackened his pace, and added : " I can readily believe that you don't wish to place yourself under any obligation to a mere acquaintance. This is no favour, I assure you. The advantage will be mutual. Say that I take a third of the profit."

" I still do not see how to work it."

"Well, you go to Larrington's. Apply for the shares——"

" Larrington knows that I haven't the private means which could justify such an order. Suppose he won't take the order without cover—what then ? "

" That will be all right. Use my name if they press. But they won't ; they'll take it for granted that you have got a backer somewhere. They prefer private buyers of your stamp. The idea is that you intend to invest—not to speculate."

"Then," said Mr. Gloucester, "do you mean to say, if I win, I take part of the profits, and if those shares go down you'll pay all the losses ? It seems too unfair."

" There won't be any losses. It's absolutely safe."

" I have always steered clear of this kind of thing," murmured Gloucester. "It would make all the difference in the world to me if I could get a little extra money now, yet——"

" You really do me an enormous favour. They might allot you every share you ask for. They want solid investors. They know me. They would think I was merely buying to sell. It's child's play.

Consult Keeping first, if you like. I know he would urge you to follow my suggestion."

Mr. Gloucester had already resolved to try his luck. Gambling on the Stock Exchange or anywhere else seemed entirely proper to the foolish, inconsistent gentleman. Nearly all the Dukes indulged in this particular amusement, which happened to be lucrative as horse-racing was, sometimes. Trade, on the other hand, still filled him with repugnance.

He drew himself up and announced proudly :

" I do not care to throw too much *onus* on Mr. Keeping." Keeping might address him as an equal but he had determined to Mister the solicitor so long as he had the power of utterance. " Mr. Keeping is too kind frequently, he is a most obliging person, most friendly, indeed, in every way, but I beg that you will consider me as a man by myself."

"Exactly!" said Catesby Bingham, in a sympathetic tone. " Keeping is willing to communicate all he knows, which, in these matters, does not amount to much. It is not for me to take the wind out of his sails. He's perfectly reliable and so forth, but——"

" Quite so, quite so ! " replied Gloucester, feeling what a pleasure it was to meet with some one in business very nearly of his own class and sentiments.

Clementine was waiting up for her father, and let him in when she heard the ring and knock, bolder than it had been for a long time, at the front door. He was good-tempered and, as he drank his glass of freshly-boiled hot water before retiring, gave a graceful imitation of Mr. Keeping, who had a marked cockney accent.

"I wish, darling, you could hear him say, 'Try a little of that port, Gloucester.' I give you an imperfect idea of the original; yet he's a well-meaning creature; never condemn any man merely because he is vulgar. Vulgar people are frequently obliging and respectable. Once or twice I felt tempted to give him a tremendous dressing, but *toutes les vérités ne sont pas bonnes à dire.* Why wound him?"

"Was he with Dr. Felshammer?" asked Clementine, surprised.

Mr. Gloucester looked annoyed at once. Since his troubles he had become irritable and uncertain.

"I couldn't dine at the Travellers'. I spent the evening with Mr. Keeping and Catesby Bingham— one of my best acquaintances. You look tired. Give me a nice new nib and some of our Eastern Acres notepaper. I must write a letter or two."

"So late as this?"

"I am not tired. Now run away to bed."

She did not sleep till she heard him mounting the stairs at midnight. The next morning she found that he had scribbled rough copies on more than a quire of paper, and had consulted the dictionary, the *Stock Exchange Year Book*, and *Every Man His Own Lawyer* in the successful attempt to write a short note to Messrs. Larrington & Co.—a name she did not know.

CHAPTER XII

THE HEART TOWARD THE HIGHWAY

MRS. OSCAR SACHS's evening party took place at her house in Prince's Gate. A number of City and professional men, with their wives and daughters, were present. All the male guests had an air of alertness and power; a few looked overworked, a few were sickly, but the crowd, as a body, seemed composed of strenuous, robust, self-satisfied, and confident individuals. The women, many of whom were handsome, wore superb jewels clumsily set in massive pendants, necklaces, and bracelets. One here and there carried a set of large diamond stars on her head; several had tiaras. Their clothes were of brocade, or velvet richly trimmed, or satin embroidered; they carried fans and pocket-handkerchiefs edged with Duchesse lace; when they talked they employed admirable English, free from slang. Felshammer, with a foreigner's discrimination, thought them dignified, virtuous, unimaginative, sincere, assertive. He did not recognise a single face he knew.

Neither Sachs nor Bickersteth, in spite of their pride
in royal and noble clients, had the smallest desire
to shine in what is known as society. They were
aristocrats themselves in the cosmopolitan world of
finance ; they cultivated their own substantial set and
were even inaccessible, except at Lombard Street, to
the numerous persons of high rank who were disposed
to regard most favourably, and attend, the entertainments given by Mrs. Oscar Sachs. Of the two
partners, Bickersteth was the more ostentatious,
perhaps because his home was desolate and his wife
an invalid. He would never have loved a Mrs. Sachs
himself, but there were hours when he recognised that
Oscar had made a wise choice, and was, beyond doubt,
a domestic man engrossed in his own family. Bickersteth was troubled by ideals of life which he was
neither strong enough to keep nor cynical enough
to renounce. He longed for changes which he did
not really want, for adventures which he was well
aware would bore him, for gaieties which were alien
to his bilious disposition. Rachel was the ennobling
element in a life which might have been easily ruined
for the sake of a half-hearted caprice, or spent in
vacillation between feeble scruples and feebler
passions.

Mrs. Oscar Sachs was the mother of two beautiful,
precocious little girls. She herself was as swarthy as
Mrs. Bickersteth, and what she lacked of Rachel's
grand air she atoned for in vivacity. The traditional

contrast between a fair woman and a dark one can never be so great as a contrast between two pronounced brunettes of different styles. Mrs. Sachs was small ; her pretty neck, round arms, and mobile face was almost brown ; so were her eyes, although they seemed as black as her silky hair ; an intense if innocent love of excitement animated every gesture, glance, and word ; her laughter rippled like a child's— when she played with her own children she was always the most boisterous and least fatigued of the three. It was her idiosyncrasy to dress invariably in plain gowns of dull colours. That evening she wore a black chiffon over white silk, diamond earrings, but no other ornament except one pink rose in her belt. By birth she was English ; her father was a wealthy cotton-spinner who had gone into Parliament. She had been christened Nadeshda because there was Russian blood in the family on the grandmother's side. Sachs told his wife many things relating to business, and when Felshammer made his appearance she looked at him with real admiration as the man who had been clever enough to make good terms with her husband.

"Wasn't it shameful about Campsey ?" she said almost immediately, opening her eyes very wide and pouting her lips. "Wasn't it too disgraceful ? An expert need not be a saint, but he must be a gentleman. It has made Oscar perfectly ill, although he won't admit that for an instant. Now, do you know any one here? I want you to enjoy yourself—a difficult thing at an English party."

She smiled gaily at her own small joke, and added: "We call this breaking the ice."

"But how ungracious it is to assume that there is any ice to break!" replied Felshammer. She put her head slightly on one side with an almost apologetic air:

"Oscar likes you very much. Yet the whole thing was unpleasant; don't you think so? People say that business men are hard. I find them, as a matter of fact, far more tender-hearted than artists and others who are supposed to be above commercial affairs. Poor Oscar feels so hurt at Campsey's ingratitude, but he is happy about you, honestly and truly. I mean it. In the circumstances that's a high compliment, because it is such thankless work as a rule to give information about some trusted person who has been deceitful."

Nadeshda seemed to him a straightforward, charming little woman, one with whom many men in his place would have certainly attempted to establish sentimental relations. To be prudent under the alluring mask of indiscretion is a rare faculty. It was the unspeakable gift of Mrs. Oscar Sachs. Felshammer had resolved, however, to avoid every danger, small or great, of the kind, because he loved Clementine, and had nothing more than criticism to bestow on others. By her youth, by her natural fascination, by her goodness, by her very indifference to himself, his affection

for the high-spirited girl had risen, gained power, and
kept it. In time the exclusiveness of that strong
feeling might have lost its vigour ; it is possible that,
as the youth waned, and the beauty of the face grew
familiar, and the precious attributes of the mind, once
proved indelible, ceased to cause wonder, he might
have sought amusement at least in studying new
creatures and their ways. But for the present he
knew her actually so little, they had met so seldom,
exchanged such few words, she was so close and
delicious in his memory, so distant in his presence,
that she engrossed every thought and emotion of his—
every hope which was not concentrated absolutely on
the money-market. But the policy of his whole
career had been opposed to friendships with women.
He did not believe in them. Had he not seen
ambitions wrecked, existences made contemptible,
hearts left void or full of bitterness for no worthier
reason than some unconsidered flirtation, begun
through vanity or self-interest, continued out of habit
or false politeness, and ending in lifelong bondage ?
No chains for him ! After he left Mrs. Sachs he
watched groups, compared manners, gaits, voices,
attitudes, marvelled at the loveliness of many of the
girls, the freshness of the matrons ; he overheard
fragments of dialogue ; one remark, offered by one
comely woman who looked like a Rubens to another
who looked like a Reynolds, made him say almost
aloud to himself :

" Just as I thought ! "

This was the remark :

" I wonder that Nadeshda invited Lady Greenslade when she must have known that Mrs. Bickersteth was coming."

It was late when the Bickersteths arrived. Felshammer did not hurry forward to meet them, nor did he approach Rachel till he saw her, haggard, inattentive, and contemptuous, sitting alone near the window, listening to the last song on the programme. The moonlight streamed in upon her through a break in the awning over the balcony; yet even these romantic beams, which, on the stage, would have seemed a deliberate, unreal, but flattering effect, could not cast any glamour over her singular personality. When Felshammer came up she showed neither surprise nor pleasure, but she looked towards a vacant chair by her side, and he received the slight movement as an invitation to sit down.

" Have I been here long enough yet ? " she asked.

" Hardly."

" Do you know why I was so late ? Ernie is rather cross with me. I was afraid I couldn't come after all. I was tired. After you had gone I ordered the carriage and called on Miss Gloucester."

He could think of nothing to say ; he flushed, his heart began to beat violently, he looked down and felt as foolish as a lovesick boy.

" I found her at home," continued Rachel, " and I

asked her to come here with me to-night, but she says
that she is not going out just now. For a girl that's
a mistake. I told her so."

Encouraging as this indirect kindness might have
been from any other woman, it was impossible for
Felshammer to regard it as more than an act of dutiful
amiability. Mrs. Bickersteth's face remained impas-
sive; she took up the programme, which she had
dropped into her lap for a moment, and began to read
very gravely to herself the following verse :

"Swallow, my sister, O sister swallow,
   How can thine heart be full of the spring?
   A thousand summers are over and dead,
   What hast thou found in the spring to follow?
   What hast thou found in thy heart to sing?
   What wilt thou do when the summer is shed?"

"How many here could understand this?" she
asked, handing it to him.

"They seem to listen to it," he replied.

"That is because Madame Cherrington is very
expensive and her voice is good. I was thinking
of the poem."

"Well, to be candid, it would not chime in
naturally with my own mood. There are too
many questions :—

   "'The world's gone, yet the world is here?
   Are not all things as they appear?'

I prefer to take that view, if I must take any, of life. You think too much. One does not go to a party in order to think."

"Evidently you are right, if I may judge by the apparent enjoyment of my fellow-revellers!"

"That's severe," said Felshammer.

"Can't you see," she said, with a sudden animation which failed almost as swiftly as it came, "that I wish I could take it all as they do? What, for instance, is your opinion of the woman over there in yellow? I heard her call this song a sweet little thing."

The woman in yellow was short, stout, frowsy, and excitable. She lounged on a rose brocade sofa, and was talking at the top of a high nasal voice about some "poor dear old Duke" to Mr. Bickersteth, who looked amused.

"She is Lady Greenslade; her father is Lord Coverley," said Rachel.

"Vulgarity, like beauty, is distributed by the gods without prejudice," said Felshammer; "it has nothing to do with one's birth. Besides, what is vulgarity but the unrestrained exhibition of too common human feelings? When we call persons vulgar we mean that they are commonplace in an artless and energetic way."

Rachel looked at him with an air of baffled adroitness.

"After all, how can it matter what anybody wonders about anybody else?" she said. Bickersteth, conscious that he was being observed, made an excuse for leaving Lady Greenslade and came over to his wife.

" You look tired to death ! " he exclaimed. "Would you like to go home ? "

Without a word she rose, and, half smiling at Felshammer, took her husband's arm. They walked together in silence till they reached Lady Greenslade, to whom Rachel bowed coldly. But her ladyship stood up.

" Have you seen Greenslade ? " she asked.

It was her method in society to ask every person she met whether he or she had seen Greenslade. He always escorted her to entertainments, and invariably left at the end of the first half-hour.

" Hasn't he gone to his club long ago ? " said Rachel, and she passed on.

Felshammer caught the question and the reply. "And yet," he thought, " women are surprised when they find they have made enemies ! "

He took leave himself soon after the departure of the Bickersteths. His evening, on the whole, had produced a painful and, what was worse, a wearisome effect on his spirits. He remembered a text which his mother, a very pious woman, used to quote, as a rule, after any festivity among her neighbours : " *The new wine mourns, all the merry-hearted do sigh.*" There had been something blighting in the atmosphere of both the houses he had visited that day—a withering, spoiling, creeping influence, which had entered every fibre of his body, every secret recess of his mind; he felt languid, callous, actually numb. A couple in the street were bidding each other good-night or goodbye as he turned the corner leading to his hotel. The woman was sobbing; the man seemed unable to speak. They clung together, parted, and returned twice for one more last touch and glance.

"How can they care so much?" thought Fels-hammer, hating himself for the sneer. But he resolved to see Clementine on the morrow. He knew by instinct that she was his necessary salvation.

CHAPTER XIII

HASTY FRUIT BEFORE THE SUMMER

CLEMENTINE was playing some Schumann the next afternoon when Dr. Felshammer called. She had tried to feel cheerful all that day, and had walked in Kensington Gardens before lunch and bought theatre tickets for herself and her father. But her mind was oppressed ; the tragic, feverish music of the Carnival found an unhappy echo in her own thoughts—perhaps because the loneliness of the young is sadder than any other loneliness. It has no memories ; its hopes are perilous, impatient, and untried. Felshammer, as he entered the drawing-room, mistook the flush of welcome on her face for something altogether more encouraging.

"You are evidently quite well again," he said, with his eyes full of admiration. "I have never seen you look better. I have come to ask why your father threw me over last night. And why didn't you accept Mrs. Bickersteth's invitation ? Do you like her ?"

"I think so. Was the party amusing ?"

He gave an account of his evening, but he walked, while he spoke, about the room, turning over the music on the piano and the books on the table.

"What's this—Byron?" he exclaimed, picking up a small blue volume and glancing at some of the poems. "I believe he is my favourite poet. Listen to this:

> "'Alas, the love of woman! It is known
> To be a lovely and a fearful thing;
> For all of theirs upon that die is thrown,
> And, if 'tis lost, life hath no more to bring
> To them but mockeries of the past alone. . . . '

That is very fine. I see you have marked it. Was your admiration impersonal or sympathetic?"

"I thought it was sad," she answered, "and I wondered whether it was true."

"You ought to have gone to the party. You are moping too much!"

"But I don't care about parties just now."

"I can't bear to hear you talk that way! You're so young; you ought to have every pleasure."

"If I were not anxious about papa, I should be perfectly happy, Dr. Felshammer."

"I'm glad to hear that. I am supposed to be selfish. My own dear mother often said so."

But he was looking at Clementine and deciding that she would still be beautiful even at sixty. He

was delighted, confused, and resolved at the same
time. He had never before spoken to her of love.
Surely there had been something fatal in the volume
of Byron !

"Yes, I am supposed to be selfish," he repeated ;
"but, on my honour, I could find my happiness in
yours. I haven't this feeling about any one else in
the world. I have never had it before. It is a
surprise to me, I own. You see, I keep nothing
back. Whatever the truth may be, you shall have it."

He had not intended to declare himself suddenly,
but the words came before he could check them, and
he caught her arm without knowing that he touched
it.

"I can't go on in this uncertainty," he continued.
"I want you always with me. I love you, Clementine. I think I could make you love me. Will you
be my wife ?"

For a moment the girl was fascinated and flattered
by his appeal. He was not eloquent in speech and he
had said nothing remarkable, but he trembled, he was
pale, the domineering, scornful, uncompromising man
seemed almost afraid of her. She had never before
received an offer of marriage, and, as she was neither
sentimental nor vain, her first instinct was one of
gratitude for his affection. In after years he often
laughed bitterly at the recollection of her reply.

"I wonder why you like me ?" She drew away
from his grasp as she spoke.

"How can I help liking yóu?" he exclaimed.
"You are everything I love; you are pretty, sweet,
kind, good, clever!"

"Good and clever come last!" she said, smiling.
"But that's because you are truthful, I suppose."

"Is that all you have to say? You can't really be
startled. You must have guessed. Women always
know. It is we men who are at the disadvantage.
I can tell nothing about you one way or the other.
Perhaps that's the charm. At any rate, I'm mastered.
I'm bewitched. I shall never be able to get
free!"

He drew a step nearer and kissed timidly her cheek,
which seemed as soft and fragrant as a leaf growing in
the sun.

"You mustn't do that!" said Clementine, with
a self-possession which would have warned a less
infatuated lover that his suit was vain. "I ought to
be angry, but I am not, because you are my best
friend. I didn't want you for my best friend, and I
used to think I could never care for you. I do care
for you now very much—oh, very much, but not in
a kissing way—even if you get vexed and say we
cannot remain as we are."

"As we are—no! Haven't I said enough? Could
we be ever again just as we were—after this? Every
time we have met there has been some difference, and
this will make the greatest difference of all!"

"That's what I meant when I said it was wrong.

I can't say now that I have never been kissed, and I wanted to be able to say that."

"To whom ?"

"To myself, I suppose.'"

"I knew you were a prude. That is one more reason for hating and loving you. A good thing, too l I like your spirit. It shows in your eyes—you could kill me. Besides, marriage demands consideration. I want you to accept me, but I don't ask you to say 'Yes' as though you had been preparing your answer for days. What have you against me ? Is it my age ? Am I too plain ? Somehow, I don't believe you would be influenced by one's looks."

She glanced away, and the Prince's handsome face rose to her memory.

"It has nothing to do with age," she said, "and I am more grateful than I sound. I think it is very kind of you to want to marry me."

"I am a fool about you l I have been begging and pleading for the last half-hour as though my life depended on your reply. Perhaps it does."

"Oh, why can't you see that you make me miserable ? I know quite well all you are offering me. I trust you. I like you. But my heart stops there. It isn't because I'm romantic. Yet I must wait. You are not the one ! I could only marry a man I loved." She blushed at the word.

"Love comes. You are not much more than a little girl l "

"Please, please say no more now!"

"I'll return to the question another time, then. I won't give up my idea—I swear I won't!"

"You must!" she said earnestly. "I should like to be your friend, if you will allow me, but this is not the way to keep friends."

The tender and profound sadness of her expression, her soft gestures, the delicate flush which rose and wavered and mounted almost to her temples while she spoke, restrained Felshammer's impetuosity, but they deepened his determination to gain the day.

"They say I always drive hard bargains," he exclaimed, pacing the floor. "Devilish hard bargains too! I am going to consider myself, and you must see life as it is. I love you and I want you, and I haven't thought of any one else for the last weeks. And if you will be my wife, I'll do any mortal thing you ask. I don't mind what it is. I wish to make you happy, that's all."

"But you cannot. Haven't I told you so? You cannot."

"I have got a strong will, and if I undertake a thing, I generally pull it through. I am plain and over forty, not a lady's man, but I'll protect you and be kind to you. I'll help your father."

"I can't do it. I can't think of it. It is not fair to press me."

"I know it isn't magnificent, but it is war," he answered. "I have set my heart on you. I don't ask you to love me—I dare not. But trust me ; believe in me." And he knelt by her side.

"I have always believed in you, but I don't love you. I cannot love any one, perhaps."

"I'll make you love me. I have fairly grovelled in the dust for you."

"It is impossible," said Clementine ; "and if I were dead and in my grave, it could not be more impossible."

"I refuse to be discouraged," he replied. But he walked away and stood at the window with his back to her as though he were looking out on to the square. Clementine, terrified by his mood, went to the piano mechanically, closed it with trembling fingers, and put her music back into its portfolio. She had been on the point of doing these things when he was announced, and now, in a kind of dream, she fulfilled the half-formed intention. Would no sound break the painful silence ? Would Felshammer ever turn, ever speak, ever go ? Each second seemed an hour. Was it all really happening ? Was the whole scene her fancy ? She touched her own face, but it was numb. She caught sight of her own reflection in the mirror—and moved her head. Yes—the reflection moved also. At last she could bear the strain no longer.

"Dr. Felshammer," she said, "I am frightened. Your thoughts are angry and cruel and bitter. I feel them all around me like knives in the air. I have done nothing to deserve this."

"No," he said, wheeling round; "but I have been a fool—a blundering fool! The moment a man is in earnest he had better cut his throat than talk to a woman. Yet you are a good little girl. I have got a reverence for you, on my soul. I am sorry if I frightened you. I will send you some chocolates. That is the thing to offer—a box of chocolates. Never love, never your whole life. Poor little pretty child!"

He took her face between his hands and smoothed back the soft brown hair from her brow, which was entirely clear and flawless. Tears sprang into his eyes as he repeated—

"Poor little pretty child! Forget all the rest."

When he had gone Clementine cried bitterly. It had been her first encounter with a strong emotion, and she began to fear that there were evil possibilities in men's love; that it was not always the sentimental heroic affection described in tales and ballads. There had been something fierce, something unsparing and implacable underlying Felshammer's manner during their interview. Had some madness beset him? She could not think that a mere girl could so affect any man—least of all one who met beautiful women constantly in society, one who had seen life in all quarters of the globe. "He sees me as I am not," she told herself; "it is some sort of accident or mistake. How could it be anything else except a mistake?"

Then she wondered what she would have thought

if Prince Paul had said all that Felshammer had said. Would it have seemed such madness? No! The instantaneousness of the response filled her whole soul with a wild joy. She stretched out her arms to greet the imagined speaker, and the lonely room had, for a moment, the charm, the fragrant stillness of a summer garden. The moment passed, but the self-knowledge gained in that instant remained. Clementine had learnt her own secret.

She was roused by the sound of footsteps on the uncarpeted stairs outside. Leonore, flushed, breathless, and excited, burst into the room.

"I ran into that Dr. Felshammer's arms!" she exclaimed. "What a fascinating man! I begin to like foreigners. They have so much feeling. But you are getting quite American. You have callers without a chaperon. It's nice to be you, I must say. He looked at my hat."

"It is very picturesque," said Clementine, anxious to divert Leonore's attention.

"Is he really in love with you?" asked Leonore, watching herself in the mirror, and deciding that she was, beyond question, the beauty of the family, although she had never received an offer of marriage.

"Has he proposed?" she continued. "He had a strange expression."

"How can you have such ideas?" asked Clementine.

"You wouldn't be foolish enough to refuse him?"

said her cousin. "You wouldn't throw away the chance of a lifetime just because the Prince has a better figure?"

"I wish you wouldn't talk about the Prince. I think it is wrong. Do I ever speak of him myself?"

"Goose! Goose! Goose! You can't deceive your little cousin. You might let me meet Dr. Felshammer again some time at tea. I see possibilities."

"I think you must be fond of flirting!" said Clementine. "I believe it amuses you."

"I hate flirting, my dear child. But I don't want to be an old maid. I have never before seen a man who had the air of wishing to marry anybody. Felshammer is in a marrying mood. He wants to settle down. I saw that at a glance. What a mercy it is that I wore this new hat! People get to like a soul, but a satisfactory hat makes an impression at first sight."

"You are more flippant than you used to be!" sighed Clementine.

"Felshammer has made me flippant," answered Leonore. "I am always what papa calls giddy when I am hopeful." She pretended to be jesting, but in her heart she was planning serious projects.

CHAPTER XIV

MR. GLOUCESTER HAS SEVERAL SURPRISES

MR. CATESBY BINGHAM was disturbed that evening in his chambers at the Albany by an unexpected call from Mr. Gloucester. Nevertheless he said pleasantly enough—

" It is nice of you to look me up. Anything very special on the carpet ? "

Mr. Gloucester, who had a drawn face, held out a letter.

" I am afraid it is very serious," said he.

" Ah, you're not used to the City yet ! "

" Well, read that," gasped the older man.

" Who is it from ? " asked Mr. Bingham, lighting a cigar. He remembered that his guest did not smoke.

" It is from Larrington's."

" I don't quite understand it," said Bingham, after he had read it, with a thoughtful air, twice.

" Oh, yes, you do," replied Mr. Gloucester, speaking rapidly—" it is terribly plain ! I applied for the shares

—shares in the East Reef, as you said—and they have gone down from twenty-eight to three and a half. The syndicate was carrying a large amount of stock on which collateral loans had been obtained. Several banks on Thursday threw out the stocks and insisted on additional security. The syndicate was seriously embarrassed for funds, and now there's a slump. But you know all this as well as I do!"

Bingham paused to admire one of his own photographs on the mantelshelf and observed—

"You must make yourself a little clearer, my dear Gloucester."

"Well, it looks to me as though—I am very sorry to say it—but it looks as though you were let in for a matter of thirty thousand pounds."

Bingham lifted his eyebrows and screwed up his mouth.

"Did you say that I was let in?" he asked. "This is a private speculation entirely on your own part, I take it."

"Why, I never knew of the East Reefs till you mentioned them to me! I merely carried out your instructions. I have no money for speculation."

"There I agree with you. But I am at a loss to account for your delusion with regard to my liability in the matter."

He surveyed his bewildered companion with an air of reproachful and injured confidence.

"What do you mean?" said Gloucester, stupefied.

"You must find the money yourself."

"Find the money myself! What are you talking about? I have no capital. Besides, you know perfectly well what you said."

"Really, Mr. Gloucester, this is too bad! It is very painful."

Gloucester by this time was frightened into courage.

"Are you going to lie about it?" he asked. "Because I am not going to stand any underhand dealings."

Catesby Bingham drew out a pocket-handkerchief scented with white rose and used it noisily.

"No heroics, Mr. Gloucester, please! Spare me heroics!" he said. "They don't answer in the City at all. You have done an extremely foolish thing—not to say dishonest—thing, and, if you had approached me in the proper spirit, I might have taken——"

Gloucester brought his delicate fist down on the table, and uttered an oath for the third time in his life.

"You yourself told me to apply for the shares in my own name. If the speculation did not turn out well, you undertook to see the thing through."

"I have not the slightest recollection of any such conversation."

"Good God!"

"It is charitable to suppose that you are the victim of some hallucination!" continued Bingham, who, as a constant patron of melodrama, employed stage

phrases when he wished to be especially impressive.
"An hallucination won't pay the deficit, and, so far as
I can see, it will not preserve you from bankruptcy, but
it will be a sop to your relatives.   As for your story,
any one would say that I am incapable of making
such absurd propositions."

"Then let me say that you are an infernal black-
guard !   If you manage to ruin me, you won't get
off scot free.   I have got a few friends in the world !"

"Will they pay up ?" asked Bingham drily.

"They will stand by me," said Gloucester. "They
are gentlemen and men of honour."   He knew, however, that they would not lend him money.   He
turned once more to study Bingham's insolent face.
"I can't think that you are in earnest !" he exclaimed.
"You can't mean to break your promise.   It's inconceivable.   Keeping spoke of you in the highest
terms."

"I deny the promise, and I deny my liability—what
is more, I deny absolutely any knowledge of the affair.
Keeping does himself rather well.   He gave us a good
dinner."

"All right.   I begin to see your line of defence—
an unworthy one, a disgraceful one.   You must be prepared to face the consequences."

"What consequences ?"

"I don't know," said Gloucester; "but I know
that there is such a thing as justice, and I know that
blackguards don't have it all their own way."

He was unnerved, shaking, livid, almost lifeless, yet there was a quality in his voice which made the stronger man quail—not with fear, but at the blind, superstitious dread of an honest curse.

"Perhaps, if you take a more conciliatory tone——" he began.

"I don't want any conciliation. I ask you whether you intend to keep your word. You know perfectly well what passed between us. You have proved yourself a liar, but you cannot prove me one."

"Mr. Gloucester! I must warn you that your expressions are becoming actionable."

"And a very good thing too! But you would no more dare bring an action against me than you would fly. I am not in the least afraid of an English jury—not in the least!"

"You are excited, sir! I decline to hold you responsible. This is the worst of admitting amateurs into business. If you will take my advice——"

"Again!" cried Gloucester, with a withering glance. "Do you ask me to take your advice again?" And, in a paroxysm of rage, he fled from the room, rushed down the stairs into the street, and walked towards the river. People were swarming on the pavement; carriages, omnibuses, cabs, and conveyances of every description were blocking the road; it was the hour when most of the theatres and large music-halls are open to the public; newsboys were shouting special editions of the evening papers; the sound of many thousand voices and all the traffic acted as an anodyne to the desperate man, and his frantic thoughts were overpowered by the roar. Twice he was nearly run over ; he was elbowed, and jostled, and trampled on by laughing couples or hurried youths ; he was exhorted to " look where he was going," and pointed at by the wild girls who, in twos and threes, trailed past him, rolling their eyes and dragging their skirts in the mud. Where should he go ? What could he do ? He had boasted to Bingham of his friends. Did he possess any ? He thought of Felshammer.

Panic and troubles had so changed Mr. Gloucester's character that he easily dismissed the remorse he began to feel at the remembrance of his ungracious conduct towards the Prince's secretary. " I didn't want to trouble him unless I was obliged to do so," he told himself ; " one has a natural disinclination to approach a mere acquaintance on such matters." No hesitation stood in his way now, however. He called a hansom and rode to Felshammer's hotel, where he found him dressing for dinner. With tears, sighs, and bitterness the old gentleman told of his disastrous experience. At the end, Felshammer turned to him kindly and said—

"I can help you. Tell your daughter I can help you, and I will."

"But Clementine knows nothing," said Gloucester ; " it would break her heart."

"Would my help," said the German grimly, "break her heart?"

"No, no! My weakness! My folly! Nothing could be more beautiful or more touching than her affection for me; it mustn't go."

"She won't alter because you have been unfortunate," said Felshammer; "and I think it is your duty to make the whole situation clear to her. But let us get things in perfect order first. Let her have the truth, although there is no reason why she should suffer any suspense."

By mortgaging his property, crippling his own resources in every direction, and binding himself to severe sacrifices, he placed Gloucester in a position, after a few weeks, to deal with Larrington's account. It was all brought to pass with so little trouble to the obliged man that, so far from realising the vast extent of his indebtedness, he forgot to be grateful. Once he told Clementine—"That fellow Felshammer is literally rolling in money. Some day I will tell something about him which I know for a fact. He can draw his thirty thousand pounds and never miss it. He has a good billet, too, at Sachs and Bickersteth's. They will make him a partner one of these days."

By this time the Romillys were at their house in Chester Square, and, as Eastern Acres was let, Mr. Gloucester and Clementine had taken unpretentious apartments in a small crescent near Gloucester Road. There the two enjoyed independence at least.

Keeping had secured a small sum of ready money by selling two villas near Blackheath, which Mr. Gloucester suddenly remembered having inherited from his godfather.

"We shall have a happy season, after all, my darling," said Mr. Gloucester; "and, if we can't be at dear Thomas's, the woman here cooks admirably. We might ask Dr. Felshammer to lunch some Sunday."

"Oh, no!" said Clementine.

"It would be a little civility to ask him," insisted her father; "he is much taken up with the City set and he may not be able to accept the invitation; but the fact is, he has done me a favour."

Her heart sank. She guessed at once the favour had reference to a loan—a loan which could never be repaid.

"Was it much?" she asked faintly.

Mr. Gloucester flushed; his complexion was still perfect and his skin transparent.

"Not much for him," was the evasive reply.

"That is why he has never called, I suppose," said Clementine. She had attributed his absence to another reason; perhaps he had come to his senses and seen that he did not love her. A vainer girl might have felt a certain chagrin at the thought of a lover cured so swiftly of his passion, but she valued his friendship, and, in her inexperience, she believed that they might come together again, after an interval, on the old

13

footing. Indeed, she had permitted herself to look
forward to their peaceful reconciliation ; yet he was
keeping away, it seemed, merely because he had lent
her father money. What a humiliating thought!
Could she bear it ?

"Oh, papa l" she exclaimed, "why from Dr.
Felshammer ? Why not from the bank ? "

Mr. Gloucester did not know how to explain that
his bankers could no longer see their way to help him
through his embarrassments.

"It was a matter of business, darling," said he. "I
shall give 5 per cent. interest. To him it was a
pure investment. Try to understand the weight of
the misfortune which has fallen upon me, and do not
add to it by reproaches."

"Reproaches !" she said, as tears sprang to her
eyes. "How could I ever reproach you? But—but Dr.
Felshammer asked me to marry him when I last saw
him. Don't you see how awful it is for me to think
that we owe him money ? "

"God bless my soul l" exclaimed Mr. Gloucester.
"How awkward ! How shocking ! I don't suppose
he meant to be presumptuous. Yet what presumption l
On the whole, I am glad that I knew nothing about
it. Of course, I cannot ask him to lunch. I am
surprised ! I am amazed l What next ? I am sorry,
in a way, that you have told me. It puts everything
in a new light. I hope he is aware that I didn't know."

" He must know that, papa."

"I am not so sure."

"But he must be certain that you would never ask a favour in such circumstances. Why, it would seem like taxing him!"

Mr. Gloucester was wondering at that moment whether his own position with regard to Felshammer was not greatly strengthened, nevertheless, by such an asset as Clementine. He had never before regarded Clementine as a form of security. The idea gave him new hopes and new courage.

"I remember now," he said, "that at the time of our transaction he mentioned you. I thought it rather bad taste on his part, and I kept him in his place. Poor fellow! I hope you never led him to · believe that there was the least chance——"

He stopped short and observed how extraordinarily attractive she had grown. He had always been a judge of beauty, and he knew the kind of charm which appealed to the best type of man. Clementine possessed that charm—it was partly composed of shyness, partly of sympathy, partly of gaiety, but chiefly of a deep, unchangeable innocence which the knowledge of evil could neither destroy nor mar. He thrilled with pride as the conviction of her assured power over the world flashed across his mind. Men and women too would acknowledge her spell. Her youth would pass no doubt, her fresh brilliancy fade a little, but the essential lovableness of her nature would last as long as she lived.

"But you are not having the right opportunities !" he exclaimed, finishing his thoughts aloud. "Something must be done before business and lawyers have demoralised me utterly."

At moments he was conscious that the terrible work of demoralisation had begun, and his one cure for the melancholy produced by this reflection was an opium pill. Long before he had sometimes taken this remedy most unwillingly for neuralgia. The prejudice in his mind against drugs was waning. Had not Providence provided a solace for the killing cares of life ? Why quarrel with benefits ?

"My darling," said he suddenly, "I wish I had never been forced to think about money. It is degrading."

CHAPTER XV

WHEN MONEY DOES NOT ANSWER ALL THINGS

MR. COBDEN DURYEE was as astonished as his knowledge of life permitted him to be at Prince Paul's demeanour in the United States. Without surprise and without effort, the young man had responded to the incalculable moods of that vast cosmopolitan democracy. But his innate character received no modification; he longed perpetually for the country of Urseville-Beylestein and the sceptre of his ancestors. An aristocrat can never alter; the traditions of caste are stronger than the strongest religious belief, and men who have changed the faith of all their ancestors have never surrendered their pride in possessing a certain rank, or their desire to exercise a once acknowledged rule. Prince Paul at his simplest never forgot that he was a monarch's son—the descendant of a great and glorious dynasty; he belonged to the Lord's Anointed—he had grave responsibilities, but also a magnificent distinction. His easy, winning manner was the result of this inherent creed. When he heard that there was petroleum in the province of Largs, he showed the first excitement which Mr. Duryee had ever seen on his handsome, occasionally arrogant countenance.

"I must know what they are doing. I must go back at once. I must be on the spot," he cried. The American, always interested in new speculations, offered to accompany him, and the two set out for Liverpool. La Belle Valentine and Mrs. Basil Hollemache, with a staff of secretaries, companions, and maids, followed them three days later. Prince Paul had grown to regard Lucie Hollemache as a most interesting young woman. She had neither the quickness of mind nor the dashing beauty of many Americans, but she was mysterious; she made no attempt to amuse or attract him; she would look far away into space when he actually tried to make himself agreeable; she was amiable enough, yet she kept him at a distance, received his compliments, charming notes, flowers, and books as mere random civilities. He had never before been so treated, and, had the indifference been assumed, it would have proved unsuccessful. But it was genuine; she cared nothing about him or any one else—so far as he could gather. She seemed an enigma, and, whereas a more common-place man would have either disliked her for her coldness or avoided her altogether as a person whom no mortal could understand, the Prince was fascinated by the strangeness of her temperament. Lucie obtained,

by not striving to do so, a great ascendancy over his
tastes ; it soon became apparent to the members of his
suite that Mrs. Hollemache's word was paramount.
He poured out to her the secrets and the ambitions of
his heart, to which she would invariably reply :

"They are too deep for me. But it is very fine to
feel like that."

He intended to offer romantic protestations some
day, although he had not yet done so, for he feared to
disturb the charm and intimacy· of their curious
relationship. Besides, he did not love her. "One
cannot love so many," he told Duryee, who had heard
the pathetic history of the Countess Sophia ; "the
days are past when, as Dumas says somewhere, one
ruined duchesses and was ruined by opera-dancers. It
would seem vulgar." The real cause of his self-
restraint was a certain haunting recollection of
Clementine. She always stood, not among his
morganatic loves possible or impossible, but among
the Princesses—one of whom he would have to choose
eventually for his wife. They were the Princess
Marie, his first cousin ; the Princess Adelaide, his first
cousin once removed ; and the Princess Olga, his first
cousin twice removed.

"Of course, I can never marry Clementine
Gloucester," he would say to himself impatiently.
Several times he thought of writing to her, but he
checked the impulse because it was too strong to be
strictly prudent. If he could not write as he felt—

and his feelings were more than kind—he preferred to remain silent.

During the voyage to England he realised that one of his first pleasures on arriving would be a meeting with the Gloucesters. The father and daughter had a homely simplicity which refreshed those who were trying to emphasise the enjoyments of life by making them its chief end. The Prince was tired now of elaborate inanities. It is true that his brain was busy with many projects. He read works on finance, and talked with Cobden Duryee from noon till the small hours of the morning about petroleum, mines, company promoting, the Stock Exchange, Trusts, and banking. On moonlight nights, when the sea had the green of dark emeralds and the bright sky was softened with small grey floating clouds, the two men would pace the deck arm-in-arm discussing the money market, till their jaws grew rigid, and their lips thin, and their eyes harsh at the thought of the determination, the sharpness, the strength needed in the conduct of business affairs.

Duryee had the name of being hard but fair in his dealings, although he had ruined thousands of unimportant persons during the course of his career.

"You must do it," he said to Prince Paul; "they are going to ruin themselves anyway—that is part of the economy of Providence. The intelligent man can always turn another man's inevitable ruin to his own advantage. That is the whole secret of success. Utilise other people's failures."

No woman's name ever passed their lips during the voyage. At Queenstown the Prince received a letter from Mr. Bickersteth, saying that he had taken the Marquis of Stokehampton's seat in Suffolk for the summer months. Would the Prince give Mrs. Bickersteth and himself the honour of a visit? Would the Prince also say whom he would like invited to join the party? Paul sent a long telegram in reply accepting the charming proposal, and suggesting that Mr. and Mrs. Sachs, Mr. Cobden Duryee, Dr. Felshammer, and Mr. and Miss Gloucester should be included in the house-party.

Felshammer, who looked to the Prince much thinner and somewhat haggard, met them at Liverpool. The three dined together at the Adelphi Hotel and talked till five in the morning about petroleum. They travelled to London a few hours later and talked on the same subject all the way. Duryee had one of his secretaries in the saloon carriage, and he dictated letters, telegrams, and cables at intervals. These last were dispatched at Rugby. Mr. Sachs and Mr. Bickersteth were awaiting at Euston Station. Each gentleman had brought a brougham and pair for the Prince's use. But, thanking them, he drove with Felshammer in a hansom to the Carlton Hotel, while Duryee went off in another cab to some chambers which he always kept in Piccadilly. The three had

arranged to meet again at dinner in order to resume
their discussion of petroleum.   The next day they all
went up to Stokehampton Hall, and in the train they
were once more able to concentrate on petroleum
without hindrance.

Stokehampton Hall, which was built during the
reign of Henry VIII., stands in a fine park, and is
surrounded by a wide moat.   The atmosphere of the
whole estate—far from the town and railways—is still
feudal, and it would not seem an appropriate background for a group of financiers bent on the formation
of a City enterprise.   A thought to this effect darted
into Prince Paul's mind as they went down the avenue
of superb elm-trees which, with the grandeur of a
Gothic aisle in an old cathedral, led to the main
entrance and the picturesque drawbridge.

The peacocks strutting over the splendid turf
screamed in terror, and the doves and rooks alike flew
towards the sky, at the sight of Mr. Bickersteth's
motor-car rushing through their beautiful, stately, and
historic demesne.   Cardinal Wolsey had read his office
in the noble garden ; Queen Elizabeth had danced as
a young girl on the lawn ; James I. had rested in the
house for two days ; Vandyck had painted portraits
there ; the great Duke of Marlborough had written
letters in the oak library ; Congreve had composed an
act of one of his comedies in a little ante-room ;
Handel had played on its harpsichord near the spinet
which had belonged to Queen Mary ; Charles I., with

Queen Henrietta Maria, had supped in the banquet-hall and slept in the wonderful tapestried rooms. The place was full of many striking associations. Its hereditary possessor, the Marquis of Stokehampton, was always ill at ease there; he had grown estranged from all the traditions of his family; he was glad to be rid of what he called "a white elephant," and he lived by preference at the Savoy Hotel, London, or at the Ritz in Paris.

All the guests had assembled to receive the Prince in the picture gallery at the top of the carved staircase. Rachel Bickersteth amazed him by her air of distinction. Mrs. Sachs pleased him by her vivacious smile and the fact that he had never seen her before; but when he discovered Clementine, standing half hidden behind an immense screen, his heart leapt, he forgot that he was being observed, and she herself trembled with joy at the delight which showed in his features.

"Miss Gloucester!" he exclaimed. "You see I have come back far sooner than Peer Gynt."

The others could not understand the allusion, but Felshammer suffered torture at the sight of the girl's happiness. When he shook hands with her, her hands felt like little birds struggling to get free; she looked away from him, and, utterly unable to speak, slipped away to her father's side. She had not wished to accept Mrs. Bickersteth's invitation to Stokehampton Hall, and the ordeal of meeting Prince Paul had

seemed too painful even for her own unusual courage.
What would happen ?   What could they say to each
other ?   Mere friendship between them was something
which she could not offer and dared not cultivate ;
indifference was impossible.   In such cases one had to
live perpetually in mask and armour, guarding every
word, look, movement, tone, only to possess at last, by
the strain of such severe self-restraint, a dead heart
which could no longer need any control.   This grim
reward for fortitude appalled her bright and naturally
gay imagination.   She wanted her heart to live so long
as she lived, and perhaps in that other world elsewhere.
But a complete separation from the Prince seemed the
best safeguard of her dignity ; it was one thing to love
in silence, without hope, no doubt, but at least unde-
tected ; it was altogether another thing to carry a
perilous secret affection in circumstances which might
compel in a hundred ways its irreparable betrayal.
Under the first rapturous surprise of his greeting, she
had forgotten every barrier between them, she had
forgotten the company, forgotten the jealous, watchful
gaze of Felshammer.   A moment afterwards, every
danger of the situation seemed magnified, and when
the men, after tea, went to the smoking-room, she fled
upstairs in order to school herself afresh for the difficult time which was to come.   They all reassembled
before dinner in a beautiful white panelled drawing-
room full of Sèvres china in cabinets.   Clementine had
dressed plainly in black, but she knew that she was

looking her best.   Her colouring had never seemed so brilliant, and Mrs. Sachs, a good-natured woman, could not help wondering whether the girl was not using paint on her cheeks and mouth.   Nadeshda had been greatly surprised when she heard that the Gloucesters were coming to Stokehampton.   She did not know them, and, inasmuch as the party was a business matter, a strictly private meeting in the pleasantest way between Messrs. Sachs and Bickersteth and Prince Paul of Urseville-Beylestein, Clementine Gloucester seemed a remarkable addition to the group.   Rachel Bickersteth hinted, however, that Dr. Felshammer was deeply in love with poor old Gloucester's daughter.

"Oh, I see!" said Nadeshda.   "That explains everything.   How kind and clever of the Prince to arrange such an opportunity for a proposal!"

Both ladies were thus absorbed in watching the progress and development of Felshammer's suit.   They were especially satisfied by Clementine's quiet, elusive manner with the secretary.   She avoided him, although it was evident that the two knew each other more than well.   She made every effort, they thought, to conceal her conquest, and did not seek to display, as many others would certainly have done, her power over the hard, almost inaccessible man.   Rachel and Nadeshda, who disagreed on every subject, were divided more bitterly than usual in their opinion of Felshammer.   While they acknowledged that he was a valuable addition to the firm, Rachel thought him sympathetic, honest, and faithful; whereas Nadeshda regarded him as unscrupulous, rather brutal, calculating, and uncertain.

"Just the one for his post," she added. "Oscar can use his brains and watch him."

This idea was odious to Rachel.

"If I felt as you do about him," she told Nadeshda, "I would not have him in my house."

Nadeshda laughed. "That's an indirect graceful compliment to all your guests," she said quickly; "you are really a dear woman."

She did in truth think her hostess a dear woman, but she disliked her cordially nevertheless. Rachel's imperial manner, contempt for the world, indifference to the pleasures of life, roused the younger woman's unwilling respect; they challenged her own fever for success, and were an incessant irritation to her restless mind. Rachel, moreover, had been a great heiress, which made Bickersteth the richer man in the firm, although he was the junior partner. To Nadeshda this seemed hard; sometimes she cried and made Oscar Sachs, who adored her, most unhappy, because, with all his wealth, he could not spend so much money as Bickersteth, or see his wife in such magnificent jewels.

At dinner, Sachs sat next to Clementine, and, while he admired her appearance, he was annoyed to think that she might marry his manager and take social

precedence of Nadeshda. Men who concentrate their
intellect on great projects, financial, imperial, and
otherwise, will often become very small in their
domestic ideas. Sachs, in the home circle, was as
petty as a little power in a provincial parish.
Nadeshda, who had fostered this capacity for silliness,
sometimes found him narrow-minded—he was too apt
to imagine that she was being slighted or placed to
some disadvantage. Such suspicions offended her
vanity and also her common sense, which really was
common to a robust degree. She smiled at Oscar
several times during the course of the dinner in order
to let him know how happy she was with the Prince.
He sat between herself and Rachel, and as Rachel said
little or nothing, although she looked regal, Mrs.
Sachs carried off the conversational honours. She was
the life of the table, and made an hour, which might
have passed in painful dulness, as satisfactory as the
unexceptionable cooking. Poor Clementine, who sat
opposite, heard, from the laughter, how greatly the
Prince was amused by the companion on his left, but
she kept her eyes fixed on her plate, because she was
afraid to look where she longed to look, and she
shrunk from encountering Felshammer's burning
glance, of which she was now uncomfortably conscious. Oblivious of the others, he barely took part
in the talk or tasted any food, but, absorbed in his own
jealous feelings and thoughts, stared, almost entranced,
at the embarrassed object of his unhappy love. There

is no granite where there has not first been fire—some
convulsive violence underneath the earth—and in the
same way Felshammer's outward hardness was due to
a volcanic nature which, ill-subdued in his early youth,
had become a merely tempered ferocity in his middle-
age.

"How I hate Paul!" he thought. "Why did
I ever admire his effeminate face? How could I
have stood his mannerisms? Why do such inver-
tebrate creatures please the best women? He is not
a man—he is *bric-à-brac*, or rather a troubadour."
But, as he felt too surely the unfairness of these
strictures, they did not console him. "How he flirts
with every woman he meets!" he reflected. "He is
gazing now at Mrs. Sachs as though he had never
seen her equal on this earth. Will Clementine have
the sense to take that lesson to heart? Paul cares for
no one but himself; he is agreeable out of sheer
vanity. I am sick to death of his conceit."

Although his old fondness for Prince Paul had given
place to a cruel and infinite resentment, he meant to
keep scrupulously loyal in the conduct of their business relations. He desired to see him dead—not to
see him fail. He had never harboured the least envy
of the Prince's position, prospects, or wealth ; he
wished him to reign over Urseville-Beylestein ; he
hoped earnestly that if he lived he would come into his
own. But he could not have Clementine. Clementine
was not for any Prince Paul.

As the ladies left the drawing-room Felshammer
fixed her with his glance, and she was so overcome by
terror at his dire and menacing expression that she
almost sank on the ground. Surely there was no love
in such a threatening look! Surely it was a kind of
madness !

"You are ill, Miss Gloucester," said Rachel, as
the three ladies went into the state saloon, which was
lit up with dozens of wax candles in rose-coloured
shades. They twinkled and floated before Clementine's
eyes till she could see nothing else.

"It is a hot night," observed Mrs. Sachs, watching
her with an amused expression. In her opinion the
girl was hysterical.

"If I may," said poor Clementine, "I should like
to go to my own room. Don't frighten papa, but ask
him to come to me presently when they begin to play
cards. He won't be missed then."

"Yes, you had better lie down," said Rachel, with
serene kindness. She saw that Clementine was not
over-interested in Dr. Felshammer.

Half an hour later, Mr. Gloucester, much agitated,
entered his daughter's room. She was standing in the
centre of the floor as though she had been hewn out of
stone and placed there. But anger had so transformed
her features that he scarcely recognised her face; it
was bloodless, quivering, and fierce; she seemed
scarcely able to breathe, and she shook with the
vehemence of her feelings.

14

"Papa," she exclaimed, "if you do not pay that man, I shall die of humiliation. He thinks I am in his power. He thinks he will break my spirit. Unless you want me to die, pay him."

"Do you mean Felshammer, my darling? What has he done? The Prince was just saying how clever and trustworthy he was."

"Pay him!" said Clementine, stamping her foot. "He takes the very heart out of my life. I can't think, I can't speak, I cannot rest, sleep, or eat till we have paid back every farthing."

"This is your fancy," said Mr. Gloucester; "calm yourself. I never knew that you had such a temper."

"I never knew it myself," she answered. "But that man will rouse everything that is bad wherever he goes. He is an evil influence. He frightens me. He is wicked!"

Mr. Gloucester sat down on the sofa and held his side.

"How can I possibly pay him?" he asked.

"Borrow it from some one else."

"I have no security."

"What security did you offer him?"

"Nothing. He behaved most handsomely. I think myself he is a rough diamond. He is one of Nature's gentlemen. He is the one man among all the hundreds I know who has helped me."

"Can I go against my own instincts? He is no

friend. Once he **was,** but something **has** changed him. Oh, what shall I do? What shall I do?"

She struck her forehead with her clenched hand.

"I feel degraded," she went on. "I feel as though I had been bought and paid for against my will."

"But what has he said or done?"

"It is in his air. He has not said one word."

Mr. Gloucester murmured again that it **was** her fancy. Yet he **was** miserable at the sight of Clementine's distress. He had never thought that she could show anger, and the unexpected revelation of her strength of feeling was in itself a shock to the languid old man. Nor was he able to persuade himself that she was wrong; on the contrary, he knew, in his conscience, that she was right.

"I will do what I can," he said.

"But what?" she asked. "I must know this time what you intend to do."

"Never mind for the moment. I have thought of an old friend—some one I knew years ago."

"I wish you would tell me who it is."

"I cannot," he said, with surprising firmness. "That is absolutely impossible. You need have no fear, however, that it will lead to unpleasantness. Now go to bed, my dear, and try to sleep. God knows I am grieved and broken."

He kissed her good-night and stole gently away. She heard the men talking and laughing in excited tones in the room beneath till the small hours of the morning. They were still discussing petroleum; Felshammer's voice dominated the others; but, when the Prince spoke, it seemed to the girl like music breaking through the growls and snarls of hungry animals. When all became silent, she got up and sat by the window to watch for the dawn. A numb foreboding of sorrow had taken possession of her once calm soul. She began to understand that she would have to fight her own battle in life, and such thoughts were hard to a nature gentle and unassertive by choice, yet capable of great endurance, determination, love, and wrath.

CHAPTER XVI

A QUESTION OF UNDERCURRENTS

PRINCE PAUL watched eagerly all the next day for an opportunity of speaking alone with Clementine. At last, after lunch, the occasion presented itself, and he asked her to show him the Dutch garden, which had been designed as a compliment to William of Orange, and was one of the most curious examples of the kind in England.

"Do you know," said Paul, looking at the girl as they walked together on the grass path, "that you are the one person in this party who seems in perfect harmony with our surroundings? I could imagine you here, the daughter of some Spanish grandee, in the court of Catharine of Aragon. They tell me she once spent a week at Stokehampton. Would you have liked a court life!"

"Court life according to Dumas," she answered, smiling. "I don't know any other kind well."

"But your Aunt Emmeline was a maid of honour."

"Please remember, sir, my Aunt Emmeline's discretion. She neither asked questions nor answered them."

"You seem to resemble her. You have not asked me, for instance, what I think about America. I will tell you. When I met the Secretaries of State at Washington, I felt as though I were dining with the northern gods—Odin, Thor, Balder, and the rest. Their look of power was stupendous. In New York I encountered fabulous kindness, unbelievable wealth, and a display which is called modern, because it is a repetition of the Renaissance without the inspiration, the taste, the genius of that period. Great riches have led at all times to precisely the same sort of extravagance. The word modern is ridiculous. New York is old Venice without St. Mark. I miss the scenery and the saint—nothing else. And now, unless you are as uncommunicative as your austere aunt, tell me what you have been doing?"

"Very little," said the girl. "I have been in London, and I have seen few people."

"You saw Felshammer?"

Clementine flushed. "He has been kind to my father."

"Felshammer is secretive; he rarely mentions his own affairs or talks about his friends. What do you think of him?"

"I think he is deeply attached to you," said Clementine, after a moment's hesitation, and they stopped to admire a tree that was cut in the shape of a boat on a pedestal.

"Do you suppose," said the Prince, "that many people are attached to me?"

"Not many."

"Why not?"

"Because many would fear lest you should think that their friendship was interested"—and she looked at another tree which was cut to resemble a bird.

"But I have little to offer any one. I am an exile. My chances of coming to the throne are remote indeed. My brother may reign, yet I doubt that too. My poor country, from all I hear, is going fast to the devil and the companies."

"If the people are happy and prosperous, you will not care."

"I cannot be so certain about my unselfishness. I believe I want my own inheritance; otherwise, where is my occupation? What is my calling? Can I become a soldier of fortune and fight for other nations —an alien always? They don't wish me in anything; I am horribly in the way here." He dropped his voice and glanced over his shoulder. There was no one in sight. "Both Sachs and Bickersteth are annoyed to find that I insist upon knowing the details of my own business. But I did not come out to dis-cuss petroleum—that is for the men. I want to tell you how much I have thought about you while I was away."

"I wonder what you thought?"

"Ah, then you have a little curiosity after all! I am reassured. I was beginning to fear I had loved an angel."

She dared not allow herself to hear this, and she called his attention to the tulips.

"I saw no one so beautiful in America," he continued.

"That is strange, because the flowers there, I have been told, are glorious."

"Nonsense! You heard what I said that time. I meant you. No one, I repeat, was so beautiful."

"This distresses me, because it is not true."

"It is true so far as I am a judge, at any rate. But why do you draw away and look pre-occupied? You make me absurdly nervous. Are you so prim?"

"Because I don't see why you should pay me compliments. I dislike them; they are flattery, and flattery might make me better-tempered than I ought to be in the circumstances."

"On my honour, I am not flattering you. I mean that I have thought almost incessantly about you, and I intended to tell you so the first time we met. I asked Mrs. Bickersteth to invite you here in order that we might talk. I need your friendship."

"But what of that. What is it when it is said?"

"I think it is a great deal; it may mean as much as you wish—more than you wish."

"No, it may not. You have no right to say such

things to me even if they are a little bit, only a little bit, true. How do you know that they don't make me unhappy."

" I hoped it would make you happy."

" How can anything hopeless and fruitless be happy ? To me friendship is a serious gift."

" I am all seriousness."

"I see no sign of seriousness at all—quite the reverse. You have an hour to spare and you want it to be as amusing as the occasion and your companion permit. But I was never good at charades. I can't improvise dialogue."

" I am not tragic—if you mean that. Just look at the day ! We might be in Italy or Greece. I did not know that you had such skies in the eastern counties. And isn't that the nightingale ! Yet you are offended because I attempt to tell you—very badly, I admit—that there is no one in the world I admire and respect as I admire you."

" And what then ? " said Clementine.

" But you are prosaic, Miss Gloucester," said the Prince, somewhat confused. "I believe that I was hoping that you had something pleasant to say to me."

"Would it gratify you to hear that I thought of no one except you ! "

"It would enchant me ; it might alter my whole career."

" It would be far more likely to alter mine ! "

" Why are you so incredulous ? "

Clementine did not know how to explain that she had once before been told that she was loved, and that the manner of the telling was very different from this. The comparison was painful. Much as she now disliked Felshammer, she knew that he had been in earnest. She saw, with wounded pride, that the Prince was trifling with his own sentiments and hers.

"He shall have a lesson," she said in her heart; "some day he at least will speak differently."

"Why are you so incredulous?" he repeated.

"I will be frank, sir. Flirting amuses you; it bores me, and, as boredom makes a deeper impression on my mind than flirting, no matter how successful, could ever make on yours, I think I must beg to be considered first." She spoke gaily, coloured, and laughed.

"Do you mean to say that I bore you?"

"Yes, sir, when you say that you think of me incessantly. If that is the truth, it may account for your dulness in dealing with the theme. I have never known you to be dull on any other subject."

"But this is enormous!"

"I think it mere tedious commonplace. Confess you have not known what to do with yourself this afternoon. You thought, 'I must turn that girl's head. It will be an easy matter, because she's impressionable, and she has seen little of the world, less of men, and she will find no reason on earth why I,

with all my thousand acquaintances, pursuits, occupa-
tions, interests, and duties, should not be absorbed for
months in the consideration, say, of her short nose!
She may possibly think my nose and profile generally
divine, but that is not my fault. Experience is good
for all of us; it will assist the maturing of her
unformed character to believe in my protestations for,
roughly, some years. She may grow to be grateful to
me in time, and she will remember, till she grows too
old to remember anything else, the lovely half-hour
we spent together in an old garden one Whitsuntide
in the country, looking at tulips and trees and each
other, and pretending to be alive!'"

"*Mon Dieu!* There is no pretence. I never
heard such a withering speech. I feel quite small.
I knew you were unusual, but I never suspected that
you could be so—so eloquent."

"But have I made myself perfectly clear?"

"Too clear. Your upper-lip is very angry."

"Your opinion of my upper-lip does not matter!
All that matters is that we should understand each
other. It is an insult to tell any woman in a flippant,
careless way, that you admire her. You see, you need
not tell her anything."

"You're very severe, but your voice is delightful,
and you look as gentle as the goddess Flora. You
can't persuade me that you are offended."

"How could I be offended over such a small
matter?"

"Ah, it is not a small matter ! You have made me miserable."

"Nevertheless," she said, smiling, "the nightingale still sings ! "

"I want you to forgive me for thinking absurdities I never thought, and saying things I never said. That may sound silly, but it is sincere. And you must believe that I did have you in my mind often, and I do like you much more than I dare tell you."

"I dare say you do like me. I like you too ; that is why we are able to talk plainly. I was hurt, that is all, when you tried to deceive me by offering me exaggerated, untrue compliments, instead of a small genuine confidence in my good sense. You don't know what love means ; you have not the slightest notion of what it means. It has never touched you, never passed you by, never been near you ! "

" Then do you know what it means? "

"I will know it when I meet it. I have not met it to-day—that is certain."

" Excuse me, it is not so certain—if you refer to me."

"Yes, I referred to you. I think I have proved my friendship amply by listening to so much as I did, and taking the trouble to explain my point of view. Now we must go in. They want to take you for a drive, I know."

He returned with her to the house and did not speak again. But he struck at the ground with his

cane as he walked, and tried to appear absorbed in
impersonal reflections on abstract ideas. He told
himself she was rather hard and unwomanly and unlovable, and he wished she would look at him once
more in order that he might return the glance with
all the haughtiness at his command. She did look
just as she crossed the drawbridge, but she took him
by surprise, and, to his annoyance, he smiled with
extraordinary affection, spontaneously.

CHAPTER XVII

LA BELLE VALENTINE HEARS THE TRUTH
AND UTTERS IT

MME. DE MONTGENAYS, wearing a Chinese robe of cherry-coloured satin lined with sable—the fur was necessary because she felt the cold even in June— Mme. de Montgenays was reclining on the sofa of her private sitting-room at Claridge's Hotel when a card, engraved with the name of Dr. Karl Felshammer, was brought to her. She read it, smiled, and asked the waiter to show the gentleman up. During the interval which passed between the delivery of this message and the appearance of her visitor, she put on a pair of unbecoming eyeglasses which she wore, as a rule, before devoted women, servants, and inconsiderable men only. Then she resumed the task of turning over letters—most of them from the grateful secretaries of the various charities to which she was a constant and munificent subscriber.

" I am glad to see you," she said, when Felshammer

came in.   "Is this a call on your own account, or do you bring me any message ? "

Having kissed her hand, he chose a seat with his back to the light, and wondered that she appeared so young, smooth, and beautiful facing it.

"I have called on my own account," he said.

"That is very charming of you.   I was longing to hear some news.   How do you think I look ? "

" Perfect 1 "

"Well, I haven't been to America, you know, since I was a little girl.   The climate braced me right up ; if you could have seen me going round the old schoolhouse again and kissing the trees I used to climb when I wanted to see Cobden Duryee just starting for college, you would have thought I was about four. Not a day more !   The tears of sorrow I have shed in those trees watching Cobden sally forth with two tweed suits and the family Bible in his grip-sack !   But you look terribly ill.   Are you suffering from insomnia ? "

" Yes, to a certain extent."

" That is too bad !   Have you made up your mind to settle down in London ? "   She fixed her piercing eyes upon his, and showed her astonishment plainly at the changes in his countenance.

" I expect to make London my headquarters, but I shall go rather frequently to Largs."

"Largs is a sound deal," she observed placidly.   " I believe in it, and I think you are the man to work it. Cobden thinks so too."

"It is kind of you to say that.   How is Mrs. Hollemache ?   Is she with you ? "

" Ah ! " she exclaimed, clapping her hands.   " I know now why you called.   You want to find out whether Prince Paul and Lucie are chums."

"It would be foolish to attempt any concealment with you.   That is why I came to the point crudely. Is Mrs. Hollemache in good spirits ? "

"She is never in good spirits," said Mme. de Montgenays, rearranging her rings ; " that is why she is so reposeful.   She is as strong as a tower of bricks, but she is naturally lymphatic.   I need some one like that with me all the time."

"I think she is an ideal friend for the Prince."

" Well, that is just what I am wondering—is she?" said La Belle.   " They get on well, but not quite well enough.   Do you follow me ? "

" Has he ever spoken to you of Miss Gloucester ? "

" Never.   Why ?   What about her ? "

"If Miss Gloucester had a touch of wickedness or a greater knowledge of men, she could influence him."

His companion burst out laughing and seemed much entertained by the humour of her own reflec- tions.   " How funny !   How funny !   I shall die l " she exclaimed, in extreme merriment.   " You don't say so !   That surprises me !   You think Clementine ought to have a touch of wickedness.   Don't worry ! I guess it will develop."

" Pardon me—I could suggest no improvement. But I noticed Paul and the girl together at Stoke-hampton.   I am opposed to their friendship on various grounds."

" This is exciting.   Tell me what you think ! "

" You are a woman of the world, madame.   You will understand me when I say that it is my earnest wish to marry Miss Gloucester."

" For Heaven's sake !   You want to marry her ! You !"   She stared at him till he left his chair and walked away.   He considered her manners atrocious and thought he had never before encountered a woman altogether without tact.

" So you want to marry her ! " she repeated. " The last man on earth, I'd swear, to marry a young green girl !   Why, you must be crazy !   It's all out of tune."

" I don't pretend to be in the running with Prince Paul," said Felshammer ; " but," he added, with a sarcastic smile, " I have this advantage over him—I could have marriage only in my mind, whereas it is the one thing which would never enter his—so far as Miss Gloucester is concerned.

La Belle Valentine showed some resentment.

" I am not so sure about that.   Couldn't it be a morganatic affair ? "

" My dear lady, how can you suggest such a thing—even for the sake of argument !   In the first place, the Prince has always had the greatest prejudice

15

against alliances of the kind ; and in the second place, the one sort of woman to whom he might be tempted to offer such a position would be the very last to accept it."

" He could renounce his right to the throne. It's pretty remote. You couldn't call it a sacrifice."

" Believe me, it is not worth discussing. I am sure that he has the deepest respect for Miss Gloucester, but I know him as you do not and cannot, and I tell you that he has no other end in his attentions than to amuse himself for the season with the most fascinating girl I have ever met or he is likely to meet. Now, for her sake, this ought to be discouraged. She is nothing to you, I know."

Valentine stared at him again.

" Then why do you want me to interfere?" she asked.

"Because it is to our common advantage, I think, that he should be so engrossed in other things that they will put love affairs out of his mind. I am too sane not to see that Miss Gloucester might be dangerously attracted by him. Would that be to her discredit? Quite the contrary! But, if he must flirt, let him flirt with Mrs. Hollemache. Surely that would suit your purpose and the purpose of Mr. Duryee much better! I am tolerably certain that Mrs. Hollemache was brought to Salso in order to amuse His Royal Highness. Your plan succeeded, and it does credit to your foresight. I never interfered—in fact, I thought it would improve him a good deal to go to America in your party. I did not oppose the project. What is more, I like Mrs. Hollemache. Her influence is good. She cures his conceit and his priggishness—faults of youth."

" Yes," said Valentine, " we have had a happy time. But you mustn't try to rush me into decisions one way or the other. I have got to think matters over. I still don't see why I should interfere."

" I can tell you why. If he once takes up this caprice in good earnest, neither you nor your friends will see him again for weeks. You must remember that I know the man. Every new and pretty face tempts him to some kind of psychological experiment, and when you have a lovely girl like Clementine Gloucester there is a certain danger in the situation."

" I am glad you call it psychological l " said Mme. de Montgenays drily. But her excellent friend Mabel joined them at that moment, and the conversation, drifting on to general topics, soon terminated in Felshammer's departure.

Later on La Belle Valentine received a still greater surprise. Mr. Gloucester's card was presented. She read his name over three times, changed her Chinese robe for a Worth teagown, and received him with much dignity, standing in the middle of the room in one of her most famous ballet attitudes—that of Aspasia receiving Pericles at a banquet. Gloucester seemed so dejected, so old, and so desperate, as he entered, that his wife could not restrain an ejaculation of sympathy.

"Why, Alfred, you look simply awful! What is the matter?

"I am in the greatest distress," he replied, speaking in gasps. "My character has been so transformed by calamities that where I might have hesitated a long while before I asked a favour of you——"

"My dear soul, sit down! Have some vermouth! Why bother to be so flowery? I don't want to give you any favours at all. I don't see why I should."

"It is not for me," said the unhappy man, hating her insolent beauty, her gorgeous attire, the perfume she used, and the pose she had adopted. "It is for the girl; it is for Clementine."

"That's a little different, but you know I am always direct. I would sooner surprise you by behaving better than you expected than by being a good deal worse. I like to say the hard things first. If I can get pleasant afterwards by degrees, why, I am willing! What is the matter with Clementine?"

And she struck another famous ballet attitude— that of Cleopatra before Cæsar.

Gloucester, who had resolved not to sit down, supported himself by leaning against one of the cabinets.

"This is the matter," said he. "Dr. Felshammer

has lent me a large sum of money—thirty thousand pounds."

" He must be crazy ! " exclaimed Mme. de Montgenays, using her favourite comment on most individuals.

" Not at all, but I found afterwards that he is deeply attached to Clementine. He had asked her to marry him, and she had refused his offer. She feels now that I have placed her under an insupportable obligation. I think it is killing her. She is too proud ; she cannot bear it. She will waste away before my eyes. That is why I am swallowing all my own pride and my dignity to implore your help. The debt is killing the child."

" Then she cannot be much like me," said Valentine, abandoning her attitudes and settling down in an armchair. " So long as she refused the man, and he knew it, and he lent you the money just the same, that lets her out. The one to be worried is Felshammer."

" But have you no delicacy ? "

" None," she replied, with good-humour.

" Can't you see that he must regard her more or less as a hostage ? "

" It sounds to me kind of melodramatic. When men pay out these large sums, it is usually, most always, on a pretty distinct understanding."

" Just so. He relies, you may be certain, on her gratitude, her sense of honour,"

" He is forty years old or more. I can't heave up a lot of sympathy for his disappointment. Does Clementine like any other man ? Because, if I know anything about girls, she would be flattered by. Fels-hammer's devotion if she had not some other ideal. Don't try to deceive me, Alfred, because everything will depend on your answer."

"She has told me nothing."

"But what have you observed ? You are not an absolute fool."

"I have observed nothing."

" Have any of your friends observed anything? Think ! Has your sister Louise said anything ? "

" Louise," said Gloucester, after some hesitation, " did mention that Leonore and Augusta fancied Prince Paul was paying Clementine somewhat marked attention."

" Well, you had a chance of seeing them together at Mrs. Bickersteth's."

Few sensations in her life had pleased her so intensely as the news of her own daughter's success in exciting admiration. Money always impressed her, and Felshammer's free tribute of thirty thousand pounds seemed irrefutable evidence of Clementine's power over men.

" I hate the idea of spying on the child," said Mr. Gloucester. " She was out for a short time walking with the Prince, that is all. I noticed that they were never alone together after that ; they barely exchanged a word. The same evening he was summoned to London to see his mother, the ex-Queen.

"She is stopping here," interrupted Valentine. "Her face is marvellous for her age, but she has lost her figure. It is the worst I ever saw. Go on with your story."

"There is none. Surely it is conceivable that a girl may refuse a man without having some other one in her mind!"

"Maybe, but it isn't likely. If there is not a real live man in the way, it is some man in a book or a play. You cannot tell me anything about girls. I know them through and through."

"They are not all the same!"

"I see very little difference once get your type established."

"Clementine's type is uncommon."

"She is my child, isn't she? I think you are the worst special pleader I have ever heard. You have not made out any kind of a case. But I am disposed to help you in this scrape. It is a freak that is going to cost me one hundred and fifty thousand dollars. Cobden would kill me if he knew it."

"It is not his money, I hope."

"No, it would be mine, but he advises me. He doesn't want me to do anything foolish or extravagant."

"Is it extravagance to help your own daughter?"

"I can answer that better when I know exactly

what I am paying for. Why do you want the money ?
What have you done ? Why haven't you got the
money yourself ? "

Gloucester, humiliated to the quick, endeavoured to
tell the squalid chronicle of his misfortunes ; but, as
usual, his memory, his pompous phrases, his habit of
repeating himself, contradicting himself, and correct-
ing himself, exasperated his impatient listener.

"If I didn't know that you were honourable by
nature I should say that you had swindled everybody
you have ever met," she said, lifting up her voice ;
" but I see it is just the other way round. You have
got in with a whole horde of scallywags, and you have
been bluffed at every turn. If I give you one hundred
and fifty thousand dollars I shall require a written
undertaking to the effect that for the future you will
hold no sort of communication with lawyers or
business men or any one who would be in the least
likely to make any demands upon your intelligence."

"I don't see why you should insult me."

"I insult you ! I like that ! I mean it in absolute
comradeship 1 "

" In my present position I cannot make terms with
you. I can only accept them."

" This is right. If you could get it through your
head, Alfred, that I am your friend and not your
enemy, there would be no trouble at all."

" We are not friends. Don't ask me to say so. I
shall never forget my wrongs."

"You were always without diplomacy ! If the girl makes a splendid marriage, I suppose you'll think better of me. You needn't be afraid of my spoiling anything. Is it likely that I should ruin Clementine's chances by telling all creation that I'm her mother? Get away with you ! Some day you'll appreciate my character. Come here to-morrow at twelve o'clock and my lawyer will meet you. Felshammer mustn't know that I have stepped into the breach. He's clever enough to guess the position. Keep me posted if you hear any news in the meantime. Goodbye !"

She kissed the tips of her fingers and dismissed him with a classic gesture. Then she wrote on a sheet of the hotel notepaper, "*Princess Paul of Urseville-Beylestein, Clementine of Urseville-Beylestein,*" in order to see how the names looked. She tried another effect —"*Prince Paul of Urseville-Beylestein and the Countess Largs.*"

"I don't care so much for the morganatic wheeze," she said aloud to herself.

CHAPTER XVIII

FURTHER REVELATIONS OF THE MATERNAL INSTINCT

" THEN what is to come next, Paul ? "

The speaker, an unusually thin woman about fifty-seven, who spoke German with a strong Italian accent, had a narrow face and a weak piping voice. She sat huddled on a chair in the corner of a bedroom at Claridge's Hotel. Her toilette had been hasty ; she wore a magnificent lace scarf twisted round her head and an opera cloak over her pink-flannel dressing-gown. Prince Paul was in the august presence of his mother, the ex-Queen of Urseville-Beylestein, cousin of two reigning sovereigns, grand-daughter of an emperor.

" Will nothing bring solace to my broken heart ? " she inquired. " Am I to understand that you utterly refuse to regard my ardent wishes ? Now that the Crown Prince has quitted me in order to attach himself to the Republicans, I must steel myself to hear that you are about to enter business with an

American and a Jew! The settlement of the times, the peace of the King's mind, the hopes of our country, will all be once more dissolved! Would that I had never been born!"

"As usual, you exaggerate, my dearest mother!" replied the young man, turning over some beautiful jewels which were scattered among the letters, brushes, flowers, newspapers, and medicine-bottles on the ex-Queen's table. "The confidential avowal of my way of thinking ought not to be turned against me. An idea, still vague, of blending the benefits of a petroleum-field with our other sources of revenue may seem new to you; it is not on that account to be despised. I shall not enter now into the merits of the proposal. The question of my marriage falls more naturally within your province. I do not wish to marry yet. Least of all do I wish to marry my cousin Marie, my cousin Adelaide, or my cousin Olga."

"You cannot always please yourself in this world," said the ex-Queen. "I am truly sensible of the very disagreeable struggles all young people undergo between duty and inclination. Did I wish to marry your father? In those days a person like Lohengrin on a Swan seemed far preferable. I feel for you in your distressing dilemma. I pray night and morning that you may be supported through the dangers of your position. Certain disgrace and ruin will come upon you if you persist in considering your own taste; friendship and connections will break; all will be lost."

"You are over-influenced by old women," said the Prince irritably. "You are quite out of touch with modern life and the spirit of the age. One would believe, to hear you, that we were still as we were during the reigns of Ferdinand and Isabella of ever-blessed memory! I wish I could feel that I knew no better than to follow your advice!"

"How often have I watched you from my window at the Villa Reale," sighed his mother, "walking alone in the garden, your arms crossed behind your back, your hat over your eyes, talking to yourself! I hoped you would prove another Frederick the Great."

"I was an affected, strutting young fool! Let me entreat you not to remind me of that ridiculous period!"

"Wretched child! My words will ring through your deserted old age, and you will vainly strive to drown the reproaches of your conscience. Leave my sight before I pronounce the curses I may regret and be unable to recall!"

She pointed one wasted finger toward the door, and the sleeve of her cloak disclosed a long, emaciated arm on which a brilliant diamond bracelet, far too large, dangled like a manacle.

"But what a fuss!" he said, in a gentler voice. "What tragedy!"

"There is nothing else for princes," was her severe response.

"Why not give me time? Why not be less aggressive?"

"There is no more time to be lost, and the exercise of authority is not aggression."

"But this is comic opera! Believe me, such expressions are obsolete."

"I have observed that you regard everything relating to your father's kingdom as the libretto of a burlesque! Go, I say, or I shall lose every atom of self-control! You are the bitterest disappointment of my insupportable life!"

"You will be calmer to-morrow!"

"True. I may be dead."

"Always these threats!"

He left her, however, and he fancied he could hear her wailing as he walked down the corridor. It was the old scene in the old, old manner. She did not understand him; she could not manage him.

An hour later he was delighted to find himself once more in Lucie Hollemache's society. The day was lovely, and he suggested a drive.

"Yes," she said, almost eagerly, "drive me out toward Acton!"

"Toward Acton!" he exclaimed, in astonishment. "Where is that? What a strange idea!"

"I know the road very well," said Lucie, showing unusual animation, "although I have not been there for many weeks."

The Prince handed her into the brougham—a

perfect vehicle lined with pale green satin. It was one which had been placed at his disposal by Mr. Bickersteth.

"I wanted to see you so much?" said Paul to Lucie, who was looking remarkably handsome in ivory crêpe de Chine and a long driving cloak. "I think I shall remain in London," he continued, "until Goodwood. I had no idea it could be so pleasant here. But it was dull, on the whole, at Stokehampton." Then he gave an amusing description of the house-party. He intended to speak out that afternoon and learn a little more of Lucie's true character. "You really must talk about yourself!" said he, after an hour's monologue. "We have been friends for ever so long, and you are more mysterious every day. What can it all mean?"

"Surely my character, sir, is quite on the surface!"

"Don't I complain of its inscrutability? Promise me, at least, that you will not be a disappointment to me! My friends lately have not been satisfactory at all. You must see how necessary it is that I should have some one creature in whom I can put implicit reliance. I want something more than a good comrade."

"I don't think," said Lucie, "that any wise person would ever want me for a comrade. I am so absent-minded."

"That may be. I wonder whether you will understand me when I tell you that my life often seems to me foolish, empty, and perhaps contemptible. This sensation comes over me when I fall off to sleep at night. I ask myself, I wonder whether death will be something like this? Nobody matters to me, nor do I really matter to anybody. It is not a pleasant thought, and when I wake in the morning it comes over me in precisely the same awful way again."

"Nothing can cure that," said Lucie decisively.

"I suppose not. But, if we are doomed to this consciousness of our solitary existence, the most delightful person is the person who can make us forget this, if only for a few hours. So far as pleasures and recreations go, I have them in abundance."

"Or rather," said Lucie, "in excess."

"But they are counterbalanced by my wretched position as an exile. There are hours, believe me, when I get desperate at the thought of my own uselessness. I had the feeling in America, where every one I met seemed absorbed in some particular occupation or devoted to the achievement of some fixed plan. How grateful I should be to any one who could make me lose my gloomy notions!"

"You seem, sir," said Lucie, "a little out of conceit with yourself to-day, but I hope you don't think it is a usual mood!"

"Don't laugh at me! I could be happy," he exclaimed, "if I lived in one of these little villas, truly hideous little villas, we are passing."

" That is nonsense."

" Ah ! I merely said that in order to find out whether you were actually listening to what I was saying. You looked so far away."

She roused herself with a start and put up her hand to tighten her veil.

" But now," she said, " you are interested in petroleum."

" I was at first. The fever has died out. I take a calm commercial interest in the affair—nothing more. I begin to feel as though I came from a generation of country bankers. I used to hear that the Stock Exchange and all these speculations were a form of madness in the blood. The history of modern times would seem to point that way, but it all leaves me cold, untouched. I have enthusiasm now for art only—art and beauty. Yet again I am no artist ; I have no executive, no creative ability. I am an amateur in that direction and in all others. What then is left me ? An overwhelming love—the capacity for a master-passion."

" Do you really think so ? " said Lucie, gazing out of the window.

" I feel it," replied the young man.

" Probably you know yourself."

" But friendship is better than love—it is more constant, more just."

" Beyond any doubt."

" Tell me something of your own heart, then ! "

" Perhaps I will presently."

" Why not now, Lucie ?   Confide in me ! "

" There is so little to tell."

" I am glad of that.   A woman should not have too much to tell about her heart.   You see, I long to hear, and yet I dread to hear.   We are such contradictions."

" You see that large square house to your left, up that road ? "

" Yes.   It looks like a home for orphans.   Pray don't ask me to admire suburban architecture ! "

" It is an asylum."

" How sad and unpleasant ! "

" My heart is buried there."

" Your heart ? "

" Basil is there.   Shall we drive back again now, or would you rather go on a little further ? "

" Your heart is there ? " he repeated.

" Yes."

" Why," he asked plaintively, " do I always like such strange, disagreeable women ?   Why did you bring me so far to look at that terrible house ? "

He ordered the coachman to return, and he maintained a sullen silence till they reached Holland Park. Then he begged her pardon.

" You were perfectly right," said he ; ." I deserved it."

CHAPTER XIX

STUDIES IN SELF-RESPECT

WHEN the Prince returned from his drive to Acton, he was summoned by an anxious lady-in-waiting to his mother's apartments. Queen Charlotte by this time had made her toilet for the day, and was wearing a handsome dress of black silk trimmed with jet. Her white hair had been arranged in a pyramid of puffs, little braids, and curls ; she bore herself nobly, and, although morbid weakness trembled in every feature, there was, nevertheless, much dignity in the mould of the sorrowful face. She was seated at a writing-table, staring with red eyes at a long document in foolscap. Near her in an easy-chair, with one of his legs over its arm, sat the Crown Prince Constantine, sucking the carved ivory knob of his walking-stick. He had a puffy countenance, a short neck, a low forehead, and bristling hair which had been cut in the German fashion and seemed to grow erect on his head. Not a bad-hearted young man, nor an effeminate one, but incurably idle, careless, and blundering—such was the official view of his character.

As Paul came into the room, the Queen, wiping away her tears, said—

" Your brother tells me, without any misgivings of shame or regret, he has made some secret treaty with Mr. Hermann Gessner with regard to Largs. The contract was signed before you went to America."

" Is that true, Con-Con ? " asked Paul.

" Don't ask him, please, in my presence," said the Queen irritably, " whether something is true of which I have already informed you ! I repeat that part of the Largs property which belongs to Constantine has been assigned to Mr. Gessner, the banker."

" My excellent, not too luminous mother is trying to tell me why I should not have done so," said Constantine, who was hard to understand because he had a thick lisp. " I needed money ; Gessner had it. I had some land which he required ; he had fifty thousand pounds which I required. Naturally we soon came to terms. If my bit of Largs is not worth so much—that is Gessner's affair."

" I think you should have consulted us first," said Paul.

" Have conferences in this family led to such satisfactory results that you recommend them ? " asked his brother.

The Queen wrung her hands.

" But a secret treaty and on a business matter—

when your ignorance of business is a matter of history and the chief source of our present situation ! "

" It is just possible," said Paul quietly, " that we can get the contract annulled."

" That would depend entirely on the means at your disposal, my dear brother. But you were always thrifty. I think myself that the sooner we embrace the fact that no one can move without a syndicate at his back, and the sooner my mother can get it through her head that ex-princes are at a discount, we shall all enjoy more dignified, more serene, and more pleasurable existences ! "

" Pleasure ! " screamed the Queen Charlotte. " Always that word ! Pleasure, pleasure, pleasure ! Pleasure and money ! Is there nothing else in the world ? Have we, God's creatures, no other aims ? Let me die, O God, before I live to see the final debasement of my accursed generation ! "

Prince Paul sighed and Prince Constantine swore. The antagonism between the latter and his parents was of the most violent kind. They themselves had quarrelled incessantly before his birth, and he seemed to both the incarnation of their mutual hatred.

" Will you be quiet ? " he called out. " Will you drop these infernal upbraidings ? "

" Not while I live ! " exclaimed the Queen. " I shall die protesting ! How can I complain of the ingratitude and folly of our people when I have brought sons into the world who justify too well the sarcasm

and contempt in which all aristocrats are held nowadays ? O bitter hour ! "

" Then don't complain of ingratitude and what-do-
you-call-it l Leave me alone and look at home ! Do
these laments help us ? Do they help anybody ?
Please remember your own extravagance, your arrogant ways, your ridiculous pride—quite out of date, I
can assure you l "

Constantine rose from his chair as he spoke and
walked clumsily to the looking-glass, where he spent
some seconds examining his tongue, the state of his
complexion, and his necktie. The necktie and his
socks were supposed to be of the same shade of olive
green ; in the light he discovered that the match was
by no means perfect—a discovery which caused him
the liveliest annoyance.

"I must get out of this climate," he muttered.
"Settle the affair with Gessner any way you please,
and you have my full authority to cancel the contract
if Gessner—or Gessing, or whatever his name is—will
agree. It matters not to me who pays the money I
want so long as I get it "—and he drew himself up,
pinched despondently his own flabby cheeks, nodded
not without a kind of affection at his brother, hurled
a glance of venomous rage at the unhappy Queen,
and marched, with the sudden assumption of a soldierly
bearing, out of the room. Queen Charlotte, as the
door closed behind him, burst into sobs and, leaning
on the table, buried her face in her hands. Situations

of this sort were over-familiar to Prince Paul because
he had witnessed little else in the royal circle from the
time he could first remember, and—apart from the
deep pity which he habitually felt for the unfortunate
lady who had brought him into the world—he was
not especially moved by her exhibition of anger and
despair.

"I never wanted children!" she gasped, between
her moans. "I dreaded them always, always!"

"Perhaps," said her son, "that is why there is not
that sympathy between us which exists, according to
tradition, between a mother and her sons!"

"I was born for the life of holy contemplation,"
she continued. "I seek for God. I want the magnificent and tranquillising thought of eternity ever
before me, not this coarse, cruel, degrading existence
among heathens in a heathen land! I 'want to press
toward the mark for the prize of the high calling.'
Not this, O God, not this!"

"And yet you cannot keep your temper!" said
Prince Paul. "There are plenty of reasons for doing
so without any appeal to religion. The news about
the contract is serious. The land will be worth double
that amount. If Gessner has paid up the fifty thousand, it can be refunded. I must go and see Felshammer at once."

"But you must be careful!" screamed his mother.
"You have not heard half of my worries this morning!
One, if not all, of us will be assassinated. The In-

spector of Police has already received information that we must be on our guard against these anarchists. You will call this comic opera also, I suppose ? "

" Have no alarm," said Prince Paul. " By brooding on these dangers one brings them to pass. I believe myself that we can actually attract misfortune and crimes by dreading them."

He kissed her bony hand, every finger of which was covered with gems, implored her to be calm, and, bound for Felshammer's office, left her hurriedly. But before he had advanced two yards down the corridor he heard his name called in a loud voice. Turning, he saw the Queen, beckoning him to return, at the door of her room. Biting his lip, he went back.

" What is it now ? " he said, struggling to conceal his impatience.

" Surely," said she, pulling him into the room and closing the door, " I am the one now to deal with Mr. Gessner ! Let me write on Constantine's account, and probably, as I am a woman, he will make less difficult terms and fewer objections."

" There is something in your suggestion," said Prince Paul, "but I doubt extremely whether your sex would make any difference. A woman can move well in business when she understands it better than most men, but otherwise she is at a positive disadvantage."

" At all events," said the Queen, " let me try.

Give me the control of the money you have promised.
That will give me confidence in approaching Mr.
Gessner."

Prince Paul laughed bitterly.   The notorious extravagance of his mother had been an early cause of their
exile, and he, as the one careful member of the family,
had been called on again and again for loans which
were never repaid, guarantees which taxed his income,
and debts of honour which stood for nothing except
an incalculable expense.

"More chiffons, I suppose ! " he said.

" My rank ! " exclaimed his mother.   " God knows
I wish I had been a humble peasant, but that was not
His Will."

" Evidently," said the Prince.   "If I make money
over this petroleum, you shall have all you want ; I
can't spare much now."

But he promised to consider the point and left her
once more.   He was not anxious to inform Felshammer
of Constantine's action, which almost amounted to
treachery, in the matter of Largs.   He had an odd
sympathy, half protective and half contemptuous, with
his elder brother.   He was ashamed of his conduct,
his tastes, and his dishonesty, but he found something
rather charming all the same in his unconcealed
selfishness.   Paul knew that Felshammer despised
Constantine, and, from a sense of loyalty, he felt
peculiarly unwilling to expose this new act of folly.
So he wrote a note to Mr. Sachs, warning him that

he might require fifty thousand pounds or more for a strictly private matter; and, although he met Fels-hammer that night at dinner, he made no reference to the circumstance.

The next afternoon he called at Mr. Gloucester's lodgings and found Clementine on the doorstep waiting to be admitted.

"I have called to see you," said he, "because you are always so unkind to me!"

"Unkind, sir! How could you think so?"

"You despise my friendship and you will not hear of my devotion. But I will not reproach you. You make me more anxious than ever to win your approbation."

The servant at this point opened the door. The Prince found himself in a narrow hall with paper imitating yellow marble on the walls, and a staircase, covered with red and white drugget, facing him.

"Our apartments are here," said Clementine, sighing, and she led the way into a small dining-room, plainly furnished but full of flowers. He sat down on a horsehair sofa and wondered why he did not mind poverty. Clementine had never appeared so beautiful. He asked himself why on earth she was not on the stage. That would have made everything much simpler.

"I hope the Queen is well, sir?"

"She is never well. She is always in trouble, and she has always too many bills. What do you suppose she wishes me to do? She commands me to marry."

"You must have known that would come sooner or later." She hoped that she controlled her voice.

" But later—as much later as possible. Does not one daughter-in-law satisfy her? Have you ever seen my brother Con-Con's wife? "

"I have seen her photograph."

" The worst is too flattering. Poor, plain, worthy, suffering creature! She is an invalid, and she is the one person in the world of whom Con-Con is really afraid. That is why he is never with her. As you know, he has no heir, and she and my mother are too much alike in disposition to be anything but enemies. When these devout women disagree, one may as well pray for a grave. Each hates the other. Great heavens! Could any one ask me to introduce another lady into our wretched circle? Are there not martyrs enough in the calendar? "

" I have always heard," said Clementine, "that the Princess Marie——"

" Don't speak of my three cousins! But I can see what is going to happen. Between them all, they will drive me into matrimony. I shall choose my own wife, however."

" Does any one suppose that you would not do so ? "

" My intention is to marry for love. In my country such marriages are called morganatic." He tried to catch her answering glance, but she was looking at the wall behind him. "Such marriages," he continued, breathing more quickly, "are usually most happy."

"For the Prince or for the lady?" asked Clementine.

"For both, I trust. My idea is briefly this—but you mustn't have that stony look while I tell you."

"I meant to look charming."

"No, believe me, it is stony. Of the three Princesses I am expected to choose from eventually, one has a lisp—a thing I hate, perhaps because it runs in our family; Adelaide has a back like a retired general's, and Olga can best be described as a good horsewoman. I won't conceal from you or myself that destiny is whipping me towards one of these."

"I see," said Clementine, with whitening lips.

"But," said Prince Paul, "before this doom comes upon me—and I can call it nothing else—I want two years, at least one year, of peace with my true companion. Surely she will not make my life harder than it is already, or stand aloof, for any motive of false pride, from a position which, in the sight of God, is the true marriage and secondary on official occasions only! You understand?"

"I don't choose to understand you," said Clementine—"you must speak more plainly."

"It must be your American blood," exclaimed

Prince Paul, "which makes you so extremely and unnaturally business-like."

"That is possible," said the girl.

"I have always sworn," said Paul, "that I would never care for an American woman. I think they are cold, independent, and exacting. I find these somewhat repellant characteristics in you. Yet, nevertheless, I am replying to your questions as though I were a child learning his catechism. It is to me inexplicable. It must, therefore, be my destiny. There can be no will in the question." He spoke half in jest, yet he intended every word as a stab.

"You mean," said Clementine, "it could not possibly be your choice?"

"In a sense, no," replied Paul, becoming irritable. "But you have not answered my question."

"What was that?" asked Clementine, looking at him.

"You want me to repeat it again? I ask you then if you will consent to a private marriage with me?"

"No!"

Prince Paul could not trust his ears. He sat gazing at her in blank astonishment.

"I am in earnest," he said.

"I did not think that you could be anything else. I don't find fault with your lack of earnestness."

"What, then, do you find fault with?"

"A false position, and therefore a false compliment. I don't care about it. How could I hear to see you married a second time? It is unthinkable!"

"Would you care so much?" exclaimed the Prince, encouraged. He had never felt altogether disheartened. Her manner, in spite of numerous peculiarities in the way of primness, was always sympathetic.

"Would you mind when you know that the—other—is merely an affair of State?"

"Yes," said Clementine, "I should 'mind,' as you say."

"But it is done every day, my dearest! Oh, let me implore you not to be so provincial in your ideas! You are spoiling the romance of my life. You have altered it so far already that you have actually reduced me to make this proposition—one which, I assure you, I could never have believed possible. If you knew my view of marriage under any conditions, if you could imagine my prejudice, you would appreciate the great devotion I have for you."

"I do appreciate it," said Clementine; "I ought to feel flattered. Still, why should all the flattery seem to come from your side? If I am worth anything at all, you ought to feel flattered by my interest in you."

"I am!" he exclaimed. "I am, indeed. You are certainly the most extraordinary girl I have ever met. I don't believe you have a heart!"

"I don't want you to believe it," said Clementine with more truth than irony.

"What more can I say—offer—do ?"

"I would marry you on one condition only. The marriage could be as quiet as you pleased and as private as you pleased, but you would have to swear not to marry any one else during my lifetime."

"But I have explained to you," said Prince Paul, "that my position does not allow me to take this purely selfish view. That is why morganatic marriages are allowed. Princes cannot always consider their own inclinations."

"They have done so often," said Clementine; "and, if a woman is worth the devotion you describe, she is also worth the consideration I ask for."

"It is your American blood," he repeated.

"I can't say what it is, but I know this—I cannot change my instincts."

"In other words," he exclaimed, "you expect me to renounce my birthright, my responsibilities, and settle down with domestic country gentlemen. And why ? Because I love you, because I admire your delightful face, your frigid character; it is clear to me that you don't know men. Not," he added hastily, "that I want you to know them. Women who understand men have, to me, lost every atom of charm and delicacy. Clementine, I am not conceited, but when I am with you I cannot help feeling that I am liked."

"You may trust that feeling," said Clementine, laughing. "I admire you extremely."

"Then why this coldness, this hesitation, this formal view, this command of language? The command of language is almost unpardonable. It is unwomanly—it is hard."

"It is best to know me as I am, sir!"

"But your looks belie you!" said Prince Paul. "You have a Southern, an all but Oriental air, which is fascinating, submissive, gracious—everything that one admires. I shall begin to think that I am no judge of your sex."

"I am sorry you are disillusioned."

"It is a shock," continued Paul. "You are not the girl I took you for."

"What do you take me for?" asked Clementine pleasantly.

"Ah, guess my opinion of you," he answered, "when I asked you to join your life with mine."

"That was very generous!" said Clementine.

"I offer you my liberty—liberty—the dearest thing a man has!"

"Next to himself," she suggested.

"I told you that I looked for all my earthly happiness in you," he continued, with a terrible glance. "What is my answer? An icy look, a lawyer's terms, a cold analysis of the position. It is not what I expected."

"I suppose not," said Clementine.

"I am glad, on the whole, that you are my friend and not my enemy, for I could detest a woman with so little impulse and so much foresight."

Clementine sighed and sat as patiently as ever with her hands clasped.

"You don't value me or my affection for you," said Prince Paul, "and you have made me bitter for life. Yes, that is the case—I am embittered. Perhaps, all the same, it is for the best."

"I am always certain of that in any event," replied Clementine, "although the best is often the hardest."

"And so," he said, after a pause, "you refuse me?"

"I refuse to place myself, to our common misery, in an equivocal position."

"But your prejudice is fantastic. Consult any one you please; refer to your own father, to your aunt Emmeline—she would tell you. Why should you, a little inexperienced girl, set yourself against the received customs of society?"

"This is a matter of feeling, and the way I feel cannot be altered."

The Prince by this time was in a bad temper.

"I think," said he, "that you have no feelings at all. I shall always speak well of you and think of you as kindly as possible—not for anything you have said or done, but because you have pretty, if misleading, manners. It would be impossible, however, to continue loving any one quite void of real sweetness and tenderness."

"I was sure," said Clementine, "that you did not love me in the least."

"That again is untrue and not well observed," said the Prince hastily. "I thought I proved my love—a foolish love, perhaps—sufficiently in the early part of this conversation. You have proofs of very unusual friendship at this moment."

But Clementine shook her head.

"I don't believe," said she, "that you know what love means."

And so the interview came to an end.

"She is a witch!" he told himself, as he walked back to Claridge's. "I had no intention of going into all these questions to-day. The *mise-en-scène* was impossible. I have never proposed before. A new experience! Well, one learns. This attitude on her part is very clever—too clever! I can see through it. I thought that coquettes were extinct. I shall tell her that this is a mere childish ruse to make herself precious. Clever of her!"

He intended to call again and arrange a theatre-party.

"I shall treat this nonsense lightly," he decided. "She will be piqued, of course, but I can't help that. It is too absurd."

That evening with Felshammer he attended a little private supper at the house of a famous composer of light music. Several accomplished and lovely young ladies from the Parnassus and other theatres were

17

present. They sang songs, danced dances, gave imitations, and apparently excelled in the womanly arts of gentleness and a limited vocabulary. But he was bored.

"I suppose the time must come," he confided to Felshammer, "when this sort of thing seems insupportably tedious. Yet is it fair to criticise any one after I have spent the morning with my dear mother? How she depresses me!"

Pride would not allow him to trace any failing of joy to his strange treatment at the hands of Clementine. But among the many voices in a man's heart, there is always one that remains incorruptibly honest. This plaintive note warned him, through his restless sleep, that Clementine had behaved, by a paradox, altogether as he had hoped.

The girl, meanwhile, was thinking in despair that she had lost him for ever. Yet she could not regret one word she had said. Remorseful fortitude is the most dangerous kind of cowardice, and it is the commonest in virtuous women. Wise virgins pray against this weakness.

CHAPTER XX

WHEN Mr. Hermann Gessner heard that there was
a hitch in the negotiations for the Largs estate, he
wreaked his annoyance on his manager, Mr. Draycott.
Mr. Draycott, in order to cover himself, began to
abuse the property in question, and, with mock
humility, confessed to Mr. Gessner that he had
committed an error of judgment in passing so
favourable an opinion upon it in the first instance.

" No one is infallible," said Mr. Draycott, who
had a face like a tortoise and very curious crawling
movements of the body ; " if I did not admit my
mistakes, I couldn't recommend myself as a safe
person for these delicate—peculiarly delicate, I may
say—investigations. The petroleum is there right
enough. I'll stake my reputation upon it. But it
isn't for you."

" We are committed up to a certain point by this
contract with Prince Constantine. I must have the

243

244 LOVE AND THE SOUL HUNTERS

whole property or leave it alone altogether," said
Gessner.

"Let me arrange it," said Mr. Draycott, moving
his lips as though he were silently rehearsing a part.
"I know all about that man Dr. Felshammer. He
may be a very good sort of equerry, but he has no
more knowledge of business than a child. And as for
Prince Constantine——"

"Oh, well," said Mr. Hermann Gessner, "I never
anticipated at any time the least trouble with Prince
Constantine. You may adopt any course you see fit—
what you want to do is to get out of the contract.
I have been informed from two or three sources that
it is not a safe deal."

Mr. Gessner was not aware that his friend Mr.
Cobden Duryee had carefully spread a cautious report
in the right quarters to the effect that Prince Constantine had got the better of the great Mr. Gessner's
great Mr. Draycott in a bargain. Duryee, with his
dry and sardonic humour, had told the story to perfection. Mr. Gessner fancied he saw smiles on
obscure faces in Mincing Lane.

"Leave it all to me," said Draycott, who was more
sensitive than his distinguished chief, a man of strong
nerves who could enjoy, after all, a small joke at his
own expense. "I will work this in such a way that
we shall have forgotten the whole annoyance in less
time than it takes to tell it!"

Accordingly, by appointment, which was fixed by

telegram, Mr. Draycott, accompanied by a young man of good family in order to give a certain tone to the forthcoming interview, set forth for Prince Constantine at the Savoy Hotel.

Mr. Draycott had lived for the greater part of his life in the Western States of America and the Colonies. He had been taught to think that bluster, brag, and insolence were impressive. Accustomed to deal with persons in pecuniary difficulties who were anxious to make bad arrangements rather than no arrangements at all, he prided himself on being able to "bounce" or "rush" any transaction in whichever direction he wished. As is often the case with individuals of this stamp, he had no very strong opinion or will of his own, and, although he knew that the Largs property was a sound investment, talk in the City had been so well manipulated by Cobden Duryee that Draycott no longer trusted his own convictions. He was extremely anxious to get out of a complication which promised to cause him serious anxiety and perhaps ruin his ally, Mr. Campsey, the expert.

On being ushered into Prince Constantine's private sitting-room at the Savoy, he was reassured to discover His Royal Highness taking an afternoon siesta on the sofa. When the Prince awoke, he rubbed his eyes, yawned, offered his callers whisky and cigars, and said that England made him drowsy. Mr. Draycott, in response to these gracious civilities, assumed an air

of sardonic melancholy. He affected a detestation
of royal and aristocratic personages, and he showed
his independence whenever he met them by exhibiting
his bad manners at their worst. The young gentleman of good family who was with him seemed a little
ashamed of his companion's demeanour, and kept the
conversation going on general topics with perfect ease
and propriety. Mr. Draycott disapproved of this, and
frowned severely at the young gentleman, who had
been brought on the understanding that he was not to
presume to open his mouth or " put in an oar."

" Business is very bad," said Draycott, in a surly
way ; "you can't get support for a single concern.
Fact ! Truth is, there's no money. Naturally, this
does not affect Mr. Gessner, who is so busy now with
Russian railways that he has hardly heard of Largs.
It's too small a deal for him ; it was taken up without
my full sanction, and now Mr. Gessner seems dis-
inclined to move. Really, if things don't alter a great
deal within the next six or seven months, I don't see
a chance for Largs. That, at least, is my opinion."

" You must have been talking to some gloomy
people !" said Prince Constantine. "I haven't heard
of this panic. You call it a slump, I suppose ?"

" There is no money in Largs—not a penny. It's
the sort of thing which absorbs thousands and hundreds of thousands. I daresay one would get it all
back in fifty years. But naturally, while there are
less speculative investments with immediate returns,

no one, not even Mr. Gessner, is especially anxious to put up any sum worthy the name for the exploitation of Largs."

"It is rather late in the day to go into all that," said Prince Constantine, "when our negotiations are settled and the first draft is signed."

"I know that," said Draycott; "your position is strong legally, and, this being the case, I just want to point out the difficulty before us."

"You wish to imply," said Constantine, "that you consider Mr. Gessner has made an injudicious investment?"

Mr. Draycott twisted on his seat and made no reply.

"I don't see, however, that this is any affair of mine," said Constantine. "The differences between Mr. Gessner and his subordinates ought certainly not to be referred to me."

"Mr. Gessner controls and directs every deal absolutely and without qualification," said Draycott; "the only one to be reckoned with in the management is Mr. Gessner. He would take over all the Largs stock and finance the deal. But it would be tempting fortune to do so at this moment. Small as the undertaking is, he won't run it as a speculative lock-up. His hands are too full just now. Later on he will do his best. He always does his best. He is a man of honour."

"Do you know," said Prince Constantine, "that

was something I had already assumed before you troubled to call? I think myself that Mr. Gessner has every reason to congratulate himself on having made an advantageous purchase."

Mr. Draycott gazed in a supercilious manner at the ceiling and his own boots.

"There is something in your manner, sir," said the Prince, "which strikes me as being distinctly discourteous. I may be wrong. I don't care for it."

"There is no discourtesy meant," said Mr. Draycott—"none whatever. I just came on behalf of Mr. Gessner to say that we do not propose to take the matter up immediately. It must stand over until some more convenient moment. When we have settled a few things with Russia, for instance."

"I see," said the Prince slowly; "that is the idea,—delay—indefinite delay."

"Roughly," said Draycott—"roughly."

"And," said the Prince, "as I myself hold a considerable right to the profits of the venture, I am expected to wait developments till Mr. Gessner can find time to proceed with them?"

Mr. Draycott once more wriggled on his seat and worked his mobile lips, thrust his hands into his pockets, and endeavoured to show his complete indifference to princes or any of the usual considerations in polite society.

Prince Constantine felt his anger rising at this intolerable conduct, and said:

"I think I can offer to relieve Mr. Gessner of that contract. I can find another market."

Draycott at this hugged himself secretly on having accomplished his object so easily, but he maintained a very sceptical air.

"Do you mean," said he, "that another firm will take it over?"

"That is what I mean," replied Constantine. He had a letter in his pocket at that moment from Cobden Duryee. Draycott attributed the Prince's independence to wounded pride.

"My one aim in coming here," said Draycott, with a triumphant glance at his gentlemanly companion, who was now blushing—"my one aim was to explain the matter fairly and squarely and to put before you the circumstances of the case and Mr. Gessner's feelings. Mr. Gessner thought this talk would be pleasanter than writing. He decided—that is, we both decided——"

"Are you a partner in the firm," asked Constantine, "or a buffer?"

He turned for information to the young gentleman, who was about to reply when Mr. Draycott, indignant at being overlooked, said with great anger:

"Mr. Merivale knows nothing of this business or any other. I am the person with whom this matter is to be settled."

"Then," said the Prince, rising, "you must express any further ideas by correspondence. In view of this other offer, I can assure you that I am entirely willing to annul the contract."

Mr. Draycott did not allow himself to believe that the Prince had received any such offer, but he considered that he had exasperated a notoriously impulsive, unwise man into some defensive attitude. He reflected on the splendid success of his method, and he thought he had never yet had a case in which he had found so little difficulty in making a person give away, as it were, his own interests under the stress of insult.

"I must say," observed Draycott, "that I have said nothing which was in the least degree inconsiderate or uncivil. If I have done so, it was entirely unintentional and you have wholly misconstrued me."

"I can but reply," said Constantine, "that, if you intended to make yourself agreeable, you have failed to convey that impression to me."

The three men stood up. Mr. Draycott opened the door, bowed slightly, and, followed by his ashamed companion, went out of the room.

"He wasn't bluffing," said Merivale timidly, when they reached the hall. "He was telling the truth."

"Don't be a fool!" replied Draycott. "I knew he would take that line. They always do."

Yet he began to feel uneasy. Men on the Stock Exchange were influenced, he knew, by every breath of criticism they received—even from the most incompetent, unreliable sources. It was absurd as generals in opposition advising each other on tactics. He himself, Ashton Draycott, had said so frequently.

"What is the Prince's game?" he now wondered.

Prince Constantine, meanwhile, was telling his mother on the telephone that he had good news.

"I have saved fifty thousand pounds," he explained in Russian; "you shall have the use of half of it at 15 per cent."

"But it is Paul's money," she answered in Italian.

"We can discuss that another time," he replied in German. He always spoke German when he remembered his brother's more careful disposition.

CHAPTER XXI

MR. GLOUCESTER DRAWS A CHEQUE

FELSHAMMER was sitting in his private office at Messrs. Sachs and Bickersteth's three days later, when he received a call from Mr. Gloucester. The old gentleman had recovered his buoyant step, and his eyes shone—not with their original mildness and faith, but with a shifting glitter. Conversation between the two was brief.

"More trouble?" asked Felshammer, in a light, reassuring tone.

"I won't take up your valuable time, Dr. Felshammer," replied his visitor, "but I want to repay that loan you were kind enough to make. I didn't expect to be in a position to return the full amount so soon, and this is a pleasant surprise for both of us."

He picked up a pen, pulled a cheque-book from his pocket, and signed, with trembling fingers, a draft on his bankers for thirty thousand pounds. Felshammer pushed back his chair, and stared first at the feeble hand of Mr. Gloucester and then at his face.

"I don't suppose," said Gloucester, making his final letter, "that you ever hoped to see the money again. That makes my obligation the deeper and your kindness the more extraordinary. But, although I have had a lot of trouble, I beg you will not think that I would have asked such a favour had I not felt that there was something behind me."

"It has been a pleasure to me," stammered Felshammer, "and I am in no hurry for the repayment if it is any convenience to you to keep this."

"No, no! I am beginning to love money as I never did when I was comfortably off. 'Blessings brighten as they take their flight'—you know the old saying. But I don't like to be in debt. You have been more than generous because, after all, we are mere acquaintances, and I haven't an old friend who could have helped me in that emergency."

It was beautifully done, but Felshammer detected a certain emphasis on the word "acquaintances." He bowed; the two shook hands and parted. One question only troubled Felshammer. Where had the money been found? Who had supplied it? He knew Mr. Gloucester's financial position, and it was certain that he had discharged one debt by incurring another. Then a surmise flashed into the secretary's mind. Had not Prince Paul drawn a very large sum, at considerable inconvenience to the firm, just two days before. For whom had he drawn it? For what purpose? As a rule Prince Paul was ex-

ceedingly open, even recklessly so, about his money
matters. He lived, however, well within his income
—a fine one—and he was not in the habit of making
heavy demands of the kind at short notice. Jealousy
now made Felshammer doubly suspicious, and he
formed a conviction that Clementine had been the
recipient of Paul's bounty.

"That is it! That is it! That, of course, is it!"
he repeated aloud, beside himself with anger. He
cursed the girl, he cursed his own madness; he
locked and unlocked the drawers in his writing-
desk, read letters blindly, wrote others which were
incoherent. At last he could bear it no longer, and,
sending for his confidential clerk, he made some excuse
and left the office for the rest of the day. He walked
the streets until the music-halls opened, then he
entered several in turn, only to find each entertainment more vapid than the last. He went to his club
and ordered supper, but he had no appetite and could
not eat. The other members bored him, and he
drove to his own chambers. But the rooms looked
desolate, small, ghostly, so he went back again to the
streets and walked along the Embankment and over
the bridge towards Lambeth, while he heard Big Ben
tolling the hours two, three, four, and five—his mind
all the time revolving the same thoughts without
variation or relief. As he was crossing Belgrave
Square a carriage full of girls returning from a ball
rolled past him in the dawn. One of these waved a

white hand to him ; it was Leonore Townshend, and
Clementine sat laughing by her side. He had just
time to catch sight of the Florentine profile. Tears
of admiration and fatigue sprang to his eyes, increasing his bitterness, and also his desire to gain the
mastery over the provoking child. He continued his
wretched walk for another two hours, and entered his
chambers when the porters were just opening the
doors, sweeping out the hall, and polishing the brass.
They looked after him as he passed ; they liked to
learn as soon as possible the habits and expressions of
a new tenant. His expression that morning was anything but pleasant ; they decided that he had lost
heavily at cards.

Later on he went as usual to the City, but, as it
was a Saturday, he was able to leave early, and it
occurred to him that the one person whom he could
bear to see was Rachel Bickersteth. There was a
London garden at the back of her drawing-room. In
the country it would have seemed small and dreary ;
the trunks of the trees were black, their dusty leaves
seldom stirred, the harsh vivid grass, growing in
sooty earth, had no vitality. The carefully planted
hyacinths—pink, blue, and mauve—were fragrant,
however, and, as Felshammer followed a servant
across the small lawn to some wicker-chairs with silk
cushions under an old elm, the place seemed
a delightful refuge. Rachel was there playing
" Patience."

"I have not seen you since you left Stokehamp-ton," she said, without a smile.

"No," said Felshammer, "I have no leisure for calling nowadays. The City turns one into a drudge."

"Prince Paul was here last night. I like him more and more each time I meet him. It seems a pity that he, too, is becoming absorbed in financial questions."

"Does he appear preoccupied?" said Felshammer eagerly.

"He talked a great deal about petroleum and some contract made with Hermann Gessner. I could not follow it because, as you know, business wearies me. I have heard nothing else all my life, and I like abstract things or beautiful ones. How I wish we could all learn to be contented on five hundred a year! Why is success measured nowadays by the money it can produce?"

"Certainly the mere acquisition of wealth is not in the least the only test of success."

"I begin to envy my housemaids," she sighed.

Felshammer remained there perhaps half an hour; he said nothing he had intended to say, yet her influence, all but sexless, was soothing. He felt certain that she was in sympathy with him, and that she realised, to some extent, the drift of his thoughts. After he had left Rachel he felt that he could trust himself to see Clementine. He drove to her lodgings and found her at home. Leonore was there, eating chocolates, and the two girls were discussing their experiences at the ball the night before. Both were flushed and excited, laughing lightly, comparing scraps of conversation. Leonore, greeting Dr. Felshammer, managed to throw him a speaking glance as though she would say that she knew all and was, with her whole soul, on his side. It conveyed also a soft suggestion that, if he should ever come to think better of wasting his time over Clementine, there were many other attractive women still left in the world. The subtlety of this glance was by no means lost on its object. Clementine, on the other hand, was courteous but constrained ; she shrank into the background while Leonore led the conversation. Balls, theatres, concerts, books, individuals—she disposed of them all with a tripping tongue and a sarcastic turn of thought. She knew that she was considered a beauty, and she had an anxiety to be thought intelligent as well. But, receiving no response from the moody secretary, she soon became tired, wished him goodbye, and, much to Clementine's embarrassment, kissed her and left. Felshammer seized his opportunity. As he could not be on the terms he sought with Clementine, the next best thing would be the exchange, he thought, of hard words.

"I have come," said he bluntly, " to quarrel. That is to say, I know it must end in a quarrel because I intend to speak the truth—the one thing which women resent."

"But," said Clementine, "as you have so often told me that I am an exception in many ways, you can hardly be certain that I should dislike honesty." ·

Now that her father had discharged his debt to Felshammer she felt free again, her own mistress, in his society. He looked profoundly unhappy, also, and this, in some way, made her forget the threatening air he still possessed when their eyes met.

"I cannot guess what you have got to say," she said, bending over a bowl of roses and lilac which had been sent to her that morning by Prince Paul.

"You will think me brutal," replied Felshammer, "but as I am fond of your father, sincerely fond of him, I want to warn you that, owing to an unsuspecting nature, he is not always careful in his choice of friends."

"What do you mean?"

"Just that. Now there are some of us who are too glad to advise or help him for his own sake, though not for his own sake entirely."

"You have proved your friendship already. I have never before had an opportunity of thanking you."

"I hate being thanked. Please let me finish without thanks. He might get involved in some nominal obligation to an unscrupulous person, and the result might be a ruin which none of us could avert. Do you follow me?"

"Perfectly."

"I have reason to think that he has been borrow-
ing money. If you remember, it was you yourself
who first spoke to me of your father's troubles. I
was proud of the confidence. Have I any thought in
the world except for your happiness ?"

He said this so earnestly, with such feeling, such
reproach, that she could find no answer.

"Do you know," he continued, "from whom he
has just obtained something like thirty thousand
pounds? I am not going to say it is a small sum,
because it is not. The richest man would think
some time before he advanced it in the ordinary way
of business—even on security which he could realise
at a few days' notice. But Mr. Gloucester has no
such security."

"I can tell you nothing," said Clementine, "because I know nothing, except this—he did obtain
money from some friend—a friend whom he has had
for a long time, and in whom he places absolute
reliance. It was a present, not a loan. This is
what he told me."

Felshammer saw that she was giving all the information in her power.

"Very well," said he, "so long as that is the case
you need not worry. I am relieved and glad. But I
have not finished yet."

"Not yet ?" said Clementine, knitting her brows.

"Prince Paul," replied Felshammer slowly, "is the

most agreeable man I know, and, without being
loveless or treacherous, he has broken more hearts,
destroyed more lives——"

"I don't think that I want to hear any tales about
him."

"You must hear them," said Felshammer quickly.
"I cannot conceal from myself the fact that he
interests you. That is natural, and he is to be
envied. I envy him. But don't let your interest go
too far. He has charm, he has grace, he has youth,
he has all the glamour of a romantic, almost tragic
destiny ; but he is a libertine. Oh, not the swash-
buckler, the villain of novels, the Lovelace ; he is a
sentimental soul-hunter, a specialist in souls. He
believes that he is in earnest, whereas he is as fickle
as women are supposed to be and are not. He has no
real affection to offer any one, and you would not
accept less than a real affection. You would not
accept less than his undivided devotion. Now, his
devotion amounts to nothing. A few delightful
letters, some enchanting conversation, some divert-
ing monologues of self-revelation, and then—he will
meet some one else. She need not be half so beautiful, she could not be so brilliant—she will have the
solitary advantage of being new. She can be twenty
years older, she may be duller than a provincial
Egeria—that will not matter. She will be a
novelty."

"You are telling me nothing I did not know perfectly well already. I don't believe he knows what the word love means. Few people do."

She looked at Felshammer steadily as she spoke.

"You could not have known all that," he exclaimed; "it is not sufficiently apparent in his manner. He deceives himself long before he deceives others. That is at once the secret and the insecurity of his friendship. To him the last face represents the abiding passion."

"Personally," said Clementine, "I feel no danger. I judge my friends for myself. What one says of the other is always worth hearing, but I don't allow it to influence me. I have my own thoughts about you, for instance, and about Prince Paul, and about my father. I may be mistaken in all of you. I don't think I am."

"You are not offended at anything I have said?"

"No; but, as you have been speaking plainly, perhaps you will let me speak plainly. I think you have more character than the Prince—many would say that you were more manly. I believe that a woman would be happier with you than with him—if happiness can be taken to mean a sense of security and the knowledge that whatever happens one will be provided for, shielded, and helped. Even then much would depend on the woman. The Prince is an egoist—not in your way. It is a light, irresponsible egoism—very easy to forgive. Your egoism is normal."

"I don't think," said Felshammer, "that you have any right to call me an egoist."

"Neither of us has any right to speak plainly, but, as you are determined to be unconventional, I, for my part, am quite willing to humour you. You didn't say that we were to talk with the simplicity of souls meeting in Paradise, but I have an idea that, if the disembodied ever do meet, they express themselves in this transparent way. It is all impersonal, surely. That is why I like it."

"Impersonal, yet—just as dissection is impersonal, I suppose."

Clementine laughed.

"You began it."

"I have made you angry," said Felshammer.

"No," said Clementine, "that is the odd part. You have not. I am always glad to talk about Prince Paul."

A dark flush swept over her companion's hard face. The scar on his cheek looked almost like an unhealed wound. He dared not answer, but he struck the table with his powerful hand, and, before she could realise the danger of irritating a jealous man, he had left the house.

CHAPTER XXII

THE CONSIDERATION OF SOULS

CLEMENTINE suffered in the struggle to 'conceal a love which she might not and would not express ; the resolution to lock up her feelings and throw away the key was not easily formed ; the cold, bantering manner which she assumed out of self-defence in all her conversations with the Prince was, for its very necessity, humiliating to her pride, and her spirit chafed at the weakness, as she saw it, of her own heart. She wondered how she could care so much for a man who, she feared, was incapable of any real affection. The fastidious hesitation which girls naturally experience in forming an attachment added tormenting thoughts to thoughts painful enough and a conflict severe enough already. It is true that Prince Paul had offered her marriage—an event she had never anticipated among remote possibilities—but the terms had been out of the question, and the manner of offering them had seemed careless, almost insolent. The most painful tears of

her life were shed after she had the right to tell herself that he had offered his love—such as it was. It
was not worth offering or accepting ; her instinct
warned her of this ; curiosity stimulated all his friendships with women—he wished to make experiments,
to observe, to transform, to trifle with tears, troubles,
kisses, and despair, to enjoy follies, vanities, reproaches,
And yet he had sent this verse with the basket of
flowers :—

"Ah, love, could you and I with him conspire
To grasp this sorry scheme of things entire,
Would not we shatter it to bits—and then
Remould it nearer to the heart's desire ! "

Surely a man who could quote that verse was not all
carelessness ? The shabby lodgings, her own poverty
had made no difference—unless for the better and
kinder—in his attitude. Was he beginning to learn
the strength, the simplicity of true love ? This faint
hope brought her a little peace, although she put away
the copied verse because she could not re-read it—the
words seemed to mock her, and she looked as seldom
as possible at the flowers. She did not wish to watch
them fade.

Prince Paul was dining informally that night with
Mr. and Mrs. Sachs. Nadeshda, in a white gown,
with white roses in her black hair, looked especially
young and innocent. She and the Prince discussed

the pictures of Burne-Jones and the dramas of D'Annunzio.

" It is a strange thing to me," said the Prince, fixing his earnest eyes on her long, sweeping lashes, " that Englishmen and Turks take no interest at all in the souls of women. We all admire physical beauty, but moral beauty exercises the lasting fascination, and as a study it is the more engrossing. Now Frenchmen are instinctively drawn toward psychology; so are Germans to a certain degree, so are Russians, Italians, and Americans. Yes, would you believe it, these practical hard-headed Americans are greatly attracted always by the feminine soul and mind ? They like to know what women think, how they feel ; they are inspired by their ideas ; but in England, if you speak of a woman's soul to a man, he supposes you must be either mad or affected. In fact, the soul is a thing which I never discuss with an Englishman."

Nadeshda replied that this was too true, and she promised herself a profound conversation with the Prince later on in the drawing-room. Her husband could be counted among those who had no patience with psychological investigations. The one other woman present was a very good-looking English actress who was more famous for her domesticity than any histrionic talent. She was always seen by interviewers watching a brass kettle boiling on an Adams hob in a little cottage at Bedford Park. Her clothes were made by a well-known firm, but she was never foolish enough to wear jewels. Her sole ornaments were bead necklaces made by a reduced peeress and sold for thirty shillings or two guineas at the most. Nadeshda called this lady by her Christian name—Amelia—and introduced her to the Prince as "my dear friend, Miss Amelia Hoyle."

"Miss Hoyle," she added, in his ear, "is about to create the part of the Queen of Sheba in a new poetical play. It is not called the Queen of Sheba on account of the Lord Chamberlain, who is afraid of offending religious people. It will be the Queen of Babylon, but it is Sheba all the same, and Solomon is to be called Solyman of Arabia. Rather clever of the author, don't you think? One must get a hearing somehow. There is to be a wonderful scene in the Desert, and we shall also have the Temple and Jerusalem, but Jerusalem will be renamed also. It ought to be a great success with one or two really good ballets. Do tell us about your part, Amelia?"

Miss Hoyle, with charming amiability, entered into an elaborate description of her five gowns. Once she referred to the merit of the poet's lines and said that the piece was "a beautiful thing." She expressed her regret at being unable to quote any part of it, but she explained all her exits and entrances, adding each time: "That is very fine you know!"

"What do you think of her?" asked Nadeshda, when she found her opportunity.

"She is handsome," said Prince Paul. "I suppose that is why she has gone on the stage."

"What do you think about her soul?"

"I have not thought about it!"

"You wouldn't believe how kind she is to all her family," said Nadeshda; "she supports her mother and two extraordinarily plain sisters. One made an unhappy marriage—that is why Amelia hates men. She has had a great many offers."

"Because she is so good?"

"Yes."

"I think it is because she is clever enough to make it clear that she never, by any chance, accepts a proposal! She begins to interest me now—such a type would be impossible in any other country."

"You must get to know her."

"Would it take very long? You see, she will be handsome for a few years only, whereas she will always remain a bore."

"Then what kind of women do you like?" said Nadeshda, resting her chin on her very pretty hand; "Do you admire that Mme. de Montgenays? I think her vulgar."

"She is a great artist all the same—very clever too," said Prince Paul. "And, mind you, for her age she is extraordinarily beautiful in an uncommon way. To be beautiful in an uncommon way is the rarest distinction possible."

"Can you understand Mr. Cobden Duryee's

infatuation ?   My husband says it is to him incompre-
hensible."

"It is a case which illustrates the fidelity of which
men are capable.   Duryee has loved La Belle Valentine ever since she was a child.   That speaks well for
both of them.   Each must be a genius in a sense.   To
do her justice she appears devoted to him."

"And then," said Nadeshda, "take Dr. Felshammer's
infatuation for Miss Gloucester."

"What!" exclaimed the Prince.   But here his
training was useful, and he succeeded in maintaining
control of his astonishment.

"He is completely infatuated," continued Nadeshda.
"The last man on earth, one would say, to break his
heart over any one.   I thought such crazes were old-
fashioned."

"I should have said so too," answered Paul, playing
with the gold fringe of a sofa-cushion ; "I have
known him for years.   Romance is not in his
nature."

"But don't you see the change in him ?   He has
aged terribly in the last fortnight.   Of course Miss
Gloucester is quite lovely ; she is intelligent into the
bargain."

The Prince did not reply immediately.

"I knew her," he said slowly, "before she came
out.   She has that peculiar genius I was speaking of—
that gift of arresting friendship or attention and keeping it."

"It is seldom," said Mrs. Sachs, "that a man can reach Dr. Felshammer's age without having formed some permanent attachment or chain. One soon gets able to recognise the chained, or rather muzzled, smile! He hasn't that air, but it is strange that he remains a bachelor."

"He is cold-blooded—quite unromantic. He is an instance of a man who cares not at all about souls."

"I wonder whether Miss Gloucester will marry him?"

"Marry Felshammer? Of course not! Why should she?"

"If she is a wise girl," said Nadeshda, "she will be thankful to get him. Her father has lost every penny of his own money and hers—which was left to her by her mother. You know what that means in society as it is at present."

"I don't think she need trouble about society as it is at present. She is an exception herself," said the Prince—"she need not remember ordinary considerations at all."

"I wish I could agree with you. But you don't know England well; you don't know the number of extraordinarily pretty creatures of good family who go nowhere, and see no one, and never get a chance to marry merely because they haven't the means to keep in the swim. The men they could get are as poor as themselves or social inferiors. So the wretched girls grow up and become faded old maids, embittered and full of fads—if they don't drift into something worse. They arrange these things differently abroad, where every girl has some sort of a dowry, and, when she does not attract suitors, she can save her dignity by becoming a nun."

"That is too cynical," said the Prince.

"Whenever one tells the truth one is called cynical."

"I think, moreover, you are mistaken about Felshammer."

"Is it possible, after all, that the affair has escaped your notice ? Why, Rachel invited the Gloucesters to Stokehampton out of kindness to Felshammer ! "

"Indeed ? " said the Prince drily.

"It was so like poor Rachel. She had no tact as a match-maker. It was much too obvious ; the girl herself saw through it, and pretended to be ill, and moped in the room."

"What small dramas go on without our suspicion ! " said Prince Paul, beginning to wonder whether Clementine cared for the secretary. "I must have this out with her," he thought. "I will go and see her again to-morrow. It is preposterous. Is she as deceitful as the others ? "

Then he had to take his leave in order to attend a very small and very select party at the Russian Embassy. He found thirty highly important personages present, including his mother and the Princess

Marie, his cousin. The Princess Marie was now seven-and-twenty. She had sloping shoulders, high cheek-bones, and an ill-formed mouth full of prominent irregular teeth, which made her lisp especially trying. At the sight of Paul an unbecoming flush covered her entire face, but her soft blue eyes sparkled —which flattered the young man and made him think her less plain than usual. She was not altogether plain at any time ; she had a sweet, winning smile always, and in full evening dress with a diamond comb in her splendid blonde hair she was not without certain qualifications to distinction.

"Ah, Paul," she exclaimed, "why are you so late ? We have been expecting you since ten o'clock. My aunt Charlotte said you would not come. I said you would come, and I was right."

Her evident delight beamed from every feature.

"She was too amiable," said Prince Paul to himself. "Dear good creature ! I wish her arms was not so red."

She looked with triumph round the room at the different privileged members of the Diplomatic Circle who were observing, with discretion, a meeting which they hoped would prove historical.

"It is so nice to be here in London," she said ; "it is too stiff at home, and here they leave one in peace. I have been shopping all day and driving in hansoms. I have bought a bull-dog. But what have you been doing, Paul ! "

"Oh, I have been in the City !" said the Prince, as they sat down in a sort of alcove near some palms and azaleas.

"Ah, to be sure ! You are becoming a kind of American millionaire. My dear aunt was telling me. Do you like the Stock Exchange ? Does it bore you as you pretend politics do ? "

She was conversing in German, but she used the English word bore because she said that there was no precise equivalent for it in any other language.

"All English people are bored," she went on ; "everything to them is 'such a bore.' I think it must amuse them enormously to be bored. When will you come to our box at the opera, Paul ? "

He was about to answer and say, "Oh, that will be such a bore !" when he checked himself and said instead, "Whenever you ask me, Marie."

He glanced up and saw his mother looking at him with an expression of approval. The Prince had paid her most pressing creditors, and she smiled as much as to say : "Marry that immense fortune. The alliance will prove extremely popular in many ways. Poor darling Marie idolises you." The ex-Queen saw, in imagination, articles in all the newspapers about a royal love-match, followed later by photographs taken of the royal home-life—the Princess playing the piano and the Prince turning over the music, with one hand on Her Royal Highness's shoulder.

"Ach, if that could be so !" thought the poor lady.

"Ach, if he would not spoil his life by foolish caprices ! "

Prince Paul did his best to entertain his cousin. She was charming, really, and what is known as a good comrade. She had been a tomboy in her childhood, and there was something virile in her vigorous hand-shake. He liked her so well that he wished she was his sister, although he could not picture her as his wife. By and by she gave him, with many blushes, a sprig of white heather from her dress.

"To remember this evening ! " she explained. "We have never before met together in London."

The dull party soon broke up, and the Prince, having escorted the royal ladies to their carriage, went home in a bad humour. He was not given to self-analysis ; his motives for action depended wholly on the sensations of pain or pleasure which they involved. A wish, due to imagination, the senses, the sympathies, or ennui, was reason enough for him. He thought of asking Cobden Duryee whether he could not go out to the States disguised and work obscurely in a mine. Anything seemed preferable to the life of artificial ideas in which he was being gradually engulfed. And then the notion of masquerading as a miner struck him as one more example of the eternal verities in comic opera.

"Comic opera," he said, as he tried to fall asleep after reading the latest Parisian success in fiction—the squalid history of a lady's-maid—"comic opera is the only true thing left in society ! "

19

CHAPTER XXIII

TWO WAYS OF PLAYING THE FOX

THAT same evening Mr. Cobden Duryee and Mr. Gessner were dining together at Duryee's flat. Both gentlemen were dyspeptics, and one was endeavouring to find nourishment in a dish of boiled rice, while the other was taking hot water with some finely-chopped raw meat. This plain food was served on gold plate, but the meal was grim—an ironical if silent comment on the strain which attends success. The two men were good friends ; both had made large fortunes, and neither had found much happiness in life. Gessner was thick-set, robust, and taciturn. His wealth had been acquired by hard thinking, laborious days, and bold, though never dishonest, speculation. Duryee was supposed to play the game of straightforwardness to the verge of eccentricity. Men, surveying his luck, attributed his ability to the devil—a vulgar error of incompetent minds. Gessner himself could never entirely overcome his distrust of American finance.

It seemed to him far too go-ahead. He was also
somewhat jealous of that curious buoyancy which
exists in America, which allows a man to gamble away
fortunes, keep his credit, and retrieve every disaster.
Failures in the United States are even a certain cre-
dential ; they prove that the man who has sustained
them is enterprising ; his courage is admired, and he
is often accepted as an expert on the very matters
wherein he may have committed errors of judgment.
It is realised there that many experiments must be
made in the proof of a new departure. When,
therefore, Duryee asked Gessner in a light tone—

"Say, Gessner, what about your contract with
Prince Constantine ? "

Gessner replied, with an air of defiance—

"I may hold on to it. I shall keep to it perhaps
without any modification."

" Is it worth your while ? " said Duryee quietly.

" Why ? " said Gessner. " Do you want it ? "

Duryee lifted his languid eyes from a plate of straw-
berries which he dared not touch, and said—

" I don't believe I want anything. I like to have
everything in my own hands or let it alone—I can do
either just as well as not. You are the same. We
have got ways beyond small deals."

" Can't we work this together ? " suggested Gessner.
He saw an opportunity of learning American methods.

" We might," said Duryee, without enthusiasm.
" But I don't think we should agree. We have both

succeeded, you must remember, on totally different lines. The policies would not amalgamate."

"What are Prince Paul's intentions about Largs?" asked Gessner.

"Well, I thought something of making him a financier, but the root of the matter is not in him. All he wants is a good time, and a good time in his own way. If I do anything with Largs, it will be on the strict condition that he remains a mere cypher. I won't touch it otherwise. Felshammer is a bright man —a little visionary may be."

"Carnegie was telling me the other day," said Gessner, "that it will cost about fifty million dollars for pipe-lines alone if I take up petroleum."

"Guess he's right."

"Did you think of working Largs on the principles of Rockefeller's Trust?"

"No," said Duryee drily. "I was thinking of the Duryee Trust! I want to experimentalise out in Largs. I may drop all I own before I'm through. You see, I haven't any wife—any family, and, instead of leaving my money to a lot of institutions after my death, I may as well have the fun of spending it now. I'll provide employment for those who are able-bodied. You others can take care of the sick and the insane and the criminals! The fact is, I'm getting so now —it may be owing to this confounded toast-water— that I watch these young fellows on the omnibus-seats, and I envy them. The enthusiasm, the ambition, the hopes, the fun, sir, of the world is right there—centred in those shabby boys."

Mr. Gessner looked at him in surprise ; he never felt anything of the kind himself, because he was passionately fond of power, proud of his fortune, jealous of his renown as one of the leading bankers in Europe. To him movement meant pleasure, and repose fatigue.

"You are a little run down," he said.

"No, I am not more run down than I was when I first started years ago. I came from a tired stock. I keep asking myself, What does it all amount to ? I have reached the conclusion that you cannot live your life fully and work the money market at the same time. As for this phase of big combinations, it is a sort of feudalism in money without any of the romance that seems to have gone with feudalism. If you have land, it is there ; you can send your labourers out on it and farm it, and you can build on it and make it beautiful. I love to read about the feudal system—the race will never see anything so perfect again."

"These are theories," cried Gessner genially— "the theories and dreams of a practical man, and, if you approach Largs in this frame of mind, it will prove very much more satisfactory as a charitable undertaking in the interests of the unemployed than as a prize for shareholders l "

He laughed at his own ponderous joke, and was so

amused that he was able to swallow some rice without tasting it.

"I will tell you what I am prepared to do," he said. "I will sell you the contract, make it over to you, and you can do what you like afterwards with Prince Constantine."

"Can I have it on the same terms?" said Duryee.

"Would that be fair to my manager, Mr. Draycott? You see, he made all the arrangements. I always insist on a clause to the effect that I can transfer any deal as I see fit."

"Just so," said Duryee, "and Draycott will expect a profit for the sake of his reputation?"

"Yes," said Gessner.

They discussed the terms of that profit, and it worked out in Mr. Gessner's favour to the extent of ten thousand pounds.

"It is purely nominal," said Gessner.

"I like to let a man feel that he has got the laugh on me," said Duryee, when explaining the interview to Prince Paul; "it makes him feel good! Gessner thinks, from the way I talked—and I must have sounded like a sick fox—that I am tumbling to pieces —losing my grip, as it were. He wants to make it easy for me to get broken. Then he'll come to the rescue and take it over. Just use the word *ideal* once in a business talk, and they'll all subscribe right away to your memorial fund. You can't tell me anything about Hermann Gessner. He's great."

Prince Paul, however, took no interest in these commercial operations; he thought them rather degrading, certainly not worth his while. He escaped from Mr. Duryee at the first lull in their conversation and drove to Clementine's lodgings. She was receiving a visit from her aunts, Mrs. Romilly and Mrs. Townshend, and the young man's heart sank when he beheld these two matrons seated in the small sitting-room. The talk which followed was trite; the aunts were absent-minded because they were considering him in every detail—his expression, his clothes, his manner. He informed them that his cousin Marie had bought a bull-dog.

"Some people are fond of bull-dogs," replied Mrs. Romilly.

"Don't you think, dear," cried Louise, addressing her sister, "that bull-dogs can be great darlings although they are so ugly, poor things? I remember Anna Sylvester had a bull-dog," and so on, and so forth.

The dust of the streets, the galleries of Florence, the Royal Academy, Beethoven's symphonies, Major Romilly's health, and Augusta's approaching marriage were discussed with vivacious gloom. Mrs. Townshend was the first to leave, because she had to catch a train, at the end of half an hour; and Mrs. Romilly followed her example fifteen minutes later with a look which told plainly her opinion that Prince Paul was compromising her niece. But, as the door closed behind her, he said to Clementine—

"I was determined to sit them out. I don't like the note you wrote me about the flowers, and I have brought it back. Just read it."

He brought her short letter out of his pocket and put it on the table.

"There is nothing the matter with the note," replied Clementine. "The flowers are beautiful, and I said so. As for the poetry, that has always been one of my favourite verses."

"We must come to an understanding," said Prince Paul. "I assure you this cannot go on. I am not absolutely blind, and I know the reason for your unnatural conduct. The man you care for is Felshammer. Oh, why didn't you tell me so long ago ? "

" Felshammer ! " she exclaimed, turning pale.

" I have not come to say anything against him, but I do think it would have been more loyal to both of us if you had given me a hint—what is easier to a woman ?—that you loved some one else."

"I am unable to explain my friendship with Dr. Felshammer," she said steadily, " but it is not at all as you think. He is nothing to me although he has been a kind friend in many ways."

"Young girls," said the Prince, "cannot have friends. That's an American custom, I believe, but it does not suit Europeans."

"In that case, sir," replied Clementine, "I can scarcely know you."

"Yes, you can, because I have explained myself. I do not pretend to these absurd so-called Platonics. A Platonic friendship is an unhealthy lie. But I am too proud to be one of a multitude. There is mediævalism in my blood. I think that the woman one loves ought to be isolated—removed from all influences. You may call it jealousy, but it is the primeval instinct of protecting the creature one owns."

"Dr. Felshammer is nothing to me," repeated Clementine.

"And what am I to you ?" said Paul.

"That is the most difficult question to answer."

"It can't be too difficult."

"You were kind enough to make a suggestion——"

"The suggestion was an offer of my whole life— nothing else," he said sarcastically.

"And I told you on what terms I could accept that offer. It won't make either of us happier to go over that ground again."

"Oh, how foolish you are ! You are driving me into that marriage with my Cousin Marie. I know and fear my own perversity. I should regret the marriage ever after. But you are driving me that way."

"I should be sorry indeed," said Clementine, "to drive you into any unhappy state."

"Marie has a heart," said the Prince, with feeling, "she has a soul, she has the affection of a true woman, whereas you seem to me almost inhuman."

" Has any one ever told you that your manners are atrocious ? "

" My manners ?   What do you mean ? "   He had always been led to suppose that they were perfect.

" I know that they are commonly considered delightful," said Clementine, " but they are not delightful at this moment."

" This is no occasion for the demonstration of one's mere manners," said Paul haughtily ; " we are talking about a matter upon which your future and mine depend.   I don't wish to regard anything except the situation, which is sufficiently serious.   I consider that you have led me on to care for you, and now I take the right to express myself with entire frankness.   I have loved you as I have never loved any one else.   I have endured rebuffs from you which, on reconsideration, I find almost inconceivable.   You have a way of speaking and looking which verges on the contemptuous.   It is insufferable really, and I think you ought to have a lesson.   You have been spoilt.   If I am fond of you, it is in spite of my better judgment and because I hope, perhaps unwisely, that your faults arise from your training—not from your actual disposition ! "

" It is very generous of you to think that," said Clementine—" very generous.   But I think it is rather justice than generosity.   There is not one word of truth in what you have been saying.   You know this.   And this is why you find you can forgive me.

Literally, you have nothing to forgive. I can't tell you how much I wish I could accept your offer."

This admission, for her, was an important step in the direction of surrender, and, as he was beginning to understand her character more thoroughly, his spirits rose.

"Why are you so impossible, darling?" said he, in his softest voice.

She smiled through her tears.

"You can't keep it up," he continued, pressing his advantage. "You make me wretched; you are unhappy yourself."

"I must not alter my terms. I must not—I must not!"

"Perhaps you need not. I love you so much that I will promise whatever you please. We can be married in a little country church and live in some villa in Italy. I will renounce every right—except the right to make you my wife. No one will come between us. I swear it."

She put her hands over her ears.

"I won't hear you. I want to, but if you break your word it will kill me. So I won't hear the promise yet. Think well about it. There is no happiness in haste. Don't see me or write to me for a month. Then, if you wish to come, come again."

"It is quite clear," he said angrily, "that you know nothing at all about men. What joy is there in waiting a month? What sense?"

"I want you to be sure of yourself."

"But I am sure already. You must think me very fickle."

"I know you are fickle."

"Then what are you ?"

"Constant, of course."

"You will let me kiss you goodbye — for a month ?"

"No! You may kiss me when you come back."

"But I want to take a memory with me."

They were both laughing by this time; there was sadness, however, under Clementine's gaiety. Would he come back? Could she believe in his protestations ?

"No," she said firmly—"no kisses."

He kissed her hand, which was trembling.

"If you were clever," said he, "you could twist me round your finger. As it is, I don't know myself when I am with you. You reverse every one of my ideas and all my experience of women !"

CHAPTER XXIV

THE DUTY OF RELATIVES

My Dear Alfred,—It is my very painful duty to point out the obvious fact that Clementine cannot receive visits from young men of high rank at her lodgings. I never heard of such a thing, and I cannot sufficiently impress upon you the importance of putting a stop at once to these improper proceedings. The fact that Clementine's mother was an American ought to make you not less, but more, vigilant in observing *les convenances*. It will be remarkably odd if the Prince does not jump to the most damaging conclusions. What on earth are you after in the City that she is so much alone? I lost all patience long ago with Clemmie's bringing up, but I have tried not to show it. I know I was averse to the idea of having a paid chaperon who would set her cap at you and piece the letters together in your wastepaper basket (as that dreadful Mrs. Weyborn did to Colonel Fletcher), yet, if you cannot be with the girl, some one else must. Louise tells me that another man, a foreigner too, was there the other afternoon. You must be mad to allow this. Clementine is of an extremely showy American type which appeals to idle fashionable men of no moral character. Be warned in time, dear Alfred.—Your affectionate sister,   Tiny.

P.S.—Don't touch salmon just now. It is neither good nor safe this year.

Mrs. Romilly always signed herself " Tiny "—the
pet name of her childhood—and added an informal
postscript about Alfred's food or his valuable life whenever she felt it her imperative duty to write him a
harsh letter.   After reading the above communication
he was at a loss whether he was more exhausted or
annoyed by its contents.   At all times a man who
resented advice, chiefly because it disturbed his indolent
mind, he did not know now where to begin or how to
act, although the fact that Clementine was at stake
urged him, as a pain urges, to attempt something.
Instinct has its surprises, and instinct, by an unexpected turn, made him think at once of his wife.
Greatly as he disliked and feared her, she had impressed
his imagination by her resource, and he saw that by
sheer force of temperament she could be of more true
service to his daughter than he with all his ineffectual
love. Valentine's positive ideas, her bewildering ability
to feel and reason at the same moment, were disagreeable in a constant companion ; but to poor Gloucester,
sinking consciously under the demoralisation of drugs,
worry, and debt, she seemed less a woman than a
bracing atmosphere, raw, harsh, cruel, perhaps, yet, in
the end, wholesome.

"I am going to pieces—going to pieces," he murmured to himself, as he drove to Claridge's Hotel.
" Some people can be good only while they are happy.
Trouble doesn't suit me. I can't stand it. My poor
mother was the same—she could not bear pain. It

made her quite devilish—poor, poor dear—quite devilish."

Mme. de Montgenays, Mr. Duryee, and Mabel were still at the lunch-table, and as Gloucester, obeying a message to the effect that Madame would see him at once, was shown into the room, Mr. Cobden Duryee, with a courtly bow, stepped out on to the balcony.   The two men felt something akin to a common pity for themselves and La Belle Valentine; on grave terms, they exchanged words seldom and never smiled in each other's company.

"I want you to read that letter from Tiny," said Gloucester, startled into directness, and refusing Mabel's silent offer of a cigarette.

Mme. de Montgenays, having perused her sister-in-law's epistle, was properly indignant.

"I wish she would mind her own affairs and leave my child alone!" she exclaimed, throwing the letter across the table to Mabel, who read it while she sipped, at intervals, a glass of port.   Admiration almost shone in Mr. Gloucester's fading eyes as he surveyed La Belle in her new character of an aggrieved parent.

"She is wonderful!   She is marvellous!   She is miraculously versatile!" he thought.

"At the same time," she went on, after her display of indignation, "from her own point of view, Tiny is right.   I don't think myself that Clementine ought to be alone, seeing men.   It isn't good form in this

country. I'm getting interested in the girl myself.
I want to know her, Alfred, and talk to her."

He put up one hand in protest, closed his eyes, and
shook his head weakly.

"She needn't know who I am. I'll pretend that I
am a friend of her mother's. There is nothing against
that, and I cannot tell how to deal with the case until
I have seen her for myself. That is necessary."

Mr. Gloucester was so relieved to have the whole
burden lifted from his shoulders that, after suggesting
a few objections to Valentine's proposal, he expressed
his willingness to fall in with any plan that she might
be pleased to make—provided always that the girl
remained in ignorance of Mme. de Montgenay's real
identity.

"You don't suppose," said La Belle, "that I want
a grown-up daughter to appear suddenly on the
horizon? But I must see her. If she is going to be
like me, I shall be sorry for your sake, and also for her
own, because the world has changed and so have
men."

"That's so!" ejaculated Mabel. "That's the truest
thing you ever uttered l"

"I don't see any modern men growing up like
Cobden," continued Valentine; "they have neither
his strength of will nor his independence."

"Clemmie is not like you," said Mr. Gloucester,
drooping. "I can't see whom she takes after; she's
like neither of us."

"Well," replied his wife placidly, "that is altogether to her advantage! Now let me call and see her now —right away. Would she be at home?"

"Yes," said Gloucester, "she is always in at this time. The poor child takes her walk early. She goes to church every morning."

La Belle Valentine smiled.

"I'm glad to hear it. This is a case for immediate action. I don't want verdure to grow all around me while I am wondering what to do next."

She joined Duryee on the balcony, held a short conversation with him, and then went to her bedroom, from which she emerged presently wearing a black dress of severe simplicity, a small plumed hat, and a very delicate black veil.

"I'm ready!" said she. "Hurry on ahead and tell them to call a hansom!"

When Gloucester left the room, Duryee rejoined the two ladies and watched Valentine draw on her gloves. He was secretly pleased to find that she took some interest at last in her own daughter. It was satisfactory also to see that she had still the charming faculty of providing astonishment to her oldest friends. She would not wait for the lift, but ran down the stairs as lightly as a fawn.

"She's got more heart and soul than you would think," Duryee observed to Mabel. "She never does herself justice." There were actually tears in his eyes as he walked about the room, picking up a handker-

20

chief, a bracelet, a sable tippet, a purse, and some stamps which La Belle had lost under various chairs during the morning. "Val," said he, "has never had fair play. Clever women have an awful time everywhere, and when they are handsome into the bargain——"

"She adores you," said Mabel; "I have never seen anything like it."

He could not trust himself to speak. A lump always came into his throat when he considered his idol at all seriously. She had given him so much sorrow and so much appreciation.

Neither Gloucester nor Mme. de Montgenays spoke during the cab-drive. La Belle had a theory that it injured her musical notes to speak much in the open air or above the noise of traffic. Gloucester, who had swallowed more ōpium, was dazed. He could not believe that he was really sitting side by side with Valentine, and that he felt altogether at ease in her society. He saw her through a vast stretch of atmosphere, and he heard his own voice, when he gave directions to the driver, as though it were a stranger speaking in the distance. Was he so attached to Clementine as he had been? He was too ill to be expected to care much for anybody, and what now seemed the most vivid recollection of his life rose up before him—blue birds in green trees, the pattern of the wall-paper on the room where Clementine was born. The blue birds sang and the green trees waved;

the whole coarse fabric of the real world vanished like fairy gold ! he was roaming in the sweet meadow of Eastern Acres. . . .

"Is this the house ?" asked La Belle Valentine, who told the cabman to wait. Gloucester opened the front door with a latch-key and let her pass him.

On entering the sitting-room, they found Clementine fast asleep on the sofa.

"Don't wake her," said Mme. de Montgenays— "I just want to take a good look at her"—and she stood there motionless, scarcely drawing her breath, holding Gloucester's arm with a grip of iron for fear he should stir or disturb the sleeper.

"She's stunning !" she said at last, in a whisper. "She is unique. The Prince hasn't made any mistake this time. Better rouse her while I look out of the window."

Gloucester called his daughter by name ; she sprang, in confusion, to her feet, and saw a woman's figure in black standing with its back toward her.

"This lady," said Mr. Gloucester, "is an American lady who knew your mother."

Mme. de Montgenays wheeled round and said, with her most gracious smile : "I implored Mr. Gloucester to bring me here to-day. Your mother and I and Cobden Duryee were schoolmates years ago."

Clementine recognised her at once as the Prince's friend—the beautiful dancing lady who had been at Salsomaggiore.

"You don't like me !" said Mme. de Montgenays, looking at her with critical but not unkindly eyes.

"Oh, please don't think that!" said Clementine. "I was startled at first, that's all."

"Why not think it, little girl, when it is so ? You are not a bit like your mother if you can't face the truth."

Clementine sat staring at her, subdued by an infinite influence which she could not understand and was unable to combat.

"Prince Paul has often told me about you," continued Mme. de Montgenays ; "he thinks the world of you. Now you are blushing! Why, my dear child, your mother had every man, young and old, in the town wild about her, and she never thought anything about it. If you think she was an angel, get that idea out of your head"—and she gave one of her rare mirthless laughs. "But I don't want to tease you. Ask me things about her—that is what I came for. I hoped you would be glad to see me."

"I am," said Clementine.

"No, you are not. Never mind."

It would have seemed profane, Clementine thought, to discuss her dead mother with this dashing, worldly individual, who had an air of wickedness, of unhallowed fascination, of unlawful knowledge. Mr. Gloucester meanwhile was moving the various trumpery ornaments on the mantelshelf, wandering about the room, passing his hands through his white hair, and muttering

incoherent phrases. He could not call the meeting
a success, and he began to be afraid lest Mme. de
Montgenays should lose her capricious interest in
Clementine. He was becoming conscious of his own
growing numbness to every duty, every tie, and he had
enough heart still left to know that the girl might
alienate, by her reserve, a strong if unsympathetic
protector. But, as on all other occasions, he mis-
calculated La Belle Valentine's moods. She was too
good-humoured to resent Clementine's indifference—
the girl's cold attitude appealed to her own peculiar
cynicism, her sense of the ironic tragedy in life, and she
promised herself much amusement in describing the
whole scene later on to Cobden. All that she saw,
heard, or learnt was invariably regarded as so much
material for the entertainment, in some form, of the
one human being whom she passionately loved.

"Well," she said, rising, "I came to gratify my
curiosity. I wanted to see Val's child. I am most
agreeably disappointed. The trouble with me has
been that I couldn't be satisfied with the two talents of
silver and two changes of raiment. Now you could."

Clementine had just time to notice once more how
superbly Mme. de Montgenay carried herself, how
handsome her face was in spite of its underlying
hardness, and then she heard the words—

"Goodbye!"

To her amazement, she saw, on looking out of the
window, her father getting into the hansom with the

visitor.   The poor gentleman was really hypnotised by
his wife's vigour.   He drove with her to Claridge's,
and when she did not ask him to come upstairs and
discuss the events of the afternoon with her and
Mabel he felt a little hurt.   So, lonely and morose,
he walked away towards the Park, wondering what
the strange creature would do next.   Her one remark
in the cab had been :

" She's a beauty, and she can keep her head.   She
will have to suffer, but she will arrive."

Gloucester, who, like all timid persons, feared anything in the nature of prophecy, had trembled all over
at this utterance.

" Please God," he had said, " it will be for the best,
whatever happens."   He repeated this as he went on
his way, finishing the pious hope with a petition to
heaven for a brown pony—a prayer of his childhood,
now remembered mechanically and uttered without
thought.   He had mumbled it at the end of the
Doxology for years.

Mme. de Montgenays had received a visit that
morning from Mr. Carrow, of the firm of Messrs.
Carrow and Hollingham, jewellers.   Mr. Carrow had
informed her, among other things, in the strictest
confidence, that a lady of very high rank indeed was
anxious to dispose by private treaty of a remarkable
sapphire necklace.

" Let me see it," said La Belle Valentine.

When, therefore, she returned from her expedition,

Mr. Carrow was waiting in her sitting-room, with a large blue velvet case in front of him on the table, talking to Mabel. The necklace was beautiful and costly—two irresistible attractions to Mme. de Montgenays. But she said she would have to think it over, and she would have to wear it first in order to see whether it suited her style.

"I have to consider my style, Mr. Carrow," said she.

Mr. Carrow, a man of taste and breeding, entirely agreed, and, on the understanding that she might wear it as an experiment that night at dinner, he left her with many polite assurances to the effect that he entertained no doubt of her success in the regal ornament.

"Regal?" she said sharply. He permitted a prudent smile to hover over his lips.

"I thought as much," said she.

Prince Constantine and Mr. Duryee were dining with her that night, and as the Prince's glance fell on the extraordinary jewels worn by his hostess he exclaimed, being impetuous and not well mannered—

"Hullo! So my absurd mother has sold them after all. It is too bad."

"Are they the Queen's?" she said softly.

"I should think so. She must be mad."

"She mustn't dream of selling them," said La Belle Valentine. "I couldn't think of allowing Her Majesty to make such a sacrifice."

"She wants the money. Some of her sleeping dogs have been roused from their slumbers!"

"If she and I could meet," said Mme. de Montgenays, "we might arrange the matter without an actual sale."

"My mother is bad at business—in fact, she is impossible in every human relation."

"Would she consent to meet me?"

"God alone knows what she will do?" said the young Prince roughly. "She lives, like my brother Paul, by caprice."

"If she would dine here, it could be kept a close secret——"

"Why on earth do you want to know my mother? She is not amusing; she is in exile, poor soul; she is *très grande dame*—if you like that kind of thing, and she will be terribly afraid of you. She is painfully shy."

"Will that matter—when I ask to meet her once only, and then to discuss an affair which is rather to her advantage than mine?"

Duryee, who was standing by, enjoyed this short conversation.

"Your Royal Highness must try and fix up the encounter," he observed. "Madame has set her heart on it."

Constantine felt tempted to say that he regarded such a desire on Mme. de Montgenays's part as a piece of extreme impertinence, but his eyes were suddenly fascinated by the flash of the Crown gems on her beautiful neck.

"She is not a bad sort," he reflected, "and why offend Duryee?"

He promised to exert his powers of persuasion to their utmost, and he undertook to obtain the ex-Queen's answer by the following morning.

CHAPTER XXV

THE DISCERNMENT OF SPIRITS

WHEN a great friendship is once broken it continues like some solid frame made for a masterpiece from which the beautiful picture has been roughly cut. The habit of confidence, the security tried by many tests, the knowledge gained by close intercourse remain, but the heart of it all is absent ; the charm, the love, and the sympathy are no more there. Felshammer saw Prince Paul almost daily, and the young man, unable to imagine the real cause of his secretary's altered manner, attributed it to the inharmonious career he had so suddenly adopted.

"The tenour of your reflections, Karl," he said gaily, "has convinced me that neither now nor at any other time ought you to have ventured into the City. Come back with me to Italy, and look at Florence from that old cemetery on the hill, and love the Botticelli Venus, and adore the Botticelli Madonnas. I used to think that marriage made men old, sour,

298

and suspicious. I find I was mistaken. It is not the wife—it is the money market."

"One cannot stroll through life merely admiring works of art and enjoying romantic scenery. The bill has to be paid!" snarled Felshammer. He called on the Queen that day and found her with her confidential lady-in-waiting, the Countess von Gundling, a person of prodigious stupidity with round hazel eyes, a dead face, and a dishevelled wig made of coarse grey hair. She worshipped her royal mistress, and once she had been disposed to protect Dr. Felshammer. That happy period had been outlived, however; now she regarded him as an upstart who knew too much altogether about the august family and probably confided facts about each member of it to the Press. It was therefore a grief to her when the Queen received him cordially as an old and trusted friend.

"This is an inspiration!" she said. "I was longing for some one who could give me good advice."

The Countess von Gundling, in consequence of this speech, melted into tears and sniffed piteously during the rest of the interview.

"We were discussing the propriety of my making the acquaintance of Mme. de Montgenays," added the Queen.

"La Belle Valentine!" exclaimed Felshammer. "I cannot imagine any circumstance which could bring that person and your Majesty together."

The Countess was so far from feeling any gratitude for this unexpected support that she snapped
out—

"Who, pray is to draw the line in these Radical
ideas? One endures every sort of impertinence from
these *parvenus* who seek to insinuate themselves into
our positions, to displace the true aristocracy by the
force of wealth, audacity, and, I blush to say it, morals
which acknowledge no sanction!"

"Do be calm, Wilhelmina!" said the Queen.
"Mme. de Montgenays has genius—she is a supreme
artist. In the case of such distinguished persons
etiquette has always been relaxed. Besides, the
meeting would be private."

"Every paper will have the news to-morrow!"
said the Countess von Gundling.

Felshammer, having perceived that the Queen had
her curiosity aroused with regard to the famous
dancer, was too diplomatic to oppose their meeting.
At the same time he wondered how her name had
been brought before the capricious lady.

"She is a great friend of Paul's, and Con-Con has
dined with her," observed the Queen, "and from all
I hear she is not so bad as many creatures in the best.
society who behave far worse with no excuse—least of
all the excuse of genius or beauty."

Felshammer owned the truth of this charitable
assertion and remembered that women of unimpeach-
able virtue were always more severe toward the

failings of those in their own class than toward their humbler sisters in the human family, and further, that they were invariably fascinated by the mysterious lives of those enchanting beings who terminate their course of folly in cruel degradation, in premature death, in comfort, in happy marriages, and sometimes in great affluence.

Several suppositions entered the secretary's brain, but he had been told nothing about Prince Constantine's contract with Hermann Gessner, and the large sum of money drawn by Paul was still unexplained. He had never guessed the relationship between Mme. de Montgenays and Clementine, and he was maddened by the unanswerable enigmas which occurred to his mind—a mind which was little used to suspense. The Queen talked for two hours about the undesirability of mixing with Bohemians and wound up, as she had intended to do at the beginning, by commanding the Countess to write a letter accepting La Belle Valentine's invitation to dinner.

"It will please Paul and Con-Con," she said, "and I think it is a mistake to hold aloof from persons who are respectful and loyal. It is also better to know how matters stand than to remain in the dark. This woman may have great power. Surely it is wiser to hear the opinions of those who wish one to succeed than to meet only, as I have done, supposed allies who are secretly anxious for my ruin!"

At this point the Countess sobbed aloud, struck her breast, and asked of what she was accused.

"Imbecility," said the Queen sharply, "and there is nothing so dangerous."

The secretary hastened to express his agreement with the royal sentiments, but he left the apartment in an ill-humour. What did it all mean? Believing, or persuading himself that he ought to believe, that, if Clementine had been flattered by Prince Paul's attentions, she was lost, Felshammer determined to make one more effort to save her. As to manner, he would endeavour to be gentle. He would conquer the girl's defiance by subduing his own love and by forgetting his own desires, and, with whatever difficulty, he would show such unselfishness that she would give him at least her trust for all time. Then, might she not learn the truth before it was too late? Might she not see that she was following vain hopes?

Mme. de Montgenays, on receiving the Countess von Gundling's letter, danced round the room, clapped her hands, played the piano, and sang at the top of her voice.

"What a triumph, Mabel!" she cried. "What a perfectly elegant time we shall have!" Mr. Duryee was enchanted by her girlish enthusiasm, and went himself to order the most perfect dinner which could be obtained in London.

When the hour struck for the royal guest's arrival, the ex-dancer, in a gown of exquisite design, without jewels of any description, was waiting to receive the ex-Queen. The meeting between the two filled the onlookers with admiration. The graciousness of the royal lady, the superb humility of the Bohemian, left nothing to be desired, and, to the astonishment of no one more than the two principals themselves, the scene, the dinner, and the conversation passed with the utmost brilliancy. Old von Gundling, who wore an air of martyrdom till she realised that her bearing was not remarked, became playful long before the third course, and permitted herself to laugh at Cobden Duryee's American stories, whether she understood them or not. The millionaire had engaged, as a pleasant surprise, a famous tragedian, a violinist, and a burlesque actor at five hundred guineas each to amuse the party after dinner. Tears of enjoyment rolled down the poor Queen's cheeks at the absurdities of the low comedian. She had never passed such a delightful evening. She heard about all the theatres, the gossip—modified—of theatrical circles, the talk—also modified—of the Stock Exchange.

"These professional people really seem to get an enormous amount of variety out of life," she observed, when it was over, to the Countess, whose countenance was now fixed in a benevolent simper. "They seem more sincere than the others and more cheerful," she added, as she looked around her dreary sitting-room. "Of course, one would not wish to be like them, because that would involve too much, but I do wish that some of our very old and dear families had equal skill in making one feel loved, and in entertaining generally. Perhaps Almighty God wishes me to do this poor Mme. de Montgenays some good by knowing her. I shall not draw back from what may be a divine mission! What was the name of that excellent *entrée* we had? Do remember it!"

La Belle Valentine meanwhile was resting on the sofa, covered with an ostrich feather rug, and enjoying the recollection of her charming success. She considered the Queen the ideal of womanly tact, intelligence, beauty, and deportment.

Mr. Duryee drawled out—

"She's a very nice lady, splendid manners, and a good deal of horse-sense back of it all. But why did you really want to know her? I have been waiting for you to tell me."

"Well," said his friend, "my idea was this—I want the Queen to see Clementine."

"What good would that do?" asked Duryee.

"It would show Ada Romilly that my child is treated with every possible consideration."

"You are somewhat elaborate in your methods," said Cobden drily, "and they cost a lot of money."

"I am very thorough," said La Belle Valentine. "I guess I take after mama. She not only chose the text and hymns for her own funeral, but also selected what the mourners should have for lunch after returning from the cemetery. I remember she ordered some-

thing hot, because it was in the late autumn, and she
didn't want any one to catch a chill."

"And she told them they would find the pickles in
the cellar," added Mabel, "and said they must be
sure to take them from the bottom of the jar, as those
underneath were always the best.   I tell you, she was
a character ! "

"She could look ahead," said Duryee.

"Well, I am like her," said Mme. de Montgenays—
"I scan the horizon."

"See here, Val," said Duryee kindly, "I hope you
are not fixing up any romance between Clementine
and Prince Paul.   There is nothing in it, believe it.
You'll get bitten, sure.   Leave the whole scheme
alone ! "

"If I had listened to you, Cobden, all my life, I
should be sitting old and forgotten at this minute in
an asylum for tired-out farmers' wives ! "

But Clementine had taken the reins into her own
hands.   She had resolved not to see Prince Paul for
a month, and she arranged with her father to leave
London that same day to visit her friend, Ruth
Hollemache, who lived at Kew.

CHAPTER XXVI

THE little house at Kew, occupied by Ruth Hollemache and her mother, was famous for its old red
barn half hidden by sycamores, and its orchard. The
dwelling itself, one of the cottages set in the midst of
a large tract of fruit and vegetable farms situated
between Richmond Park and the Thames, had once
sheltered the great Cromwell. Two centuries later
Wesley preached there, and the Emperor Louis
Napoleon, during his first exile, had used to sit on
the fence of an adjoining field, smoking and drum-
ming his heels as he dreamed of his future plans, and
chatted, in neighbourly talk, with Ruth's great-
grandfather. Railways and disfiguring villas have
now obstructed a view which had extended to the
river and beyond it ; the well-cultivated land has been
cut into small holdings ; the starlings still chatter, the
blackbirds whistle, and the thrush sings, but the
nightingales which once sang in the groves have
gone. There was in the garden a lilac thicket which,
presenting a splendid mass of colour, grew almost as

high as the window of Ruth's bedroom. A large
walnut-tree, a plum-tree, a pear-tree, and an apple-
tree had been planted on the stretch of lawn bordered,
on one side, by laburnum, white acacia, and maple,
and on the other by a privet hedge and beds of Mary
lilies, purple flags and purple iris, syringa and jessamine.
Clementine used to sit under the maples facing the
ivy-covered porch which led to the quaint panelled
kitchen; to the left she could see the aspen pollard
quivering by the front gate, and to the right there
was the orchard, which, especially beautiful in the
blossoming-time, now, if less vivid during June,
presented a lovely design of young bright leaves
against the sky.

Mrs. Hollemache, who had inherited the house
from her father—the last of a long generation of
gentlemen farmers—was an invalid. Ruth, a girl of
six-and-twenty, was engaged to be married to a
lieutenant in the Navy. She was a sweet, rather
pensive creature, with a pale oval face and soft dark
eyes which seemed to be expecting a happiness which
was not yet attainable. As a distant relation of Basil
Hollemache, she had been able to tell Clementine the
little she had heard from members of the family about
poor Lucie. Hollemache gossip on the subject was
unfriendly, and Clementine found one more reason for
grieving about the Prince and his conduct.

It was Saturday afternoon; the girls were seated in
the garden; Ruth was engaged in some plain needle-

work, a garment intended for her own simple trousseau, while Clementine, weary of town, sat with her hands in her lap, breathing in the soft air and enjoying the fragrance of the flowers.

"I wonder what you will really do with your life, Clem?" Ruth said abruptly as she surveyed her companion's mobile face. "Ever since you were a child I have always thought that you would have some kind of a romance. Mamma thought so too."

"You don't seem to have been right so far," said Clementine.

"But your friendship with Prince Paul is extraordinary—you don't seem to realise that."

"It isn't satisfactory," replied Clementine; "it is a friendship which spoils one for other friendships; it may be very slight, and yet it comes between all others and interferes with them. You may remember that I wanted nothing in the first place. There are days now when I almost wish I had never seen him at all."

Ruth was not in perfect sympathy with her old playmate on this point, because she was contented herself, and she could imagine no better lot than to be the wife of her breezy lieutenant. She had a placid, sensible mind, and, although she was too loyal to discuss Clementine with Augusta and Leonore, she had often acknowledged, in conversation with her own mother, that Clem's life had already been spoilt more or less by these gaudy celebrated acquaintances in a society beyond her proper sphere. Clementine

had never told her about the last interview with
Prince Paul, but Ruth felt by instinct that some
strange excitement was stirring the girl's heart. She
had a new and startling beauty — the evanescent
charm of dawn with its changing lights, its melting
promises, its intangible glow, and, for the moment,
she seemed enveloped in an atmosphere which
separated her from the pollution of the ordinary
world. Ruth was about to ask a few discreet
questions when they were both disturbed by the
sound of cab-wheels. The vehicle stopped at their
gate, and Dr. Felshammer stepped out.

"Is that the Prince?" said Ruth.

Clementine, turning pale, explained who it was as
he crossed the pathway and, unannounced, came
toward them.

"I cannot pretend that I do not see you," he said,
with assumed ease; "you forgive the informality?
What a delightful spot! It makes me careless of
all my troubles."

Ruth remembered that she had an engagement at
the parish-room and soon left them. Already she had
decided that such a suitor ought not to be discouraged.

"You are angry with me for coming," said he,
when Miss Hollemache had gone, "but they gave me
your address at your lodgings, and I drove here
immediately. What is the use of denying it? I
can't keep away."

"I am very tired of London," replied Clementine.

"As I told you before, I wanted to escape to Touraine, or some old French town. This was nearer, but——"

"You cannot escape your fate," said Felshammer huskily. "I believe you are trying to hide, but, wherever you go, it will follow you and find you out."

"Even so. Then let it find me in peaceful sur-roundings—with those I can love and trust."

"Well, you can trust me, although you will not love me. I won't surrender. Why should I? You are the one thing on this earth I want. You are little more than a child; you see life and men in an artificial light. In a year's time you will be laughing at many of the notions you have now."

"Then I must wait for the ebange. If it is to come, it will come."

"Why waste a whole year? Take my word for it."

"You don't understand. I am happier this way than I could be in any other way that you could suggest."

Felshammer felt to the bottom of his soul that the self-willed girl was desperate. There was evil round about her, temptation in prospect, the cynical and the unscrupulous were in her path. How could he best display the mockery of egoistic love?

"You used to know Mlle. Savary, the actress, and all her friends, when you were a child?" he asked suddenly.

"Yes."

"You could not have understood her life, but you

must have seen that it was not enviable. And take the lives of girls of another caste. Brieux and Sudermann have written plays about them. They are born with pretty faces and good brains ; they surpass all their relatives ; they grow to despise the rough fellows of their father's set ; they attract men of higher position. They either return to their own class and their own people, or they die, when they are sensitive, of broken hearts. Those who are not sensitive are below consideration. They know their way through a world which they find entirely congenial. Now, I do not compare you with Mlle. Savary or with these girls I have just described. But the same difficulties —less squalid, perhaps, yet just as painful—occur in every grade of society. There seems to be no remedy."

"There is no remedy while the girls themselves are willing to accept a false position," said Clementine ; "their own conduct justifies, in most cases, the misery which they have to suffer."

"Women are so afraid of loneliness," said Felshammer. "Existence can so soon become for them dull, barren, grey, and inane. And they drift into these hopeless, terrible attachments ; they do not see that they were not made to give love but to accept it. They squander their devotion on a sex which requires devotion in its infancy, or in illness only. A prudent woman will permit herself to be worshipped, protected, provided for ; she keeps a close guard over her own affections."

"I agree with you."

"Then what have you against me?" he said passionately. "I don't ask for your love. I haven't Paul's manners and ways, but I am a man of my word. When I offer you my whole life, I mean my whole life. And I am so afraid for you—so horribly afraid!"

"Why?" said Clementine. "Why? And what do you fear?"

"Everything that is most tragic," he replied. "He will make you believe in him because he will believe in himself. But his sentimental mistake will be your eternal sorrow. Sorrow—that's what I fear for you."

"You have said that I can't escape my destiny."

"Let us suppose," he said, "that I am your destiny. We need not stickle for petty points of romance. You are beautiful; you carry romance with you. You see what an awkward fool I am at compliments, but you know what I mean."

"Isn't it always a failure when we try to meet as friends and talk about indifferent things?" said Clementine, speaking even more coldly than she wanted to.

"Well, romance wouldn't suit me, nor would I suit romance," he continued; "you are heartless, you are proud ——"

"I don't think so—at least, not now. I may have been proud once."

"I daresay I am a brute, yet I can understand a few

things. You are fretting about Paul. Oh, I can see
it! He is written all over your face, and he is written
in your eyes. It is Paul—Paul—Paul—everywhere I
look. And the whole time I can hear your thoughts
running on Paul—Paul—Paul—no matter what you
are saying or what you are doing. It takes some
nerve to stand it when one is an impatient man—as
I am."

"But you have no right to feel impatient with me.
My thoughts are not your business."

"They have become my business unhappily. I
cannot help myself. Therefore I should be a very
weak fool to give in—a very weak fool!" He could
not bear to be beaten. The desire for supremacy was
stronger in him than any other, and he was fighting
as much for his own way as for what he took to
represent his happiness.

"It is hopeless," said the girl firmly, "and, if I
were dead, it could not be more hopeless."

"You said something of the kind once before,"
replied Felshammer, "but our wills seem well
matched. You call out the best in my soul and
the worst in my temper. You are pale and your
hands are cold. I can't bear to see you look sad. It
hurts me if I think you are suffering."

"I must beg you to leave me at least—if you cannot
avoid these scenes," said Clementine; "they exhaust
me—they humiliate me."

"That's true—you misunderstand all I say. Well,

I beg your pardon. You must forgive me. If you would only trust me a little—I love you infinitely; I would not annoy you or wound you by a word or a look—but life without you begins to be insupportable. Men do not like to have their lives disturbed and disorganised. You say that you can never live with me, and I cannot live without you. We have reached that stage. How will it end? I am not to blame for any of this—there is no one responsible. Perhaps I am your curse, and you are mine. That first day when you came into the church I felt as I had never felt before. I have known hundreds of pretty girls ——"

She glanced with terror at the love which was almost hatred in his excited face and especially in his threatening eyes.

" You imagine," she faltered ; " you persuade your-self."

" You may as well tell a man who has a knife in his heart that he feels no pain. I have worn you out, however, and, as usual, I have injured my own cause. I believe I am possessed. I don't pretend to know myself in this character. But I cannot help it. I struggle against it as a weakness, as folly, as madness, and the more I struggle the deeper I get involved. Poor child, the fault is in human nature—not in either of us l "

There had been so much truth in Felshammer's words, and he spoke with such sincerity, that Cle-

mentine felt completely dominated by his mind
although he had no power over her heart. She seemed
almost magnetised by the spell of his fierce mood,
which, like all manifestations of real strength, whether
in ideas or in emotion, made its own law and over-
mastered every deterrent. The man's obstinate conviction that Clementine was being gradually drawn
into the most appalling mistake possible to an
impetuous and chivalrous woman gave a note of
peculiar fervour to his voice.

"The spirit of revolt is in you," he continued;
"you do not see why things should be as they are.
You do not see why you should sacrifice your
dreams, your pride, your youth to a tyrannical
etiquette. For it is a question of etiquette—not
morality, not heaven, not hell. All the conditions
are worldly in the narrowest sense—the human vital
conditions are wholly disregarded. Prince Paul may
have been pitchforked out of his country; they may
have changed his residence—they cannot change his
hereditary prejudices. He feels, in spite of himself,
that his flesh and blood are vastly superior to ours;
the sentiment is possibly unconscious, but it is knit up
in his very bones."

Clementine remained immovable, oppressed, irresistibly subdued, yet in utter opposition.

"But," she said presently, "if I refuse to acknowledge or accept those conditions—what then?"

"You may refuse, perhaps you will refuse, them—

but it will embitter you. Every day I meet men and
women who have withstood the cramping social laws,
but what is the result? They become ironical or
contemptuous toward others who have had neither the
strength, nor the inclination, nor the courage to do
the same. And that is what I dread for you—either
a ruined life or a spoilt nature."

"Whatever happens," said Clementine, "I must
bear it alone. You cannot help me."

"Am I to regard that as your final decision?" said
Felshammer, with a hard laugh. "My dear child,
you cannot dispose of me so easily. Tell me one
thing—has the Prince made any proposition to you?
For his sake, tell me."

The girl hesitated ; then she replied :

"I have no fault to find with him. I do not think
him weak, selfish, or vain."

"That is not the truth!" exclaimed Felshammer,
in anger. "I repeat, that is not the truth. You
know that he is all three; you are trying to make
him out a hero. You forget that I am his most
intimate friend."

"It would be a difficult fact to remember at the
present moment!" said Clementine drily.

"I daresay you think I am disloyal, but you are
moie to me than he has ever been or could ever be.
I see plainly that he has spoken to you and gained
your confidence. I am trying to save you, although
you won't let me. There's the eternal woman—you

are all the same. I wish you were dead." He looked
her well in the face, studied each feature, sighed
deeply, and repeated :

"Yes, I wish you were dead. If you were dead, I
could be just to you. As it is, there are hours when
I believe you are capable of anything, any deceit, any
folly. It is not your fault. It is my unspeakable
curse. And so, I wish you were dead."

Then he turned away, and, smiling quietly to
himself, as men do who are sustained through ridicule,
disaster, and persecution by a fixed sublime or insane
belief, he left the garden.

Ruth and Clementine were sitting at supper that
same evening when the maid announced a visitor for
Miss Gloucester. He had written his name on a
card which was enclosed in an envelope.

"At this hour ? " asked Ruth, glancing at the clock.
It was past nine. "What a strange time to come !"

She felt dismayed, even alarmed, on her friend's
account, and feared that Clementine had fallen into
the easy customs of Bohemian society. She saw, too,
the girl's agitation, the sudden brilliant light in her
eyes, the flush of joy which mounted to her cheeks.

" Oh, Clemmie," she exclaimed, when the servant
had gone out, " if it is Prince Paul, don't see him !
Why should he call at this time in the evening?
What can he mean ?   Doesn't it show that he is
selfish and inconsiderate ? He compromises you and
you don't seem to care ! Try not to like him ! Try

to be firm! There are no **two** loves possible for you —if you once give yours to him, you will have none left for any one else. In the end you will just be broken."

Clementine looked impatient, but Ruth caught her arm and held her back.

"I do want you to see what all this means," she persisted; "this is not life—this is exceptional; you must look more carefully where you are going. You have that uncommon vein in your character which ought to make you cautious; you know, too, that you are very handsome. Handsomeness won't last, Clementine, and a man like the Prince wouldn't care for anything else. What will you do when you grow older?"

"I can die," said Clementine defiantly.

"Oh no, you won't!" said Ruth. "That is the tragedy of every woman's life. She is pretty for a few years and old for a great many. If you want to be happy, you must love some one who takes love in a solemn way."

"Men who tell one that they take love solemnly are almost always superficial," replied Clementine, "and they are constant, in many cases, merely because they are lazy, or because they have neither enthusiasm nor imagination. I want to be loved recklessly while I am loved, and when I am no longer loved—as I have said—I can die. Your warnings are too late, Ruth."

Nevertheless, she did not go at once to Prince Paul. Ruth heard her running lightly upstairs, and she followed, because, having entered her protest, she now felt at liberty to enjoy the excitement of seeing Clementine prepare for the forthcoming interview.

"I don't want to keep him waiting so long that he will think I am changing my dress," said Clem, as she put some flowers in her belt, while Ruth opened the box which contained her best hair-combs—old Spanish ones made of tortoiseshell, amber, gold, and enamel.

Prince Paul was trying to interest himself in the pictures on the wall of the small drawing-room when Clementine opened the door.

"Surely," he explained going to meet her, "you did not expect me to wait a month? You are not surprised to see me?" He seemed nervous, and he talked rapidly.

"Don't you think it ought to surprise me—to find you unwise?"

"Ah, *chère amie!* I have quite done with wisdom. What a charming little house! I like to see the blue night outside the window. The sky is full of stars. It reminds me of that evening at Salsomaggiore— when we stood on the balcony and talked about Peer Gynt. I remember every word you said, every movement you made—it is unforgettable. Oh, how happy I am to be with you again—yes—I am perfectly happy! And you?"

"I am happy too."

"That is right. You are the one being in the world who seems able to idealise life for me. I cannot, I will not take it as it appears ; I have burnt my ships ; I have put everything away from my existence, my future, my duty, my ambition—everything except you. I need you always. The love I feel for you is not ordinary love at all. You are part of myself— the other half of my soul. A chance—a divine chance—brought us together. Such good fortune does not come to one man out of five thousand. And you ask me to think about it for another month ! Impossible ! "

"What am I to do ?" answered Clementine. "I am poor ; I am not a Princess."

"Haven't I just said, dearest, that you are part ot myself ? "

"I should like to think so," she replied, smiling.

His handsome face lit up with triumph and un- feigned joy. He was so glad that he had burnt, as he said, his ships. It had all been decided in a moment. One morning he woke up and said to himself, "Of course I love Clementine, and no one else matters to me in the least." Prolonged thought, for a period of years, on the subject would have brought him to the same conclusion. Here, clearly, was the advantage of a mind impatient under psychological analysis, or the imaginative tricks of a dreaming temperament. He was no dreamer—a reason, beyond doubt, why he attracted irresistibly the women in whom sex was a pure quality undisturbed by artificial sentiments. Clementine felt no surprise at his abrupt dealing. When two beings love each other their emotions are in such true accord that the normal, if unconscious, struggle for supremacy which continues in all mere friendships does not exist. Delays, misunderstandings, and reproofs between lovers arise from some fault, some deficit, some real cause for doubt in the actual affection of one or the other. But as soon as a devotion is recognised as absolute all smaller thoughts, all common human fears vanish, and the heart for the first time shows its original simplicity. Clementine saw and felt that Paul was at last in earnest. He was still selfish, still undisciplined in the enjoyment of his own intelligence, sensations, and sentiments—even love cannot alter a man's essential character—but he was serious, sobered ; he spoke the truth in his own way ; when he said that he cared more for her than for any one else in the world he meant it, he believed it, and it was the case. He no longer questioned himself in the matter, and she did not question him.

"You see——," he stammered, suddenly losing his command of words.

"Yes," she said, "I see. I think we can help each other. I think we belong to each other. But don't call it a mere chance."

He kissed her forehead and her hair, restrained by a reverence and moved by a stronger, more intimate feeling than the common impulse to touch some one who is beautiful or charming. She seemed to him a creature apart from all he had ever known. Her eyes, which were always direct and peaceful in their glance, had none of the uncertainty, the morbid defiance, the restlessness, the reproach, the desire almost beseeching and incessant for admiration which had attracted him so often in those of other women. It flattered his egoism to detect in that self-reliant girl the profound and tangible expression of the best in his own secret nature.

"You wanted all or nothing," he said, "and now I offer all I have—it seems too little. I can't be idle; I could not lead the life of the rural English duke, and I may not meddle in politics. The one career open to me is in the financial world. I shall work under Cobden Duryee."

He was surprised to find himself able to speak quietly at such a moment of plain affairs. He had imagined many romantic, passionate love-scenes between Clementine and himself; serenity of this kind was, perhaps, not to be imagined. He felt already that they were united for ever; that they had never been separate; that they were in spirit and body identical. So he drifted gradually into a conversation which was the literal utterance of his thoughts as they came—plans for their marriage and their common future. When the clock chimed ten he apologised for the lateness of his visit.

"But I couldn't wait," he said; "it had to be

settled.   To-morrow you shall meet my mother and Con-Con ; I'll observe the strictest etiquette ! It is absurd, yet I know one must think of these things."

Five minutes after he had left the house, Ruth ran, with a white, scared face, into the room where Clementine still stood entranced with happiness.

"Did you hear that shot," she exclaimed—"a pistol-shot ?"

"No," said Clementine, "I heard nothing."

"I may be fanciful, but I am sure some one has been hurt," said Ruth ; "there was a sort of cry too. It was terrible.   Did the Prince drive away ? "

"He walked to the station."

The girls stared at each other.   Clementine put out her hand and the two hurried out into the garden. All was quiet.

"Shall we go a little way up the road ? " suggested Ruth, peering and straining her eyes.   Clementine nodded, but her fingers were too numb to lift the gate latch.   Ruth opened the gate ; they passed through, and some distance down the lonely road they saw a dark object lying in their way.   "I am afraid," said Ruth, and she hung back.

Clementine went forward.   Presently Ruth heard her calling :

"Ruth ! Ruth ! "

The object in the path was the body of Prince Paul.

CHAPTER XXVII

DR. FELSHAMMER WRITES HISTORY

EIGHT days after the news of the attempted assassination of Prince Paul of Urseville-Beylestien had been called from every street corner and talked of in every club throughout the civilised world, Felshammer sent the following letter to his old friend Frank Hollemache at Berlin :

You may well ask for the true facts of this curious affair. The newspapers are extraordinarily well informed on many points—indeed, I am amazed at the details which they have been able to discover and publish—but, as usual, the whole impression given is a false one. Far too much, for instance, has been made of the point that the Prince was fired at in a lane not more than fifty yards from the residence of Mrs. Gerald Hollemache, where he had been calling on Clementine Gloucester, who actually found him later lying on the road. Ruth Hollemache was with her. The natural inference is that the unknown assassin was an anarchist, who, having followed Paul to this lonely rendezvous, seized the opportunity to attack him on his way homeward. An element of scandal, wholly misleading, uncalled for, and cruel, has thus been introduced. Here, I think, the Prince himself deserves blame. When he recovered from the first shock, he pretended that his injury was a slight accident, insisted on escorting the girls back to the house, refused all help, and then walked a long distance to some livery stable, where he hired a conveyance. At last, barely conscious, and suffering severe pain, he reached Claridge's Hotel, where, after a consultation, the surgeons, who had been hastily summoned, decided that his chances of recovery were not out of the question. He kept calling out for Clementine—this after his senseless precautions—and from the odd phrases he dropped from time to time in his delirium these people readily gathered that he was involved in some love entanglement. The Queen and Con-Con showed their genuine grief in characteristic fashion. Her Majesty disturbed the patient by sobbing and praying at the top of her powerful voice all night long. Princess Marie had to sit in a room on the floor below chewing her pocket-handkerchief and shedding torrents of tears. Why do women almost invariably add a grotesque note to tragedy? Sachs and Bickersteth loitered in the corridor, seeing journalists, messengers, doctors, and official personages. Need I say that the ladies-in-waiting lost their nerve, and Mme. de Mont-genays, with her unfailing genius, proved a friend in need to the poor Queen? The Queen cannot exist out of her sight, and La Belle, whose manners have become incomparably courtly, rules her with a rod of iron. A case of infatuation. Paul is dangerously ill, and, if he pulls through, he cannot hope to be the man he was. Shall I confess that his folly in this present case has taxed my patience to the breaking-point? What has Miss Gloucester done that she should be compromised in this way? No one can see her; she is prostrated; her family are indignant; the Queen does not hesitate to say that the poor girl lured Paul to his ruin and was in league with the anarchists. I quote this to illustrate the imbecility of ordinarily intelligent people. Mme. de Montgenays, on the other hand, defends Miss Gloucester.

"Majesty," said La Belle to the Queen, "I know all about Alfred Gloucester's daughter. She is a beautiful, sweet young creature. Her mother was a friend of mine. The Prince has often talked to me of Clementine. He loves her."

"He must be mad!" sobbed the august Charlotte. "Who but an idiot would fall in love with a *jeune fille?*"

When I want the brutal rhetoric of common sense I listen to ladies of blameless virtue. And tell me this— was there ever, at any time, a real note of the grandiose in anything? One hears that religion once was able to invest even hypocrisy with a kind of grandeur. Hypocrisy, however, ¯is slowly dying out, and the candour of modern souls would be sublime if the souls themselves were not, for the greater part, squalid. One would prefer them to be less truthful. I am grieved, disenchanted with the world, sick, not of life as I could feel it, but as I see it manifested around me. You will say that the strain of the last week and the poison of the Stock Exchange have told on my nerves. Possibly. Yet beyond and above any physical *malaise* there is death in my heart. I begin to suspect that I see the world as it is, and that it is in every respect ignominious. Our greatest passions can be traced to our meanest instincts, and the fine names we have invented for successful selfishness mean no more in reality than the base ones which we contemptuously bestow on the selfishness which fails. I'll add no more now. But let me assure you in conclusion that this is no mood. All that existence holds for me now is distress, agony, and nausea.

When he had signed this, he sealed it in an envelope and locked it away with many others, also sealed, addressed to one or two individuals, and unsent, in a despatch-box. It was Sunday afternoon, and he had formed the habit of calling weekly at Carlington House to see Rachel Bickersteth. Sometimes she was too ill to receive him, but, as a rule, she gave him tea in the still garden, where the lawn looked like the lifeless grass which grows in old cemeteries. An Indian client had given Mr. Bickersteth a present of some beautiful white peacocks, and these alien birds moped in the tree near Rachel's chair. Felshammer was beginning to regard the Quakeress as his only true friend, and he found a peace in her society which could usually restore his temper or his spirits to something resembling contentment. This day he hoped, as he had never hoped before, that she would be well enough to talk to him. He caught himself murmuring, " Thank God," when, with the customary pomp which no longer excited his ridicule, he was ushered into the octagonal boudoir at the end of a gallery and three large saloons. Rachel was reading a book on financial matters by Paul de Rousiers, and she flushed slightly as Felshammer expressed his surprise at her choice.

"A new departure for you," said he; "what does it mean?"

"I begin to feel my ignorance of these things," she replied.

Then she noticed that his hair had turned grey, that his face was drawn, that he had the air of one who was on the brink of a serious crisis.

"You take Prince Paul's illness too much to heart," she exclaimed, speaking with a vehemence which was altogether new in his experience of her character; "but why are you so anxious? He is getting better. Surely you do not fear that there will be further attempts upon him?"

Felshammer looked at her strangely and said with terrible irony:

"Who can tell? Now that he knows that he is a marked man, he can never feel safe so long as he lives."

"And have they no suspicion—no clue?"

"Nothing whatever. You see, that road by the Hollemaches' place is deserted; it might be in the heart of the country although it is so near the station. One could well say that it looks as though he had been preordained to go straight to his doom there."

"I suppose an anarchist shot him," said Rachel; "it could not have been by any chance a private enemy."

"An enemy?" repeated Felshammer,

"Yes. Hasn't he been reckless in the past—especially with regard to women?"

"It is strange that you should think of this possibility," said Felshammer slowly; "an idea of the kind occurred to me. But, frankly, it won't hear analysis."

"Jealousy," said Rachel, "can excuse many crimes. A jealous man would have made more sure of his death—that is, if the whole thing were planned. There might have been no plot. The Prince may be able to throw light on the subject when he is better."

"There are moments when the gruesome, hideous business seems a nightmare," said Felshammer, sitting with his hands clasped and his head bowed; "I can tell myself it is not true, it never happened. When I go into Paul's room and see him lying there on the bed, with his ghastly face and all the atrocious paraphernalia of surgery about him, the nurses and doctors, the poor Queen wailing and the boy himself moaning and calling in his delirium—even then, with my eyes on all that, I am sometimes able to say to myself—'You will wake up!' I used to love him better than any one in the world. I thought him so handsome, so brilliant, so romantic. Imagine me caught by romance! I made myself blind to all his faults, I would not admit that his follies were more than the picturesque audacities of youth."

"What made you change?" asked Rachel.

"He disappointed me. I began to see, little by little, perfidy, a colossal loveless egoism, a consuming vanity; perhaps I was as bad, even worse, myself, but he seemed able to indulge his nature whereas I had to control mine. I had admired him for what I took to be his superiority to myself; he sank to my level—lately I was able to consider him too often as my inferior. And I hate my inferiors. They show me my own lowest possibilities too clearly. I am drawing my spirit in pleasant colours, I know. But, for some reason, I don't mind your hearing the truth."

"Has Miss Gloucester seen him yet?"

"She can see no one. Wouldn't it be humorous if all this killed her?" He laughed, and looked, with despair in his features, at Rachel.

"Does she care—so much?" asked Mrs. Bickersteth.

"Body and soul. I am certain of that."

"Poor child!" said Rachel, tightening her grasp on the book she still held.

"Poor child indeed! Do you wonder that I cannot forgive him?"

"Could he have guessed," said Rachel, dropping her eyes, "that you were especially interested one way or the other?"

"We never discussed her. Besides, latterly he and I were estranged. He became secretive."

"And she—did she say nothing?"

"She took pleasure in wounding me whenever his name came up between us. The best women are cruel when they wish to defend the men they love. I never blamed her."

"How long is it since you saw Miss Gloucester?"

"It was that very day," he replied huskily; "I went down in the afternoon."

"And the Prince called in the evening?"

"So I gather," he said, after a short pause. Neither of them spoke for some minutes. But, as she lived so much alone, she had kept the faculty of hearing unuttered thoughts—a faculty which is wrongly thought supernatural, because it becomes either dead or dissipated in the traffic of constant affairs. Her countenance suffered a dreadful change, the book fell from her fingers, she stood up and went with outstretched hands toward her wretched companion. He remained rigid, although he accepted her pity, and, unflinching, met the awful question in her eyes. Then she moved away, picked up the dropped book, placed it on the table, and went back to him, taking his hands and looking into his face once more.

"He isn't going to die," she said; "it wasn't to end like that. They used to tell me when I was a child that God was full of compassion. I thought so till I lost the boys. Then I said it was a lie. But I begin to understand now. I have sorrowed so much that you can believe me and you can trust me. Paul will not die."

"Do you think I want him to live?" he asked.

"I know you do," she answered gently.

CHAPTER XXVIII

FELSHAMMER SPEAKS

ANOTHER week passed. Prince Paul's case had excited a great amount of interest ; no ear was closed to the whispers which made every attendant circumstance sensational, and the season, which had been in a number of ways dull, received a certain importance from the fact that, during its course, an Urseville-Beylestein had narrowly missed a violent death. Although Clementine had never been allowed to attend merely fashionable gatherings, she was known in society as a singularly beautiful girl belonging to one of the oldest families in the kingdom. Rumours of an astonishing, even malicious, kind spread from club to club and from circle to circle till Mr. Gloucester found himself harshly criticised on the serious ground that he had permitted his young daughter to be compromised in a most deplorable way. The anger of his relatives (and among them many remote connections now classed themselves), while . violent, rhetorical, and just, was somewhat assuaged it must be owned by the fact that the erring lady's name had been associated with that of an exile Prince. On all sides one heard people ·murmuring : " It's awful ! That cousin of mine, Alfred Gloucester, must be mad. What will become of Clementine?"

Clementine, who had sunk at first under the terror and anxiety caused by the Prince's misfortune, took nevertheless such confidence from the knowledge of his love that the world seemed to have lost its power to wound her. Whether for happiness or sorrow, she saw the work of God in all that had occurred, and resolving to be the mistress at least of her own movements, she offered no reply to the questions which filled the air. Paul asked for her constantly, and at last the physicians agreed that if some meeting could be arranged between them his chances of a swift recovery would be greater. Under pressure, with tearful misgivings, and fortified by the advice of Mme. de Montgenays, Queen Charlotte gave her consent to the proposal, and Mr. Gloucester was astonished to receive an autograph letter from the august lady herself asking him to bring his daughter privately to visit the Prince.

. Gloucester took the communication at once to La Belle Valentine, on whom he called frequently as possible now in the hope of securing even five minutes of her valuable time. In boundless good-nature she would listen to his complaints about his health and his mistakes, meeting them always with some shrewd counsel based on her unemotional yet soothing philosophy. After reading the Queen's communication, she observed :

"You don't want anything better than that. The marriage will have to take place. That is what Paul is playing hard for. He's a man. I like him. So does Cobden. The marriage will take place."

Mr. Gloucester, unable to grasp this thought, sat shaking his head and repeating :

"That will never do—never! Horace Walpole had a niece who married a royal duke, and then, of course, there was Mrs. Fitzherbert, but the times have changed."

"You are way behind the age, Alfred," replied his wife. "You don't see that a reaction against snobbery is coming. The world is getting much more healthy ; it still thinks far too much about money, but all the strong folks are coming right along in splendid style. Clementine is among the strong ones."

"But," gasped Mr. Gloucester, "how could a girl of quiet tastes be happy with a man in Prince Paul's position—with the fear, too, of assassination ever before him."

La Belle looked wise, pursed up her mouth and said :

"I am not talking any more to-day. I have an idea about that anarchist. I do not worry about him."

Clementine was in the garden at Kew when her father came to her with the Queen's message.

"I knew he would send for me," she said quietly, "and I know, too, that he will get well."

"Has he ever paid you any addresses, my dear?" asked Mr. Gloucester, much agitated.

Clementine blushed and began to laugh.

"Should I go to him, papa," she said, with a charming smile, "if we did not understand each other?" She saw agreement written on Mr. Gloucester's comforted and radiant face.

Felshammer happened to be waiting in the corridor outside Prince Paul's apartments when Mr. Gloucester and Clementine arrived. The unhappy secretary, whose eyes still kept their look of angry suffering, conquered his inner trouble and made an effort to speak. But the girl was so absorbed in the ecstatic prospect of seeing Paul again that she passed by, lovely in her trembling joy, without noticing a single bystander. Felshammer watched the two visitors admitted : he saw the door closed again, barring him out, as it were, for ever from the lives to whom he had given every passion of his soul. He went away to find Rachel, and broke down completely in her presence.

"All I have done," he said at last, "is to bring them nearer together and make their marriage all but a necessity. What am I to do? I cannot remain here; I cannot bear to see them together, and I cannot bear myself alone."

"I think," said Rachel gravely, "that you will

never be able to rest till you have told him the truth."

"What!" he exclaimed.

"I think," she repeated quietly, "that you ought to tell him."

Felshammer looked furtively round the room, and then lowered his voice till it was all but inaudible.

"Do you want me to give myself up? What would be the use? It is pure sentimentality to imagine that I feel the least remorse. I do not."

"I want you to let Paul know as much as you know."

"You are like all good women," he said roughly; "you ask too much."

But he could not forget her wish. It followed him through the days and nights—an invisible companion. At last he heard that Prince Paul had formally renounced his right, such as it was, to the throne of Urseville-Beylestein. The enraged ex-Queen sent for Felshammer and poured out curses on the ruined careers of both her sons.

"Self-indulgent and miserable fools!" she screamed. "Heaven in its wrath will smite them to the earth. Unworthy of their calling! Heedless of my voice! Let them rush to their well-merited doom! Their girls and their horses, their cards and their dissolute friends are the talk of the whole world! I have brought forth manikins—not men."

The Princess Marie, who was present, wearing a

very tight tailor-made dress, stifled a bitter cry, and looked, with overflowing eyes, at the secretary.

"People do not care any more for the old ideas," she began, but her voice broke, and, for fear she should lose every atom of self-control, she bit her lip, the clumsy lip of her famous race, till it bled.

"Marie and I represent the great traditions of Europe," said the ex-Queen. "Our hearts will break in silence and we may be forgotten before our epitaphs can be engraved. But, bless God, Who is above all, He is our Support." She paused and added: "Come, my poor child, with me to Biarritz!"

The Princess smiled even through her grief at this absurd anti-climax. A season with her aunt at Biarritz rose before her mind; she heard the wild conversation, she saw the ridiculous train of religious and artistic impostors who followed in Her ex-Majesty's wake—the spiritualists, the Christian scientists, the false prophets, the cackling old nobles with their wives, sisters, and daughters, the loyal adherents to the exiled family, the jewellers, dressmakers, duns, parasites, and bores.

What would the days be? Long drives, irregular, interminable meals, harangues, hysterics, fits of melancholy, explosions of temper, exhausting parties—these, alternating with attacks of church-going, convent-visiting, and the like, would fill the useless hours. And in the evenings! There would be the worst kind of sentimental music—silly sacred songs, facile

23

and overstrained melodies on the violin, arpeggios of too familiar chords on the harp, calls from depressed and tiresome officials. But, on the other hand, she would be able to hear, perhaps, authentic news of Paul.

"Oh yes," said Marie cheerfully, "let us go together to Biarritz!"

"The Empress will be there," added the Queen, "and the Empress is my one friend!" She no longer cared so very much for Mme. de Montgenays.

The Prince was sitting up in a chair by the window when Felshammer, after leaving the royal ladies, joined him. The change wrought in the faces of both men was in one case a purification, and in the other a scarring disfigurement. The lines in Felshammer's countenance had deepened, his features had grown heavier, his complexion was darker; he looked old and hunted and careworn. Paul put out his hand with his usual frank gesture of trust and affection; the other accepted it, but dropped it almost immediately.

"I wonder whether we can be here without interruption for a short time," said he, standing with his back to the light.

"I will give orders," said Paul, touching a bell at his side as he spoke. After the servant had entered, received his instructions, and retired, Felshammer came close to the Prince's chair.

"I want to make a statement," he said firmly. "I have never told you, and probably you have never guessed, that Miss Gloucester made a profound impression upon me the first time I met her. The peculiar power which she exercised, and exercises unconsciously, over me simply illustrates one of those secret influences we call fate."

The Prince sighed and kept his glance fixed attentively upon Felshammer, who continued speaking.

"I became jealous of you. I blamed you. I thought you were trifling with a woman who deserved very different appreciation. Mr. Gloucester, meanwhile, after your departure from England, got into money difficulties. I was able to relieve his embarrassment. I lent him a sum of money which he repaid in circumstances which forced me to suspect that he had discharged his debt to me by placing himself under some heavy obligation to you. I don't know now whether I was right in this surmise."

"You were altogether wrong," said Paul. "I have never helped Mr. Gloucester in the slightest degree, and I had never given Miss Gloucester so much as a little present till the other day when she accepted our engagement ring."

Felshammer grew livid and remained silent for a few seconds.

"I presumed to offer marriage to Miss Gloucester," he said bitterly, "and I need not tell you with what result. When she left London, in order to avoid me, as I thought and possibly also to escape from you, I followed her to Kew. I repeated my offer. From various remarks she made I felt certain that there was some understanding between you. I regret to own I thought you were deceiving her. I went home, but later I returned and watched her house. I did not see you go in. I saw you come out."

Paul sprang to his feet, and the two men surveyed each other.

"I saw you come out," said Felshammer. "I followed you a short way down the road and I shot you. When you fell I hoped you were dead, and I thought you were dead. Otherwise I would have fired again."

"I have often said," replied the Prince, after a long pause, "that you were quite capable of killing me, but not of deceiving me. My instinct, it seems, was perfectly sound. Do you intend to make a second attempt ?"

"No," said Felshammer; "no—that is all in the past. I put myself in your hands. If you wish me to repeat this confession at headquarters, well and good."

Paul shook his head.

"This is a very strange business, Karl," said he. "I forgive you, and the matter is buried—so far as I am concerned. But we must never meet again. That is the one request I make."

Felshammer bowed, turned on his heel in the military fashion, and walked straight out of the room. He was conscious only of a suffocating hatred for the man who had spared him.

CHAPTER XXIX., AND LAST

THREE POINTS OF VIEW

IT was Mr. Bickersteth's wish that an entertainment should be given at Carlington House in honour of Prince Paul's fortunate recovery and betrothal. Rachel, therefore, overcame her constitutional repugnance to the part of playing hostess to a multitude, and gave a party which was called small because it occurred at short notice. There was a dinner first for sixty distinguished persons, followed by a concert at which Paderewski played, and Mme. Bernhardt recited, and Mme. Melba sang. The company had been selected chiefly from among Prince Paul's own acquaintances in London. Rachel's own small circle of friends made up a delighted chorus of spectators for the stream of exhausted, dishevelled, well-meaning, and nervous aristocrats who talked loudly during the music and ate whenever it ceased. Clementine and the Prince, who were too happy to be critical, were amused by the assembly, and charmed by the trouble which had evidently been taken to give the function that shallow brilliancy which is associated always with any exhibition of great wealth. Nadeshda Sachs, who had been chagrined at first to find that her own house was not considered important enough for such a festival, lost her ill-humour on becoming, as usual, the most admired, the most vivacious, and the most successful woman present. No one paid much attention to Rachel, who stood superbly at the head of the staircase, looking ill, and smiling with absent-minded courtesy at each arrival. She had watched for Felshammer the whole 'evening, and, although he came last of all, she seemed to lose some of her weariness at his approach. Mme. Bernhardt was declaiming at the moment a poem of Victor Hugo's, and the conversation in the rooms was perhaps less animated than it might have been had her voice possessed the power of a musical instrument. Bicker-steth was doing his best to suggest silence out of respect to the great actress, and Oscar Sachs was laughing at the banker's effort to enforce good manners on his noble guests. They gabbled, stared, giggled, whispered, yawned, spoke loudly, and gesticu-lated with a freedom which was more genial than elegant. Felshammer smiled bitterly and said to Rachel, as he looked through the doorway at Paul and Clementine, radiant in the distance—

"Are they going to end, after so much, in this mob? Will she come down to the feverish vulgarity of a life spent in public? The soul-hunters have caught them after all. They may marry for love, but they will soon forget that in the scramble for money and pleasure."

"You must not exaggerate," answered Rachel. "Remember the many things you have often said to me about the dangers of misanthropy. You have taught me a great deal."

He was still glancing toward Clementine, and he seemed lost in his own emotion. "In time," he said presently, "I may be able to forget all this."

"You are quite right," she answered, trying to speak with calmness, although her heart sank with a new weight. "You are quite right, of course. You must forget all of us. What have you decided to do?"

"There is work for me in Urseville-Beylestein."

"Oscar Sachs tells me they may elect you some day President of the new republic out there. Wouldn't that be a strange development?"

"To be a President at sixty? It is too dull a prospect to be unlikely."

"You will become a President, and the Prince will turn financier, working with Cobden Duryee in America! What would be more extraordinary?"

"And, as you are in a prophetic mood, will the two be happy?"

"Yes," she replied. "They love each other. He will give her trouble, no doubt, but he will never love any one else so much."

"And that is to satisfy her?" he said.

"She isn't inquisitive. A woman without curiosity
is already among the happiest of her sex."

At that instant Nadeshda came out of the music-
room with Leonore Townshend. The girl smiled
rather slyly, and Felshammer turned to glance again
at her pretty face.

"She is attractive," he said—"why didn't I love
her instead of the other?"

The recitation had come to an end, and a murmuring restlessness at once affected the company.

"I must go now," said Felshammer hurriedly,
"before they can see me. I shall leave England
early to-morrow morning. Think of me sometimes.
Goodbye!"

She gave him a cold hand, murmured "Goodbye,"
and turned to answer a question about the weather
which some conscientious gentleman thought his
mere duty to offer any hostess, whether he knew her
well or not. When she moved again in Felshammer's
direction he was at the foot of the staircase. Would
he look back? She waited; she hoped; she held her
breath. But he went straight out. For a long time
she remained in a reverie from which she was roused
at last by Prince Paul, who picked up the fan she had
dropped.

"I shall never forget this evening," he said.
"Clementine and I were just thinking that we could
not have a happier memory to take away with us
to the New World. I have never before met

so many kind people, nor heard such perfect music."

Rachel's eyes rested on the joyous faces of the two young creatures transfigured by love, hope, and extreme contentment. She held out both her hands because she could not speak.

" Every one is too kind," replied Paul ; " I'm beginning to understand what life can be ! "

June 1899—June 1902.

24

The Gresham Press,
UNWIN BROTHERS, LIMITED,
WOKING AND LONDON.

T. FISHER UNWIN'S NEW BOOKS.

MOTOR CARS AND THE APPLICATION OF MECHANICAL POWER TO ROAD VEHICLES. By RHYS JENKINS, Memb. Inst. Mech. Eng. With over 100 Illustrations. Medium 8vo, cloth, 21s. net.

THE BARBARIAN INVASIONS OF ITALY. By Prof. PASQUALE VILLARI. Illustrated, and with Three Maps. Two vols. demy 8vo, cloth, 32s.

IN THE LAND OF THE BLUE GOWN. By Mrs. ARCHIBALD LITTLE, Author of "Intimate China." One vol. medium 8vo, with over 100 Illustrations, 21s. net.
[*Second Impression.*

SAND-BURIED RUINS OF KHOTAN. By M. AUREL STEIN, Indian Educational Service. With upwards of 60 Illustrations. Demy 8vo, cloth, 21s. net.

LOMBARD STUDIES AND IMPRESSIONS OF LAGO DI GARDA. By the Countess EVELYN MARTINENGO CESARESCO. Demy 8vo, Photogravure Frontispiece, and many other Illustrations, cloth, 16s.

AUGUSTUS. Life and Times of the Founder of the Roman Empire (B.C. 63–A.D. 14). By E. S. SHUCKBURGH. Demy 8vo, cloth gilt, 16s.

THE CONFESSIONS OF A CARICA- TURIST. Being the Autobiography of HARRY FURNISS. With over 300 Illustrations, many made specially for this work. New and Cheap Edition. One vol., cloth, 10s. 6d.

NEW FAIRY TALES FROM BRENTANO. By KATE FREILIGRATH KROEKER. A New Edition. With Coloured Frontispiece and 8 Illustrations by F. C. GOULD. Fcap. 4to, cloth, 3s. 6d.

THE MODERN CHRONICLES OF FROIS- SART. Told and Pictured by F. C. GOULD. With special Cover Design, Decorated Title, and 44 Illustrations. Fcap. 4to, 3s. 6d.
[*Fifth Impression.*

MEDIÆVAL WALES. Chiefly in the Twelfth and Thirteenth Centuries. By A. G. LITTLE, M.A., F.R.Hist.S. With Maps and Plans. Crown 8vo, cloth, 2s. 6d. net.

THE DAWN OF DAY. By FRIEDRICH NIETZSCHE. Translated by JOHANNA VOTZ. Demy 8vo, cloth gilt, 8s. 6d. net.

LONDON : T. FISHER UNWIN, PATERNOSTER SQUARE, E.C.

T. FISHER UNWIN'S NEW BOOKS.

A LITERARY HISTORY OF PERSIA, from the Earliest Times until Firdawsi. By EDWARD G. BROWNE, M.A., M.B. Demy 8vo, 16s.

THE WELSH PEOPLE : Their Origin, Language, and History. By JOHN RHYS and DAVID BRYNMOR JONES, K.C., M.P. Demy 8vo, cloth, Third Impression, Revised, 16s.

LABOUR LEGISLATION, LABOUR MOVEMENTS, AND LABOUR LEADERS. By GEORGE HOWELL. With Frontispiece Portrait. Demy 8vo, cloth, 10s. 6d.

THE BEGINNING OF SOUTH AFRICAN HISTORY. By Dr. G. M. THEAL, Author of "South Africa," &c. With Maps and Illustrations. Demy 8vo, cloth, 16s.

THE AMERICAN WORKMAN. By R. LEVASSEUR. Translated by THOMAS S. ADAMS, and Edited by THEODORE MARBURG. Demy 8vo, 12s. 6d. net.

IN BIRDLAND WITH FIELD-GLASS AND CAMERA. By OLIVER G. PIKE. With Photogravure Frontispiece and over 80 Photographs of British Birds. Cheap Re-issue. Crown 8vo, cloth, 2s.

RANCH LIFE AND THE HUNTING TRAIL. By THEODORE ROOSEVELT, President of the United States. New Impression. Royal 8vo, cloth, 10s. 6d.

THE COLLECTED POEMS OF A. MARY F. ROBINSON. Crown 8vo, cloth, with Frontispiece, 7s. 6d.

THE HEART OF THE EMPIRE : Studies in Problems of Modern City Life in England. Large crown 8vo, cloth, Cheap Edition, 2s. 6d. net.

TALES ABOUT TEMPERAMENTS. By JOHN OLIVER HOBBES, Author of "The School for Saints," &c. Cloth gilt, 2s. 6d. net.

HOOKEY : A Cockney Burlesque. By A. NEIL LYONS. Small crown 8vo, cloth, 2s. ; paper, 1s.

LONDON · T. FISHER UNWIN, PATERNOSTER SQUARE, E.C.

T. FISHER UNWIN'S NEW BOOKS.

"STORY OF THE NATIONS" SERIES.—New Vols.

With Maps and numerous Illustrations, cloth, 5s each.

WALES. By O. M. EDWARDS. Also published bound in half-morocco, full gilt, 10s. 6d. net.
[*Second Impression.*

MEDIÆVAL ROME: 1073–1600. By WILLIAM MILLER, Author of "The Balkans," &c.

THE PAPAL MONARCHY: from Gregory the Great to Boniface VIII. (590–1303). By WILLIAM BARRY, D.D.

CONWAY AND COOLIDGE'S CLIMBERS' GUIDES.

New Volume, 10s.

THE BERNESE OBERLAND (from Gemmi Pass to Monchjoch). By G. HASLER.

JAPAN: our New Ally. By ALFRED STEAD. With an Introduction by the Marquis ITO. Fully Illustrated. Crown 8vo, cloth, 6s. net. [*Second Edition.*

THE EPISTLES OF ATKINS. By JAMES MILNE. With 12 Illustrations from War Sketches. Crown 8vo, cloth, 6s. [*Second Impression.*

PEN PORTRAITS OF THE BRITISH SOLDIER. By the Rev. E. J. HARDY, Author of "How to be Happy though Married," &c. Demy 12mo, cloth, decorated cover, 1s. Illustrated.

CAPTAIN JOHN BROWN OF HARPER'S FERRY. By JOHN NEWTON. Fully Illustrated. Crown 8vo, cloth, 6s.

THE "FREE TRADE" EDITION.

THE LIFE OF RICHARD COBDEN. By the Right Hon. JOHN MORLEY, M.P. Popular Re-issue, Abridged. Demy 4to, paper covers, 6d.

THE WELSH LIBRARY. Edited by OWEN EDWARDS.

THE MABINOGION. In 3 Vols. Vol. I. now ready. Fcap. 8vo, cloth, 2s.; paper, 1s.

FROM SLAVE TO COLLEGE PRESI-DENT. Being the Life Story of Booker T. Washington. By G. HOLDEN PIKE. Illustrated. Crown 8vo, 1s. 6d.

LONDON: T. FISHER UNWIN, PATERNOSTER SQUARE, E.C.

NEW SIX=SHILLING NOVELS.

BREACHLEY, BLACK SHEEP. By Louis
Becke. *[Second Impression.*

**MISTRESS BARBARA CUNLIFFE (THE
COMBERS).** By Halliwell Sutcliffe.
[Second Impression.

THE PASSION OF MAHAEL. By Lilian
Bowen-Rowlands.

BLUE LILIES. By Lucas Cleeve.
[Second Impression.

A GIRL OF THE MULTITUDE. By the
Author of "The Letters of Her Mother to Elizabeth."
[Second Impression.

**FOMA GORDYEEFF (THOMAS THE
PROUD).** By Maxim Gorky. With Portrait of the
Author. *[Second Edition.*

THE DEEPS OF DELIVERANCE. By F.
Van Eeden.

HIGH POLICY. By C. F. Keary, Author of
"The Journalist."

THE LAKE OF PALMS. By Romesh Dutt,
C.I.E. With Frontispiece.

THE POET AND PENELOPE. By L.
Parry Truscott.

THE INSANE ROOT. By Mrs. Campbell
Praed. *[Third Impression.*

THE YELLOW FIEND. By Mrs. Alexander.
[Second Impression.

A LION'S WHELP. By Amelia E. Barr.
Illustrated.

THE MATING OF A DOVE. By Mary E.
Mann. *[Second Impression.*

THE FIRST NOVEL LIBRARY.

No. 1. WISTONS. By Miles Amber.
[Third Impression.

No. 2. THE SEARCHERS. By Margaretta
Byrde. *[Third Impression.*

London : T. FISHER UNWIN, Paternoster Square, E.C.

MRS. KEITH'S CRIME

BY

MRS. W. K. CLIFFORD

**With a Portrait of Mrs. Keith by the
Hon. John Collier.**

Sixth Edition. Crown 8vo., cloth. **6s.**

" Is certainly the strongest book that Mrs. W. K.
Clifford has given to the public. It is probably too the
most popular."—*World.*

" It is charmingly told."—*Literary World.*

" A novel of extraordinary dramatic force, and it will
doubtless be widely read in its present very cheap and
attractive form."—*Star.*

" Mrs. Clifford's remarkable tale."—*Athenæum.*

" Will prove a healthy tonic to readers who have
recently been taking a course of shilling shocker mental
medicine. . . . There are many beautiful womanly
touches throughout the pages of this interesting volume,
and it can be safely recommended to readers old and
young."—*Aberdeen Free Press.*

EFFIE HETHERINGTON

BY

ROBERT BUCHANAN

Second Edition.   Crown 8vo., cloth, **2s. 6d.**

" Mr. Robert Buchanan has written several novels. . . . . but among those which we know, there is not one so nearly redeemed by its ability and interest. . . . The girl is simply odious ; but Mr. Buchanan is a poet—it would seem sometimes *malgré lui,* in this instance it is *quand même* — and he dowers the worthless Effie with a rugged, half-misanthropic, steadfast lover, whose love, never rewarded, is proved by as great a sacrifice as fact or fiction has ever known, and who is almost as striking a figure as Heathcliff in 'Wuthering Heights.' "—*World.*

11, Paternoster Buildings, London, E.C.   *b*

T. FISHER UNWIN, Publisher,

THE RAIDERS

BY

S. R. CROCKETT

Eighth Edition. Crown 8vo., cloth, **6s.**

"A thoroughly enjoyable novel, full of fresh, original, and accurate pictures of life long gone by."—*Daily News*.

"A strikingly realistic romance."—*Morning Post*.

"A stirring story. . . . Mr. Crockett's style is charming. My Baronite never knew how musical and picturesque is Scottish-English till he read this book."—*Punch*.

"The youngsters have their Stevenson, their Barrie, and now a third writer has entered the circle, S. R. Crockett, with a lively and jolly book of adventures, which the paterfamilias pretends to buy for his eldest son, but reads greedily himself and won't let go till he has turned over the last page. . . . Out of such historical elements and numberless local traditions the author has put together an exciting tale of adventures on land and sea."
Frankfurter Zeitung.

SOME SCOTCH NOTICES.

"Galloway folk should be proud to rank 'The Raiders' among the classics of the district."—*Scotsman*.

"Mr. Crockett's 'The Raiders' is one of the great literary successes of the season."—*Dundee Advertiser*.

"Mr. Crockett has achieved the distinction of having produced the book of the season."—*Dumfries and Galloway Standard*.

"The story told in it is, as a story, nearly perfect."
Aberdeen Daily Free Press.

"'The Raiders' is one of the most brilliant efforts of recent fiction."—*Kirkcudbrightshire Advertiser*.

11, Paternoster Buildings, London, E.C.

THE GREY MAN

BY

S. R. CROCKETT

Crown 8vo., cloth, **6s.**

Also, an Edition de Luxe, with 26 Drawings by
SEYMOUR LUCAS, R.A., *limited to 250 copies, signed*
by Author. Crown 4to., cloth gilt, **21s.** *net.*

" It has nearly all the qualities which go to make a book of the first-class. Before you have read twenty pages you know that you are reading a classic."—*Literary World.*

" All of that vast and increasing host of readers who prefer the novel of action to any other form of fiction should, nay, indeed, must, make a point of reading this exceedingly fine example of its class."—*Daily Chronicle.*

" With such passages as these [referring to quotations], glowing with tender passion, or murky with power, even the most insatiate lover of romance may feel that Mr. Crockett has given him good measure, well pressed down and running over."—*Daily Telegraph*

T. FISHER UNWIN, Publisher,

RECENT ISSUES IN THE
GREEN CLOTH LIBRARY

In uniform green cloth, large crown 8vo, **6s.** *each.*

The Wizard's Knot. By WILLIAM BARRY.

"A romance of rare intensity of pathos. Of tragic power in the delineation of passion and its consequences, and of exquisite tenderness in its treatment of love and sin and suffering. . . . There has been nothing finer for a long time in imaginative fiction. No truer hand with more exquisite touch has fingered the stops of Irish human nature."—*Scotsman.*

Among the Syringas. By MARY E. MANN.

"It is long since we have seen a story so full of human interest woven out of materials so simple. . . . The authoress has written clever stories before, but none, we think, which shows such a matured power."—*Manchester Guardian.*

The Lost Land. By JULIA M. CROTTIE.

"The most remarkable Irish novel we have had for many years."—*Bookman.*

The Rhymer. By ALLAN MCAULAY.

"One of those gems of fiction which are not easily surpassed."
Oban Times

Black Mary. By ALLAN MCAULAY, Author of "The Rhymer."

Evelyn Innes. By GEORGE MOORE.

Sister Teresa. A Sequel to "Evelyn Innes." By GEORGE MOORE.

The Two Standards. By WILLIAM BARRY.

Shameless Wayne. By HALLIWELL SUTCLIFFE.

Edward Barry: South Sea Pearler By LOUIS BECKE. Author of "Ridan the Devil," &c

The Maid of Maiden Lane. By AMELIA E. BARR.

11, Paternoster Buildings, London, E.C.

T. FISHER UNWIN, Publisher,

WORKS BY JOSEPH CONRAD

I.

AN OUTCAST OF THE ISLANDS

Crown 8vo., cloth, **6s.**

"Subject to the qualifications thus disposed of (*vide* first part of notice), 'An Outcast of the Islands' is perhaps the finest piece of fiction that has been published this year, as 'Almayer's Folly' was one of the finest that was published in 1895 . . . Surely this is real romance—the romance that is real. Space forbids anything but the merest recapitulation of the other living realities of Mr. Conrad's invention—of Lingard, of the inimitable Almayer, the one-eyed Babalatchi, the Naturalist, of the pious Abdulla—all novel, all authentic. Enough has been written to show Mr. Conrad's quality. He imagines his scenes and their sequence like a master; he knows his individualities and their hearts; he has a new and wonderful field in this East Indian Novel of his. . . . Greatness is deliberately written; the present writer has read and re-read his two books, and after putting this review aside for some days to consider the discretion of it, the word still stands."—*Saturday Review*

II.

ALMAYER'S FOLLY

Second Edition. Crown 8vo., cloth, **6s.**

"This startling, unique, splendid book."
Mr. T. P. O'CONNOR, M.P.

"This is a decidely powerful story of an uncommon type, and breaks fresh ground in fiction. . . . All the leading characters in the book—Almayer, his wife, his daughter, and Dain, the daughter's native lover—are well drawn, and the parting between father and daughter has a pathetic naturalness about it, unspoiled by straining after effect. There are, too, some admirably graphic passages in the book. The approach of a monsoon is most effectively described. . . . The name of Mr. Joseph Conrad is new to us, but it appears to us as if he might become the Kipling of the Malay Archipelago."—*Spectator*

11, Paternoster Buildings, London, E.C.

THE EBBING OF THE TIDE

BY
LOUIS BECKE
Author of " By Reef and Palm "

Second Edition. Crown 8vo., cloth, **6s.**

" Mr. Louis Becke wields a powerful pen, with the additional advantage that he waves it in unfrequented places, and summons up with it the elemental passions of human nature. . . . It will be seen that Mr. Becke is somewhat of the fleshly school, but with a pathos and power not given to the ordinary professors of that school. . . Altogether for those who like stirring stories cast in strange scenes, this is a book to be read."—*National Observer.*

PACIFIC TALES

BY
LOUIS BECKE
With a Portrait of the Author

Second Edition. Crown 8vo., cloth, **6s.**

" The appearance of a new book by Mr. Becke has become an event of note —and very justly. No living author, if we except Mr. Kipling, has so amazing a command of that unhackneyed vitality of phrase that most people call by the name of realism. Whether it is scenery or character or incident that he wishes to depict, the touch is ever so dramatic and vivid that the reader is conscious of a picture and impression that has no parallel save in the records of actual sight and memory."—*Westminster Gazette.*

" Another series of sketches of island life in the South Seas, not inferior to those contained in ' By Reef and Palm.' "—*Speaker.*

" The book is well worth reading. The author knows what he is talking about and has a keen eye for the picturesque."—G. B. BURGIN in *To-day*

" A notable contribution to the romance of the South Seas."
T. P. O'CONNOR, M.P., in *The Graphic.*

T. FISHER UNWIN, Publisher,

TROOPER PETER HAL-
KET OF MASHONALAND

BY

OLIVE SCHREINER

Author of " Dreams,"
" Real Life and Dream Life," &c.

Crown 8vo., *cloth*, **2s. 6d.**

" We advise our readers to purchase and read Olive
Schreiner's new book 'Trooper Peter Halket of Mashona-
land.' Miss Schreiner is one of the few magicians of
modern English literature, and she has used the great
moral, as well as the great literary, force of her style to
great effect."—*Daily Chronicle.*

" The story is one that is certain to be widely read, and
it is well that it should be so, especially at this moment;
it grips the heart and haunts the imagination. To have
written such a book is to render a supreme service, for
it is as well to know what the rough work means of
subjugating inferior races."—*Daily News.*

" Some of the imaginative passages are very fine. . .
The book is powerfully written."—*Scotsman.*

" Is well and impressively written."—*Pall Mall Gazette.*

11, Paternoster Buildings, London, E.C

Lightning Source UK Ltd.
Milton Keynes UK
UKHW021420010219
336575UK00014B/975/P